To Alice Tillman—
hope you enjoy these
stories
Judy Budnitz

FLYING LEAP

JUDY BUDNITZ

PICADOR USA ≈ NEW YORK

PICADOR® IS A U.S. REGISTERED TRADEMARK AND IS USED BY ST. MARTIN'S PRESS UNDER LICENSE FROM PAN BOOKS LIMITED.

GRATEFUL ACKNOWLEDGMENT IS MADE TO THE FOLLOWING PUBLICATIONS IN WHICH THESE STORIES FIRST APPEARED: *PARIS REVIEW*: "DOG DAYS"; *STORY*: "SCENES FROM THE FALL FASHION CATALOG," "FLIGHT," AND "COMPOSER"; *GLIMMER TRAIN*: "HUNDRED-POUND BABY." "PARK BENCH" APPEARED IN *25 AND UNDER/FICTION* (1997), SUSAN KETCHIN AND NEIL GIORDANO, EDITORS.

LIBRARY OF CONGRESS CATALOGING-IN-PUBLICATION DATA

BUDNITZ, JUDY.
    FLYING LEAP / BY JUDY BUDNITZ. — 1ST PICADOR   USA ED.
    P. CM.
    ISBN 0-312-18097-7
    I. TITLE.
    PS3552.U3479F57   1998
    813'.54—DC21   97.36088
                                           CIP

FIRST PICADOR USA EDITION: JANUARY 1998

10 9 8 7 6 5 4 3 2 1

ACKNOWLEDGMENTS

I would like to express my thanks to the Fine Arts Work Center in Provincetown and the Rona Jaffe Foundation. I also wish to thank my agent, Leigh Feldman, my editor, Reagan Arthur, and my teacher and friend Jill McCorkle for their encouragement and support.
My thanks go out to my teachers at Harvard and New York University, and to all the friends and family who made this book possible.

CONTENTS

CONTENTS

FLYING LEAP

DOG DAYS

The man in the dog suit whines outside the door.

"Again?" sighs my mother.

"Where's my gun?" says my dad.

"We'll take care of it this time," my older brothers say.

They go outside. We hear the shouts and the scuffle, and whimpers as he crawls away up the street.

My brothers come back in. "That takes care of *that*," they say, rubbing their hands together.

"Damn nutcase," my dad growls.

But the next day he is back. His dog suit is shabby. The zipper's gone; the front's held together with safety pins. He looks like a mutt. His tongue is flat and pink like a slice of bologna. He pants at me.

"Mom," I call, "he's back."

My mother sighs, then comes to the door and looks at him. He cocks his head at her. "Oh, look at him, he looks hungry," my mother says. "He looks sad."

I say, "He smells."

"No collar," says my mother. "He must be a stray."

"Mother," I say. "He's a man in a dog suit."

He sits up and begs.

My mother doesn't look at me. She reaches out and strokes the man's head. He blinks at her longingly. "Go get a plate," she tells me. "See what you can dig out of the garbage."

"Dad's going to be mad," I say.

"Just do it," she says.

So I do it, because I have no excuses, there's nothing left to do, no school, no nothing. No place to go. People don't leave their houses. They sit and peer out the windows and wait. Outside it's perfectly quiet, no crickets, no katydids.

I go back to the door and lay the plate on the stoop. My mother and I watch as he buries his face in the dirty scraps. He licks the plate clean and looks up at us.

"Good dog," my mother says.

"He's a *man*," I say. "Some retard-weirdo."

He leans against my mother's leg.

My mother doesn't even look at me. "Not a word to your father, Lisa," she says, and she goes inside and slams the door.

I sit down on the stoop. The man sits next to me. He smells dirty and sweet, like garbage on a hot day. His eyes are big and brown. His face is lost in tangled hair. He scratches himself. I sit there and breathe his smell and wonder if he has fleas. Finally I reach out and touch his head. The fur is matted and stiff. I touch a ragged ear, then give it a yank. He doesn't even blink. Of course. It's not his real ear. I pat his head, and stroke it, and his eyes sort of melt and blur on me the way a dog's eyes will when he's happy.

Then I stop and give him a shove, then a kick, then I chase him away so my father won't find him when he comes home from hunting.

It is so deathly quiet. I can hear him panting, his four-legged scamper scuttling on the sidewalk for a long time.

*   *   *

Last February was when things started happening. The plant closed. That meant my dad was out of work and sulking around the house all day. He'd sit and drink in front of the TV, his face big and red and his eyes all tiny from the drinking. He'd sit all scrunched up in the chair, his big head right on his shoulders like he had no neck at all. He'd watch the morning news, the news at noon, the evening news. "Aren't you going to look for another job?" my mother would ask. My dad would point to the TV screen and say, "What's the use?"

Then March came. Some of the stores in town closed up, and the movie place, and two of the gas stations. No new stock coming in, they said. The government needs supplies, they said. Gasoline shortage. You understand.

April: My school closed early for summer vacation. So did the high school my brothers, Eliott and Pat, went to. For a while they enjoyed it. Then they got bored and tried to find summer jobs. But no one was hiring. Later even more stores closed up, and restaurants. Downtown began to look like a ghost town. For a while Eliott and Pat and their friends liked to drive around at night, smashing windows and things. Then gasoline ran out.

My friend Marjorie lived two and a half blocks away and I went there. Marjorie had two long ponytails and always thought of things to do. She taught me to hang by my knees, and how to make a grass stem buzz between my thumbs. Once we drew faces on our stomachs and made them talk to each other and kiss.

Then came June. The electricity went. No air-conditioning, and it was just beginning to get hot. We missed the TV. We still sat around it sometimes and stared at it like it might all of a sudden come to life. Then one night Dad got angry and kicked the glass screen in. Now he sits and reads the paper—every word of it, even the ads.

It's all because of the war, they say. Roads are closed off. For government use only. And the power—they say the government shut it off so the enemy can't trace it with their radars and bomb us. I think the government's hoarding it for themselves; they're all holed up in Washington watching TV, one giant slumber party.

There's nothing to do; it's deathly quiet. No cars running since the gasoline ran out. People stay in their houses now. Nobody goes out. When you do, you can see people watching you from their windows, from behind curtains, all up and down the street. Everyone sits and waits. That's the worst of it, sitting and waiting. For what? The attack? Should we look at the sky? Should we look down the road? Dad keeps the news in the paper to himself. The government delivers the paper, once a week. Dad says you can't believe a word of it anyway. But still he reads it and chews his lip.

I have nothing to do because Marjorie is gone. Her family went to stay with her grandmother who lives in the city. They left in June, just before the roads closed. These days my dad says I should stay near the house, but when he is away, I walk over to Marjorie's old house and just look at it. I'm afraid to hang by my knees without her. I might fall on my head.

The worst of it is the animals. Sometime in July, they all went away, every one. You don't think about it really, until they're gone. Then the silence. No birds singing. No squirrels doing acrobatics in the trees or knocking in the attic. Even the crickets—gone. The pets have disappeared. My mother's cat, Polka Dot, wandered off long ago. She cried about it for days. Pets that couldn't get out died in their cages. My pet goldfish, belly-up in the bowl. Are they all dead, all those missing animals? Or did they all go somewhere else, a great exodus in the middle of the night? The flock, the pack, the herd, the horde of them. Two by two down the road? To somewhere safe? We'll never know.

"Rats deserting a sinking ship," says my dad. "They know something we don't know."

So we wait and watch the skies, watch the roads, watch the ground—who knows, they could tunnel straight through the earth and surprise us that way, where we least expect it. Technology, the technology can do anything these days, my father says. I picture technology as a big transformer robot crushing cities, slicing the sky. Germ warfare, Dad warns us. When I drink water, I try to filter it through my teeth, screen out the germs. Surely they are big germs, heavily armed. We try to hold our breath.

I think radiation, when it comes, will rain down glowing like the juice inside neon signs.

No one seems to know who we're fighting. Pat says it could be anyone. America has been number one for too long, and now all the little countries are ganging up on us. Anyone could be an enemy. Your next-door neighbor could be a spy.

Pat says, "Your own *sister* could be a spy, even."

"Am *not*," I say, and hit him in the gut.

"I was just *kidding*, sport," he says, and whacks me a hard one. Pat has straight greasy brown hair. It hangs in his face. He hasn't had a haircut for a long time.

Eliott doesn't like to talk about who we're fighting. He is almost old enough to get drafted. My dad says they haven't started drafting people yet, but they may, soon. He keeps telling Eliott to walk around barefoot all the time, so then maybe he'll develop flat feet and they won't want him in the army. I can't tell anymore when my dad is kidding. His eyes are always shiny. He watches us all without blinking. My mother says he has begun to grind his teeth in his sleep, keeping her up all night.

In August the beggars started coming around. My mom calls them unfortunates; my dad calls them bums. They don't have anywhere to live; they don't get government rations. They came wandering from I don't know where. First they came around asking for work, a night in the garage. Now they ask for food, scraps, even a glass of water. Now there's nothing left, and still they come by. All they seem to want is the human interaction—a little attention, some eye contact, conversation. Even when you yell at them, they seem to like it.

This one is the dog suit is a new thing.

He comes back again the day after we feed him that first time. It is almost nice to see an animal again, even if it's not a real one. He's well trained. He sits up and begs. My mother puts a morsel in his mouth. He rolls over.

"How adorable," says my mother.

"He's trying to look up your skirt," I say.

"You'd better look out; he's some nut," says Pat. "Some crazy. Some loony who hasn't seen tail in a long time. Yeah, and I don't mean a *dog* tail, either."

My mother turns around and stares at him. "Where did you learn to speak like *that*?" she says. Pat hunches over and slinks away without answering.

I could tell her where Pat learns things. Pat and Eliott spend their nights sitting in the basement reading old *Playboys* by the light of the moon. There's a curfew now at night, so everybody has to be home, inside, before dark. Army trucks patrol the streets.

My mother strokes the man's head for a moment. Then she goes back inside. She finds things to do—she cleans the house; she keeps busy. We haven't gotten mail for months, but she still checks the mailbox. There's nothing to do, but still she bustles around all day, stays on her feet, is exhausted by evening.

My dad reads the paper every day, then goes out with his gun. He's looking for anything: a pigeon, a rabbit, a squirrel, someone's pet chicken. There's nothing out there.

Pat and Eliott keep to themselves. They don't talk to me. They wear the same clothes, day after day. Back in May they traded most of their clothes to a friend for some joints. I heard them talking about it. Now they wear the same sour-smelling jeans and T-shirts. When I go down to the basement, they chase me out.

That is why I sit there on the stoop after my mother goes back inside. I sit next to the man in the dog suit. I tell him things. He cocks his head at me like he's listening, but he doesn't really understand—which is okay.

I stroke his head. It is a hot day. His nose is shiny with sweat. He pants.

It must be hot in the dog suit.

He smells worse than before. His teeth are yellow and his gums are black.

After a while I push him away. He looks back at me, wiggling his stump of tail. I chase him away again. He crawls off, whining and sobbing.

I go inside and find my mother straightening up closets. "Why does he do that, Mom? Why does he pretend he's a dog? Is he crazy?"

My mother sighs and sits back on her heels. "If he thinks he's a dog, why can't we let him think that? If that's what he wants, is it so hard for us to go along with it? It's the polite thing to do, don't you think?"

"I guess," I say, though it doesn't seem *polite* to me, exactly.

"If he thinks he's a dog, then he *is* a dog," my mother says, in a way that means, That's final.

"Okay," I say. Then I look down and see what she's doing. She's sweeping out little dried carcasses from the back of the closet. Dead beetles or roaches or something. Dozens of them, curled up and hollow, legs in the air.

Now it is September. Now the man in the dog suit comes to our house every day.

My mother feeds him bits and crumbs of things. Then I play with him, tell him things. He is a good listener. I show him the bruise Pat gave me the day before, pushing me out of the basement. They don't want me down there, but sometimes I sit at the top of the stairs and listen to their voices.

I tell the man in the dog suit all this, and also about the limp dark hairs on Eliott's upper lip. And about the dark cloud that always settles in the room where my father is. I tell him about Rick Dees, my favorite DJ on the radio, before the power went out. Rick Dees, I tell him, has a slick, handsome voice and he must be a slick, handsome man, with sunglasses and movie-star eyes.

The man in the dog suit nods.

I decide to give him a name. Prince.

I tell my mother and she says, "Good. That's a good name for a dog."

Then the day comes when my father comes home too early and finds Prince on the front steps, and my mother and me stroking his back.

"What's this?" says Dad, his face going darker than ever. He's got his gun pointed at Prince, at us. His shirt is unbuttoned, so I can see the tuft of fur peeking out. Prince freezes.

"Oh, Howard," says my mother, "he's not hurting anything. Really."

"What's that you're giving him?" Dad says.

"Just trash," my mother says. "He's helping me clean up."

"He's dangerous. He could hurt you," says my dad, aiming with the gun.

"He keeps the other beggars away," says my mother.

This is true. Since Prince started coming, the other beggars have avoided our house. "Like a guard dog," I say.

My dad looks at us, squinting, like he's aiming.

"Howard, let him stay. He's not doing any harm," says my mother.

"Please, Dad," I say.

And Dad—I don't know why—cocks his head and says okay and stomps into the house. A moment later he calls to my mother to find him something to eat.

I sit on the stoop with Prince. We listen and wait. We watch the sky.

October now. We're still holding our breath, waiting. Nothing happens. It is still hot. Nobody tells us anything: how the war's going, or when school will start, or how many people are dead. I think the war is getting bigger, coming closer. No one has told me this, but I can feel the waiting, the tension buzzing in the air around my head like a hornet.

I think people are moving away. I don't see our neighbors peering from behind their curtains anymore. "They're dead," says Pat, "The government comes with trucks and clears them out in the middle of the night, when we're asleep." I think he's teasing. Maybe not.

I play in the yard with Prince. I throw the ball. He chases it, brings it back to me in his mouth.

My dad, watching us, says, "He's not a dog, he's a man, for God's sake. Treat him like a man."

But we ignore him. I throw, Prince fetches. We are having an all-American good time, just like Dick and Jane and Spot in the reader. After my dad leaves, I sing all of Rick Dees's favorite songs for Prince. Prince likes that. He barks with me.

I tell Prince all kinds of things. I know he won't laugh, like Eliott, or punch me, like Pat does. He presses against me, all warm and furry. He would never hurt me. I am taller than he is anyway.

His face is so kind: warm, wet, blank eyes.

I have little pink bumps on my legs. Fleabites, I think, but I won't tell my mother.

"If he ever hurts you, tell me right away," says my dad.

Prince would never hurt me.

My dad thinks everybody thinks like him.

One day I see my dad in the yard, talking to Prince. "You're a human being, for God's sake. Stand up like a man. Listen to me! Take off that Halloween costume shit. I'll give you my own clothes if you'll take it off and stand up like a man and talk to me. I know you can talk. Come here, you." And he grabs for the dog suit, tries to pull it off. Prince runs away.

One night Eliott says, "Well, you know what they say. Man's best friend."

Pat says, "Don't let him touch you. You want to end up with a litter of puppies?"

He and Eliott snigger and lean in together, their faces all twisted. Pat's face is rotten with pimples. He doesn't have any cream to put on them, so they are getting worse and worse.

Sometimes at night I creep downstairs and out on the porch, and

Prince is there sleeping or waiting. I curl up beside him and bury my face in the rough, sick-smelling fur. Prince gives my hand a lick. That is his way of saying good night.

November: The army trucks, with their ration packages and bottles of water, stop coming.

The sky is a curdled yellow color. It seems like most of our neighbors have gone on vacation, or died or disappeared or moved away, or something.

We seem to be losing.

The silence is deafening.

In December Eliott and Pat break into some houses at night, looking for food. An army patrol brings them back. If they do something like this again, they will be taken away for good.

"Taken away where?" I say. No one will tell me.

My father has a dark look all the time now, as if a black mildew is growing and spreading on him.

"Maybe it wouldn't be so bad, to get out of this shithole," says Pat. But he and Eliott stay in at night.

There is nothing to eat. My mother has scoured the house. She tries making us a salad of grass and things. It makes me throw up.

I find a bottle of Flintstones chewable vitamins in the back of my drawer. I don't want to share. I eat a whole handful and it gives me a horrible stomachache.

My legs are nice and thin now. And my bones stick out of my face in a nice way. I look like the models in the magazines. I know this because I spend a lot of time in my room now, looking in the mirror. I don't want to be with my parents, or Pat or Eliott, so I sit with the mirror to keep me company. The mirror behaves. We have conversations. Sometimes if I squint really hard into the mirror, I can see Marjorie there, in the mirror room, smiling at me.

I've been writing things down in my diary, month after month. I'm beginning to lose track of the days. They all run together. I remember when every day was different: Monday was music day at school; Wednesday I had piano lessons; Friday I went to Marjorie's house. Now they are all the same.

Sometimes I look in my closet and it surprises me to see all the clothes hanging there. Now I always wear the same shirt, and some pants all bunched up with a belt. There's no reason to change. I remember my mother used to yell at me to put on clean underpants every day. Now they are all dirty and she is too tired to yell.

Every day I go downstairs and sit on the porch. Prince is still curled up there, shivering in the cold. My dad won't let him in the house. And Prince won't leave, even though we can't feed him anymore.

He loves me. I can see this in his soft brown eyes.

I scratch him and sing to him. His fur is loose and baggy on him. I tell him secrets. Sometimes I pretend he is Rick Dees and we are on a fashionable date in his fancy car. Prince plays along, though he doesn't really understand. Rick Dees and I have a romantic dinner at a fancy restaurant.

My mother stays in bed most of the time now. She asks that we not disturb her. Maybe she is imagining that she is somewhere else, someone else. But who else would she want to be? She's my mother, she can't be anything else.

My brothers stay in the basement. They are making plans down there, I think. They are stroking the magazine pictures, trying to pretend they are real. I know that by now the magazine pages must be all withered from their pawing. Looking at the fleshy naked women all day must make them hungrier.

Only my dad still goes out, every day, with his gun. He walks unsteadily, hanging on to things, but still he goes. He still seems to think there is something out there, something to put in the pot.

There's nothing left. There hasn't been for months. But he refuses to believe it.

Then suddenly it gets colder. Is it because of the war, because of a bomb? I wonder. Or is it just a very cold December? My mother comes downstairs, my brothers come upstairs, and we all settle in the living room. The bedrooms and the basement are too cold. It is warmer with all of us together, and the living room is better insulated. We hardly speak to one another. My brothers seem to speak by looks: They snicker suddenly, together, at nothing. And my parents speak with stares and shrugs. Me, I don't look at anybody; I stay in my corner with my winter coat and my blanket. Two of my teeth are loose. They shouldn't be.

I still spend a few hours a day with Prince on the porch. Most of the time he stays curled up against the side of the house, trying to steal some of the warmth. Once in a while he crawls around the yard, trying to warm himself up.

I'm too tired these days to sing. Just opening my mouth gives me a headache.

Prince understands. He is the only one who understands me.

Then one day I come in from the porch. It's starting to get dark so early, now that it's winter. I go into the living room and it's all in shadow. I can't see anyone's face clearly; all I see are their teeth shining.

It is so quiet. Then I hear their breathing, each one of them separately, like singers not in harmony. They are all waiting for something.

"I wish I had a steak," says Eliott, his voice strained and high.

A pause.

"In Africa they eat grubs and things. Maybe there are worms in the backyard," says Pat.

"You can eat dandelion greens. I've heard of a dandelion salad," says Eliott.

Pat says, "I heard in Korea people eat dogs."

No one says anything. I can see the room get darker.

Then my dad stands up.

"What are you doing?" my mother says. He doesn't answer.

"Where are you going? Howard—don't—don't—"

My dad is reaching for his gun. My brothers stand up.

"What are you doing? How can you even think of—"

They are walking slowly to the door.

"He's a man, Howard! A man! You can't—" my mother screams. "He's a dog," says my dad. "He's an animal."

And then I see the door swing open, see Prince lift his head expectantly. I see my dad lift the gun and aim. I'm trying to get over there; I can't get there fast enough—the air is too thick. They're framed in the doorway, my dad and my brothers, and beyond them I see Prince pause, showing the whites of his eyes, wind ruffling the fur on his head. Then he's running, galloping on all fours across the yard, his tongue hanging out like a pink streamer. A shot rings out, echoing in the silence, but it misses him. He keeps running, and then he's up, up on his hind legs, lurching away two-footedly, front legs pawing the air, and then another shot rings out, shaking the world, and he's down, down, splayed out on our front lawn, nose in the dirt, tail in the air, wind whipping his fur around, his legs quivering, then still.

I try to go to him, but it's too late. My dad and Eliott and Pat beat me to him.

They run across the lawn, the pack of them, and fall upon him snarling.

G U I L T

"What kind of son are you?" asks Aunt Fran.

Aunt Nina says, "Your own flesh and blood!"

"What your mother wouldn't do for you . . ." Aunt Fran goes on. "She'd do anything for you, anything in the world."

"And now you won't give just a little back. For shame," says Aunt Nina.

"Now I'm glad I didn't have any children; it would hurt me too much if they grew up as hard and selfish as you!" Aunt Fran cries and shudders. The heat is stifling, but she pulls her sweater closer.

We're sitting in the hospital waiting room, Aunt Fran and Aunt Nina and I. My mother suffered a heart attack this morning. An hour ago we talked to the doctors. They told us her heart is in bad shape. It's tired, they said, and erratic—a senile old dancer lurching from a tango to a two-step, stumbling to a halt and starting again. We're waiting to see her, the aunts and I.

The doctors told us her heart won't last much longer. Her old ticker is ticking its last, unless something is done. "What can be done?" the aunts cried.

"We can't fix it," the doctors said. "She needs a new one, a transplant."

"Then give her one!" the aunts cried.

"It's not that easy," said the doctors. "We need a donor."

The doctors went away. The aunts looked at me.

"Arnie," Nina said, "what about your heart?"

"My heart!" I shouted. "Are you crazy?"

That started them both off on what a bad son I was. It's impossible to argue with Nina, especially with Fran to back her up. They see no reason why I should not donate my heart to save my mother's life.

The doctors still won't let us see my mother. So we sit here waiting on the green vinyl chairs in the waiting room. It is empty, but we can see the ghosts of other bodies imprinted in the vinyl, others who sat waiting here for hours.

I sit in the middle. Aunt Fran clutches one arm, Aunt Nina the other. They wept at first, but now they sit grimly. A Styrofoam cup of coffee steams next to my foot, but I can't reach for it. The aunts don't care; they are amazed that I bought it, amazed that I can even think of coffee at a time like this.

Aunt Fran wears a bally sweater and sensible shoes. Her lips are pressed tight. She taps her feet nervously. On my other side, Nina licks her lips again and again. She has high blood pressure, so when she's upset, she becomes flushed and overheated. Even now I can feel the creeping heat of her thigh touching mine.

I try to pretend it's Mandy sitting beside me, clutching my arm the way she does at horror movies.

"I saw it on *Sixty Minutes*," Aunt Fran announces. "They put the heart in a cooler, a regular Igloo cooler like we have at home, and they rush it in a helicopter to the hospital, and they put it in, connect up the pipes—it's just like plumbing."

"You must be your mother's tissue type, too. I'm sure you are," Aunt

Nina puts in. "You're young. You're strong. You have a college education! Your heart is exactly what she needs."

"It looked like a fist—a blue fist," Aunt Fran goes on. "It wasn't heart-shaped at all; I wonder why. . . ."

"You shouldn't have started smoking, though," Aunt Nina says. "It's so bad for the heart. You should have thought of that when you started."

"But what about *me?*" I blurt out finally.

"That's what we're talking about—we're talking about your heart," Nina says.

"But what happens to me?" I say again.

"I can't believe he's thinking of himself at a time like this." Aunt Fran sniffs.

"*I* need my heart! You want me to die so my mother can live?"

"Of course we don't want *that*," says Aunt Fran. "Sylvie loves you so much, she'd want to die herself if you died."

"We can't both have my heart," I say.

"Of course not," says Nina. "You could get one of those monkey hearts, or that artificial heart they made such a fuss about on the news awhile back."

"Why can't Mother get one of those? Or a transplant from someone else?"

"Do you want your mother should have a stranger's heart? Or a monkey's heart? Your poor mother? Do you remember how she never used to take you to the zoo because she couldn't stand to see the filthy monkeys? And you want her to have a monkey's heart? It would kill her!" Fran cries.

"She's so weak, she needs a heart that will agree with her," Aunt Nina adds. "Any heart but yours just wouldn't, wouldn't do. But you— you can handle anything. You're young. You're strong. You—"

"Have a college education," I finish for her.

Aunt Nina glares and says, "Your mother worked herself to the bone for you, so you could go to college. She nearly killed herself so you could go and study and make something of yourself. And now what do you do? Out of college four years already, and all you do is sit in front of a typewriter all day, call yourself a writer, smoke those cigarettes, never get a haircut—"

"And the first time your mother needs you, you turn your back on her!" Aunt Fran finishes. They both tighten their grips on my arms.

I don't remember ever wanting to go to college; it had seemed like my mother's idea all along. I went because I thought it would make her happy.

"I do things for Mother all the time—" I begin.

"Only half the things any normal son would do. And I thought you were raised to be better than an average son!" Aunt Fran huffs.

"Oh, Isaac must be just turning over in his grave right now," her sister moans. Isaac is my father. I never knew him.

"You're so lucky. I wish I'd had the chance to save my poor mother," Aunt Fran says.

One of the doctors appears at the end of the hall. As he approaches, my aunts rise, pulling me with them. "Is she all right?" demands Fran when he is still twenty feet away.

"We've found a donor!" Nina announces.

The doctor greets us. He is a small man, completely bald. The eyes, behind thick glasses, are sad. He strokes his scalp as he talks, savoring the feel of it.

"She's all right. She's being monitored," he said. "We will look for a donor, but there's a long waiting list."

"We've got a donor. Sylvie's son. He's in the prime of health," Aunt Nina says.

"This is Arnie," Fran explains.

The doctor studies me carefully.

"Surely you don't do that sort of thing?" I say incredulously.

He gazes at me. "It's very rare, very rare indeed that a son will be so good as to donate his heart. In a few cases it has been done. But it's so rare to find such a son. A rare and beautiful thing." He takes off his glasses and polishes them on his sleeve. Without them, his eyes are small, piggish.

He puts them back on and his eyes are sad and soulful once more. "You must love your mother very much," he says, gripping my shoulder with a firm hand.

"Oh, he does," Fran says. I shift my feet and knock over the cup of coffee and it spills on the floor, a sudden ugly brownness spreading over the empty white.

A nurse leads us to the intensive care unit, where my mother is lying attached to machines and bags of fluid. The room has no outside windows. There is an inner window, through which I can see a nurses' station, where they are watching our every move.

Aunt Fran rushes to one side of the bed, Aunt Nina the other. I shuffle awkwardly at the foot of the bed. I touch my mother's feet.

"Sylvie!" "Are you all right?" the aunts cry. They are afraid to touch her because of the tubes snaking into her arms, the needles held by strips of tape.

My mother opens her eyes. There are purple circles around them. She looks pale, but not so different from usual. Hardly on the verge of death. "I'm fine," she says, gazing at them.

I look at them, the three sisters. To me, the aunts are just variations on my mother. Fran, the oldest, is like my mother, only stretched— tall, hair strained tightly back, thin drawn-on eyebrows, cheekbones jutting up under the skin, long front teeth resting on the lower lip. And Nina is my mother plus some extra—her cheeks are full, her chin sags, and her eyes are heavy-lidded.

My mother is just my mother. Not a young woman, but not an old one. Gray hair spread on the pillow. She's young for a heart attack, I suppose; she's still got many years to go. She smiles dully at her sisters. "Oh, Sylvie, you look wonderful! Just the same!" they say. Then she raises her eyes to me.

"Oh, Arnie, you look terrible," she says. "That jacket—I told you to throw it away. I'll find you another. There's no reason to go around looking like a mess."

"Arnie has some good news," Nina says.

"Then why does he look like a thundercloud?" says my mother. "Arnie, is something bothering you?"

Fran says, "Arnie wants to give you his heart."

"I never said that—" I cry.

There is a pause.

"Of course, Arnie, you shouldn't. You don't need to do that for me. Really you don't," my mother says. She looks terribly sad. The aunts' faces have gone stony.

"You have your whole life ahead of you, after all," my mother says. She looks down at her arms, at the branching veins that creep up them like tendrils of a vine. "I never expected anything from you, you know," she says. "Of course nothing like this."

I look down at her feet, two motionless humps under the blanket. "I'm considering it, Mother. Really, I am. I want to find out more about it before I decide, that's all. It's not as simple as changing a car battery or something." I force out a laugh.

No one else laughs, but the aunts' faces melt a little. My heart is pounding. My mother closes her eyes. "You're a good boy, Arnie," she says. "Your father would be proud."

A nurse comes in and tells us we should let my mother rest for a while. Aunt Fran and Aunt Nina head back to the waiting room. They sit down in the same seats and look up expectantly, waiting for me to sit between them.

"I think I'm going to take a little walk. I need to stretch my legs," I say.

"He probably wants to go call one of those tarty women he runs around with," Nina whispers loudly. "Tart" and "run around" are as close as she gets to profanity.

I walk up and down halls of dull white where patients shuffle in slow motion, wheeling their IVs along beside them. I can feel in the floor the buzzing vibration of motors churning away somewhere in the heart of the building. I take the elevator and wander through more humming white halls until I find a pay phone.

I call up Mandy. She picks up on the first ring. "Hi," she says. "Where have you been?"

"My mother had a heart attack this morning," I say. "I'm at the hospital."

"Oh, I knew this would happen," Mandy says. "I burned my hand on the radiator this morning, and right away I thought, Uh-oh, an omen, something bad's going to happen. How old's your mother?"

"Fifty-seven," I say.

"Ooh, that's young for a heart attack. And she wasn't fat or anything. I feel like it's my fault; I should have warned you or something."

This is how I met Mandy: One day last spring she got some take-out Chinese for lunch, including a fortune cookie that told her that she would soon meet a mysterious stranger in a blue coat. That afternoon I happened to take my car to get fixed at the garage where she worked. Lucky thing: I was wearing the old blue jacket my mother hated. Mandy asked me out to dinner right then and there. That doesn't sound like a sound basis for a relationship, but for some people it is. Mandy believes in signs and predictions the way some people believe in religion. She's usually right about things. She sure did a lousy job on my car, though.

Mandy's asking me something, but I can't hear because the woman next to me is sobbing Spanish into the phone. Mandy says again, "Where did it happen?"

"At the bank. She was working," I tell her. "There was an ambulance, and her sisters are here, and I got here as soon as I could. Mandy, could I—"

The woman next to me is screaming. "I need to ask you something," I shout into the phone.

"What—what?" Mandy's voice calls.

Finally I tell her to come to the hospital and she says all right and hangs up. I don't need to tell her where to go; she always seems to be able to find me. She says she just follows my smell.

I wander down toward where I think the entrance of the hospital is. I stop some stretcher attendants and ask directions, but I can't understand their English.

Mandy never gets lost. And she never has to wait in line. Strangers on the street talk to her. Jobs fall in her lap. She's nice-looking: freckles on her nose, good straight teeth. She keeps telling me that my signs indicate that my life will be on a big upswing soon and that I am just in a transition period right now. I hope she's right.

Lately she's been dropping hints about getting married. And Mandy drops hints like she's dropping a load of bricks on your foot. My mother hates Mandy. She doesn't put it that way; she says Mandy is "untidy," "irresponsible," and "has no future," but I get the message.

I finally reach the lobby, and just as I do, Mandy comes bursting through the doors, beaming at me. She doesn't smile; she beams. Not like sunlight. Like lasers. She has these eyes like headlights. "I knew I'd find you," she says. "How's your mother? Have you seen her?" Her breath in my face is like pine trees and toothpaste.

"Yeah, she's all right for now. Come on, let's go outside for a minute. I want to ask you something."

Outside, the afternoon is darkening to early evening. The hospital breathes and shudders behind us. We wander in the parking lot, among the cars, talking softly, like we're afraid we'll wake them. It's cold. The wind sends trash and dry leaves scuttling along the ground. I keep looking back to see if anyone's following us.

"They say my mother's heart is bad. She needs a new one. They want me to donate *my* heart. What do you think of that?"

Mandy stops, her eyes and mouth open. Wind whips her frizzy hair around her face. She looks shocked. I breathe a sigh of relief: at last, someone who can see reason.

But then she says, "Oh, Arnie. How wonderful! Can they really do that? That's so wonderful—congratulations!"

"You mean you think I should do it?"

"Isn't technology incredible?" Mandy says. "These days doctors can do anything. Now you can share yourself, really give yourself to someone else in ways you never thought were possible before. Your mother must be thrilled."

"But it's crazy—"

She takes my hands in hers and looks up into my eyes. "Frankly, Arnie, I didn't think you had it in you. I'm really impressed. Really, I am."

"Mandy, I thought you could be realistic about this. What about me? Do you want me dead? What am I supposed to do without a heart?"

"Oh, I'm sure they could fix you up. The important thing right now is to help your mother." She unzips my jacket and presses her hands against my chest. My heart twitches, flutters like a baby bird in her hands.

"What about *your* heart? If I give my mother my heart, would you give me yours?"

She draws away from me suddenly. All the lights in the parking lot click on simultaneously and her face is flooded with white. She presses her knuckles to her mouth. "Now that's not fair," she says.

"There! Now you see! When it's your own heart in question, you change your mind, don't you?" I cry, waving my arms around.

"You're not being fair," she says again, her lower lip quivering. "*You're* the one who doesn't want a commitment. You're the one who can't even say the word *marriage*. A few months ago I would have given you my heart, and gladly, but you didn't want it. But now . . . well, if I gave it now, that wouldn't be fair to either of us, don't you see?"

"No, I don't. Maybe it's time we thought about getting married. You could come share the apartment; we could share things—"

"Oh, you're just saying that. You're just thinking about yourself, what *you* need; you don't care about me. I think I'd better go—"

"But Mandy! Wait! What am I supposed to do?"

"Arnie, you know what the right thing to do is. You should get back to your mother now. Give her my regards."

"You hate my mother."

"No, I just feel sorry for her. She has a bad aura. She's had a hard life, and it's not all her fault," Mandy says. She pats my arm. "You know what you should do. She's your mother."

I try to kiss her, but she turns away and I get a mouthful of hair. "Why don't you call me after you make a decision?" she says. "Then maybe we'll talk." I'm reaching after her, wanting to grab hold of her hair, the belt on her overcoat, anything, but she's too quick, a few steps away already.

I watch her go. Brisk, determined steps, like a schoolteacher. "But Mandy!" I bawl. "Mandy—this may be the last time you ever see me with my heart! Next time I could have a different heart! A different heart! What about that?"

She doesn't even stop, just calls over her shoulder, "Who knows, it might be better than the old one."

I find my way back to the waiting room. Someone has mopped up the coffee.

"Feel better?" Nina asks.

"Made a decision yet?" Fran says.

"Yes . . . no . . . I don't know," I say.

They are both quiet.

Then Aunt Nina says, "She carried you for nine months. More than nine months! You were late. Do you remember it?"

"Of course he doesn't," Aunt Fran says.

"She didn't mind it, of course. She loved it. But it couldn't have been easy," Aunt Nina says. "She was a frail woman."

"What are you talking about?" I say, though I can guess.

"There was a time when her heart beat for both of you." She sniffs. "I don't see why you can't do the same for her."

"He said he's thinking about it," Aunt Fran reminds her. Fran turns to me. "Arnie, think about this: The heart's a little thing really. Less than a pound. It's just a muscle. You've got muscles all over the place.

Can't you spare one?" She looks earnestly into my face. "Can't you spare a little bit of flesh?"

"Your mother's dying in there!" Nina blurts out. She heaves a shuddering sigh, then another. "Don't you care?" she says, and then they are crying, both of them, drops sliding down the wrinkles in their faces.

My mother's dying in there. Dying? She looked all right just a little while ago, I remind myself. But I have to sit down. A coldness sinks and spreads through my gut. I want to call someone, talk to someone. I want a drink badly.

Later we go visit my mother again. She looks worse, but perhaps it is the fluorescent lights draining color from her face. I stand again at the foot of her bed. I can see the veins and tendons on her neck. So delicate, so close to the surface, you could snip them with scissors.

"Arnie," she says softly, "you should go home and get some sleep. And shave. You look terrible. So tired. Go. I'll be here tomorrow, I'm not going anywhere."

"You see?" Fran hisses at me. "Sick in the hospital with a bad heart, and all she can think about is you!"

Nina strokes my mother's head and tells her she'll be fine. I look at my mother lying there and I try to think of her as organs, blood, cogs and springs and machinery. I remember a time when I was small and she hugged my head to her. My ear pressed into her stomach and I could hear the churning, gurgling workings within.

"Go on, now. Get some sleep. I'll be fine," my mother says weakly, and closes her eyes. We shuffle out.

Fran and Nina say they will stay awhile longer, in case anything happens. I leave, but promise to come back soon.

I drive home in the dark. I go up to my apartment and turn on the lights. I take a shower and try to shave, but my body does not want to work properly. I stub my toes, jab my elbow, and poke a toothbrush in my eye. When I look down, my body looks strange and alien, hairier than I remembered, and larger. Looking in the mirror gives me a chill;

as I shave I have the feeling the face in the mirror will start to do something different from what I am doing.

I go into the kitchen and put a frying pan on the stove. I put in a dab of margarine and watch it slide around, leaving a sizzling trail. I think of eggs. Scrambled? No—fried, sunny-side up, half-raw and runny. I get two eggs out of the refrigerator. I crack one into the pan. There's a blob of blood mixed in among the yellow.

I dump everything in the sink and run the garbage disposal, trying not to look at it too closely.

I want to call Mandy. Then I realize I don't want to call her at all.

Usually my mother calls in the evenings to tell me about TV programs and weather changes.

I turn off the lights and sit in the dark. I look at the ceiling, at the smoke detector. It has a blue light that pulses and flickers with a regular beat like the blip on a cardiograph.

Early the next morning, at the hospital, I tell the doctor, "I want to do it. Give her my heart."

He gives me a long, steady look, eyes huge behind the glasses. "I think you've made the right decision. I do," he says. His eyes drop to my chest. "We can get started right away."

"But what about a transplant for me?" I say. "Don't you need to arrange that first?"

"Oh, we'll take care of that when the time comes. I want to get your heart into your mother right away, before . . . before—"

"Before I change my mind," I say.

He hardly hears; he's already deep in his plans. His scalp is shiny with sweat.

"Is it a complicated kind of operation?" I ask.

"Not really," he says. "Making the decision is the hardest part. The incision is easy." He claps me on the back. "Have you told your mother yet? Well, go tell her, and then we'll get your chest shaved and get started."

This is what I've realized: All along I thought I'd publish a book.

Lots of books. Get recognition, earn lots of money, support my mother in style in her old age. Give her gorgeous grandchildren. I thought that was the way to pay her back everything I owe her.

But now it looks like I have to pay my debts with my heart instead. Under these circumstances, I don't have a choice. I'm almost glad; it seems easier this way. I'll just give her a piece of muscle and then I'll be free of her forever, all my debts paid. One quick operation will be so much easier than struggling for the rest of my life to do back to her all the things she thinks she's done for me.

It seems like a good bargain.

When I tell my mother the news, she cries a little, and smiles, and says, "Oh, I didn't expect it. Oh, not for a minute. I wouldn't expect such a sacrifice from you, Arnie, I wouldn't dare even to mention such a thing. It's more than any mother could expect of her son. I'm so proud of you. I guess I did a good job raising you after all. You've turned into such a fine, good person. I worried that I may have made mistakes when I was bringing you up, but now I know I didn't."

On and on she goes.

And the aunts. They cry, and clutch my arms, not so tightly as before. They say they doubted me but they never will again. "What a good son," they keep saying. Looking at them now, they seem smaller than they did before, shriveled.

I call Mandy, and she dashes over to the hospital. She kisses all over my face with her cherry-flavored Chap Stick, and she hugs me and presses her ear against my chest. She tells me she knew I'd do the right thing. I'm feeling pretty good now; I light up a cigarette. She takes it away from me and mashes it beneath her heel. "That belongs to your mother now," she says.

They all give me flowers. I feel like a hero. I kiss my mother's cheek.

I hop on a stretcher. They wheel me out. They sedate me slightly, strip me, shave me.

And then they put the mask on and knock me out good; it's like I'm falling, falling down a deep well, and the circle of daylight above me grows smaller and smaller and smaller, until it is a tiny white bird swooping and fluttering against a vast night sky.

How does it feel to have no heart? It feels light, hollow, rattly. Something huge is missing; it leaves an ache, like the ghost of a severed limb. I'm so light inside, but so heavy on the outside. Like gravity increased a hundredfold. Gravity holding me to the bed like the ropes and pegs of a thousand Lilliputians.

I lie at the bottom of a pool. Up above I see the light on the surface. It wavers, ripples, breaks, and comes together again. I can see the people moving about, far above, in the light. I am down here in the dark, cradled in the algae. Curious fish nibble my eyelashes.

After a while I see a smooth pink face above me. The doctor? "Arnie," he says. "The operation went very well. Your mother is doing wonderfully. She loves the new heart." His words begin far away and drift closer, growing louder and louder, until they plunk down next to me like pebbles.

"Arnie," he calls. The pool's surface shivers. His face balloons, shrinks to a dot, then unfolds itself. "Arnie, about you—we're having a little trouble. There's a shortage of spare hearts in this country right now. We're looking for some kind of replacement. But don't worry, you'll be fine."

Later I see Aunt Fran and Aunt Nina. They lean close; they're huge. Their faces bleed and run together like wet watercolors. "Your mother's doing so well!" they call. "She loves you. Oh, she's so excited. She'll be in to see you soon!"

And later it's my mother gliding in, her face pink, her hair curled. "Arnie . . . Arnie . . . you good boy . . ." she calls, and then they wheel her out.

They leave me alone for a long time. I lie in the deep. It sways me like a hammock. There is a deep, low humming all around, like whales moaning. My mother does not visit again. When do I get to go out and play?

Alone in the dark, no footsteps, no click of the light switch.

Then the doctor looms above me. "Your mother," he says, "is not doing well. The heart does not fit as well as we thought. It's a bit too small." He turns away, then leans over again. "As for you, we're working on it. There's nothing available at the moment. But don't worry."

And then Fran and Nina are back. "How could you?" they scream, their voices shattering the surface into fragments. "Giving your mother a bad heart. How could you? What kind of son are you? She's dying—your mother's dying, all because of you." They weep together.

For a long time no one comes. I know without anyone telling me that my mother is dead. It is my heart. When it ceases to beat, I know. A high keening rises from the depths.

The doctor comes to tell me how sorry he is. "She was doing so well at first. But then it turned out the heart just wasn't enough. I tell you, though, she was thinking of you when she died. She asked for you." He sits quietly for a moment. "We haven't managed to find a heart for you. But you'll be fine. We've shot you up full of preservatives. You'll stay fresh for a while yet." He goes away.

Aunt Fran and Aunt Nina no longer visit.

Mandy? Gone.

I lie listening to the emptiness in my chest, like wind wailing through canyons.

These days the doctor comes in often to chat with me.

One day he tells me a story: "You know, when your mother died, we managed to save your heart. It was still healthy. We thought about giving it back to you. But there was a little girl here, about eight years old, and she needed a new heart, too. Cute little blond girl. One time a basketball star came here to visit her and there were TV cameras and photographers and everything. She was in the papers a lot. Kids were always sending her cards. Anyway, we decided to give her your heart. She's only a kid, after all; she's got a whole life ahead of her. Why should we deny her that? I'm sure your mother would have wanted it that way. She was such a caring, selfless woman. I'm sure deep down *you* want her to have it, too, don't you?"

Of course I do.

.

SCENES
FROM THE
FALL FASHION
CATALOG

Our new fall collection has something to suit every woman. We've reinvented the fashions of the past to create clothes that never go out of style. Our catalog contains everything today's woman could possibly need, from lingerie to shoes to jewelry and accessories, as well as an easy-to-use order form on the back page.

I. PRAIRIE DRESSES
Choose from among several colorful prints in washable wrinkle-free fabrics.

The woman lies spread-eagled across the tracks, beneath the noonday sun in the middle of the prairie. The sage ripples in the breeze. Her breasts heave; the sweat trickles down between them. Her dress is lace-trimmed, scattered with flowers. The skirt rises, and falls, and flaps in the wind. A bleached steer skull leers in the grass nearby. Above, a vulture circles and stares with red eyes, cocking his bald head. His shadow passes over her face. Her eyes are closed; she doesn't notice.

The land fades into the distance, rolling and overlapping, like giant tangled bodies under bedclothes. The sky: baked, hazy. Thunder rumbles far away, It rolls like smoke, thick and uncoiling. A mosquito buzzes and lands, drawing a perfect drop of blood from the smooth inside of her arm.

I should add, I suppose, that her hair is golden, her cheeks are flushed, and her eyes are blue. But I think you know that; you have seen this picture before. You know already the way her hair blows, and her neck arches, and her body writhes against the tracks.

The metal of the tracks is warm against her wrists and ankles. The tracks stretch out unbroken on either side of her; they lie snugly against the ground's curve, a belt holding the earth's fat belly.

The splintery wooden ties prick through her petticoats. Her mouth is firm and resolute, but her brows are drawn and her lashes tremble. Flowing tresses, trickling sweat, relentless sun, woman trussed to the tracks. And finally a tremor, the slightest sizzle in the hot metal touching her wrists.

There. In the distance the column of smoke appears, like a tornado leashed and dragged forward by the great engine. There are whistles and snorts, the grind and pulse of machinery, metallic thunder and lightning. She hears the noise and raises her head.

The train approaches; its cowcatcher and round one-eyed face loom ever larger. The noise engulfs her; the tracks rattle beneath her. The engine man, with mustache, striped cap, and bandanna, peers ahead and spots the obstruction. Heavens! Word spreads quickly through the passenger cars. Frantic heads pop from windows on both sides; the news even reaches the heaving, bleating livestock car, where one cow is groaning in labor, a calf's hoof dangling between her hind legs, swaying with the motion of the train.

The train hurtles forward at breakneck pace. She stretches her neck in silent entreaty, but everyone knows brakes are useless at such a speed. The train roars onward. The engine man throws up his hands, then hides his face in his bandanna. The passengers must look on helplessly as the train approaches its doomed target. She stares up at the sky, resigned, expectant. Children kneel on the train seats to see better. The monstrous engine snorts and squeals and rears. Grisly death is moments away. The wind again lifts her skirts; her fair legs flash in the sun.

But wait! Far in the distance, there is an answering flash of white! The passengers shade their eyes and hold their breath.

Here he comes, on his silver steed, galloping twice as fast as the train. He emerges from clouds of dust: broad-shouldered, graceful, impeccably dressed. Tanned cheeks, strong chin, a smooth shave. Bright teeth flashing—they fill his mouth neatly as bathroom tile. The eyes are far-seeing, surrounded by squint lines. Thick curls show between the buttons of his shirt; he is blessed with a full head of hair and none on his back. His boots are expensive, his gun large. These qualities are apparent even from a distance; all the spectators murmur in relief. The circling vulture spots him, sighs, and flaps away.

He gallops hard to the lucky damsel. The show is nearly over now. He leaps from his loyal horse; he bends over her and drizzles her with manly sweat. The train passengers are treated to a view of his muscular hindquarters in tight leather pants. He snips her bonds and tears her limp body from the tracks in the nick of time. The engine screams past with a defeated roar. She reaches for his face; he cradles her in his protective arms; they share a hearty but tasteful kiss.

And they are surrounded suddenly by hundreds of cheering spectators. It is uncertain whether they jumped from the train or sprang spontaneously from the empty grasslands, but it does not matter. There is much cheering and cap tossing and backslapping. The man is borne aloft as a hero. The woman in the flowered dress is borne to the marriage altar. She is speechless, seems bewildered by her good fortune.

So they are married right there with much fanfare, amid the jostling good-natured crowd. He holds her tightly—a bit too tightly, actually, making it difficult to breathe—and his gun digs into her side. But everyone tells her how lucky she is, and what a handsome couple they make, and many pictures are taken. In the pictures her head hangs down, hair hiding her face. His smile is dazzling. What big teeth he has.

People find the whole affair so fine and romantic that they try to imitate it. All over the country, women are tied to every available stretch of track, usually by an obliging gentleman in black with a curling mustache. Then, in quick succession: sunset, train, white horse and rider, fade-out. The scene appears in novels and on movie screens, and all the viewers relish the heroine's horizontal wiggle, the train's shuddering approach, the happy union drenched in surging music, kisses for everyone.

Everyone knows the ending of this scenario. The funny thing is that almost no one knows the beginning of the story.

The beginning—you can imagine it if you retrace your steps through the story, rewind the film so that horses gallop backward, the sun rises in the west, and people's mouths open and close as they swallow their words. Backward to the time before she came to be lying on the tracks.

Our woman with the flowered dress and golden hair lives in a small town. She wears an apron. She cooks; she sews. She makes butter. You've seen pictures of this in your history books: the butter churn, and the heavy dasher, which the woman holds in both hands and jerks up and down until the cream breaks. She knits socks; she quilts. She smells clean. She is wonderfully domestic. Her mother has trained her well.

One day her father calls her outside and introduces her to the man who has asked for her hand. This man has a round, low-slung belly and a shiny wetness all around the mouth. He has brought three cows as a gift. These stand in the yard, ignoring the conversation. They are dull-eyed, coarse-haired animals. The udders sag; the teats are raw and chapped.

Her father looks pleased. Good milkers. He runs his hands over the heavy heads.

That night after her suitor leaves, she tries to speak to her father.

He raises his voice and slams his fists on the table. She goes to bed sullen but not cowed.

In the dark hour before dawn she leaves her home and runs away across the fields.

She runs to another town, but it is not so different from the first. She finds work baking and churning and pickling. But the town's women all tell her to pinch her cheeks rosier, fasten her corset tighter. The men all talk of trade and domestic animals. One day while sewing she is startled by a man's groping hands. She pricks her finger, and the drops sprinkle on the cream waiting in the churn, so that the butter is pink that day.

During the night she runs to another town, but it is more of the same. She moves from place to place, like a pencil following a connect-the-dots picture. With each town there are more horses and cows and dogs, and chickens wandering the streets. You might picture the swing-door saloons, the piano player, sneering men and shiny guns. Clouds of dust. Men who proposition her, who press and prick.

You can call her Caroline—that is a nice name and appropriate for the time period—but you could just as well call her Virginia or Evangeline, or Mary Lou; she doesn't care. You can stare at her, but her face will not come into focus. She would rather be left alone.

Eventually she tires of the faded towns, the men who bellow for their dinners and a back rub. She leaves the latest town and walks the grasslands. Here she comes: hopes dashed, battered, bitter. She stumps along until the train tracks cut snakelike across her path and give her an idea.

High above, the vulture with the sunburned head circles and watches her arrange herself on the tracks. She fastens herself to the rails with shoelaces and stay strings, tightening the knots with her teeth. Then she lies back to wait, sun warm on her face.

Of course the train appears, then the shining horse with its rider. The hero with the chiseled chin leaps from his steed with the train fast approaching; the spectators hold their breath. The woman on the tracks groans and thrashes in frustration. No one seems to notice her face; no one hears her scream at him to leave her alone, to just let her be. He tears her loose in the nick of time. The train crashes past, cheers and confetti pour from the windows, and as he holds her triumphantly aloft, she watches her own hands rise and reach for him, not in a grateful embrace, but to rip his eyes out.

II. CIRCUS EVENING WEAR
We took our inspiration from the circus, to bring you everything from sequined thongs to tent dresses.

One day my neighbor approaches me and says she has a date the following evening; would I mind baby-sitting her seven-year-old daughter?

Phil appears at my door on the arranged night, dressed in red overalls, scratching scabs. Her name is Phyllis, but she likes to be called Phil. She smells of childhood, of sweet milk and graham crackers. The hand she offers me is sticky. I don't know how to entertain children, so I've arranged for us to go to the circus.

The circus appears not in a tent but in a large indoor theater, which holds in the smells of elephant dung and gunpowder and the sugartainted spit of a thousand children.

I buy Phil a T-shirt and cotton candy. It is light and feathery on our lips, and then it turns to sweet nothing on our tongues. We eat it in handfuls until the opening parade, with the elephants and clowns and stilt walkers. The Siamese Twins. The Thin Man. And the Fat Lady.

The Fat Lady reclines on a float drawn by twenty straining horses. She rolls her eyes at us, too languid to wave. Her body is all one large rippling mass, rubbery and inflated. The features are lost in the puffiness of her face. She looks so familiar; she is someone I have seen or been in a nightmare. I take the cotton candy away from Phil and flatten it beneath my shoes. Sticky mess. Phil whines.

Next are the dancing bears, the dogs jumping through hoops, the monkeys riding motorcycles. The lion tamer does his thing in the center ring. He has platinum hair, meaty pectorals, a big whip. When the tigers and lions get too close, he cracks the whip at their noses. The animals have sullen faces and beautiful hair; they are sulky and aloof, like runway models. They drag their paws the whole time. Phil yawns.

Next is the Knife Thrower. He spits on his hands while his gold-spangled assistant straps herself to the round target, which begins to rotate. Her body spins like the hands of a mad clock. She wears a smug, expectant look. The Knife Thrower sweats; he hesitates, staring straight ahead at her bare spinning stomach and the rhinestone pasted to her navel. There is an odd tension between them. He begins flinging the knives, with rapid precision. The knives sink into the target, neatly outlining her arms and legs. The knives land between each finger and toe. Knife handles form a halo around her head.

The bristling target. Her dangerous smile. Scattered applause, oohs and aahs. For the final knife, he blindfolds himself, stretches his arms at the sound of a drumroll, then kisses the blade and lets it fly—straight at her face.

The audience gasps; hands hide eyes. Her body within its metallic outline is electric. The world stands still as the knife screams through the air; her head snaps in a sudden sickening way—and then a fanfare bursts out of the sound system, trumpets and cymbals. The assistant smiles more brightly than before. She has caught the knife in her teeth.

The Knife Thrower turns and bows to the audience. We clap uncertainly. Then the target halts and the assistant steps down. The applause swells; we all rise to our feet. The Knife Thrower we applaud merely for his manual dexterity. The woman we applaud for her courage. She is brave to the point of foolishness.

The Knife Thrower has a dark look. I'm sure that in the deep coilings of his mind is the thought that he would like, just once, to see a knife veer off course. He would like this, but he will never let it happen. Without her, he is nothing, a pizza slicer in tights. The assistant knows his conflict; this is why she smiles and thrusts out her belly-button bull's-eye.

The assistant now smiles brilliantly at the crowd. I've heard she once had teeth of her own, but after a few months of the act they were so broken and jagged that they tore her tongue and frightened small children. So the teeth were pulled out and now she wears false teeth like an old woman. The new teeth are flawless and indestructible; they leave little semicircles of dents on the knife blades.

The drama of the knife-throwing act has left me queasy. I stand up to leave, but Phil begs to stay a bit longer. She wants to see The Lady Who Hangs by Her Hair. I sit down again.

Soon she appears—the Lady. All the little girls in the audience clasp their hands and gaze upward. The Lady wears only heavy makeup and sequins in strategic places. Her hair is knotted on the top of her head and she clips herself to a cable. She leaps from the platform and hangs by her hair; she swings with a tight, strained smile and her eyebrows inching up to her hairline. She twirls high above the floor, then swings to and fro, to and fro, toes pointed, with a dreamy, pendulous motion. Phil is kneeling on her seat, entranced.

There is a terrible accident. The Lady Who Hangs by Her Hair is swinging and then abruptly she drops out of the spotlight. In a sudden flash and crinkle and crumple of sequins she is lying on the ground. Shreds of sawdust and elephant dung cling to her skin. I hear her harsh unrehearsed cry, and then she is whisked away on a stretcher.

A murmur rises from the crowd. Children wailing. Hostile mingled voices. "Ruined the whole show," mutters a woman behind me. "Great—now the kids will have nightmares," says another.

Someone says, "It was bound to happen. She had split ends, don't you know. They say she'd been putting on weight, wasn't taking care of herself."

A child's voice says, "Is she Rapunzel?" And her mother answers, "No, honey. In the Rapunzel story the lady sits in a tower, and her lover climbs up her hair. This lady here, she hangs from her hair her own self." The child says, "Why did she fall?" And the mother: "That's what she gets for trying to change the rules like that."

The lights switch on and I see that Phil has thrown up all over herself. The stuff is pink and smells sickly sweet. She holds her wet shirt away from her chest. Her face is teary-slick, but she twists away from me. "I want my mother," she says with dignity.

So I take her home.

A few days later I knock on the door and ask about Phil. "Still a little sick," her mother says, and eyes me suspiciously. She's wondering what I've done to her daughter that's made her afraid to get out of bed.

"Can I come in and see her?" I ask.

Her mother says, "No, I don't think so, not right now; she's very busy watching cartoons."

She shuts the door in my face.

III. KITCHEN WEAR
Aprons for every occasion.

Do you remember: being knee-high, living in a world of pant cuffs, skirt hems, and the undersides of things?

Your mother stands in the kitchen. She cooks for your father: *fondue, meringues, shish kebab, chutney. Gefilte fish, lotus, lo mein, ravioli. Tabouli, tortilla, moussaka, succotash* and *goulash.* Your aunt wears high heels and goes out at night. She dances for men: *salsa, samba, chacha, meringuee. Lambada, salome, tango, fandango, disco. Jitterbug* and *hokey-pokey.* Your mother holds the bowl tightly against her stomach; she beats and beats with a wooden spoon. Your aunt practices the tricky steps, heels pounding the floor; sweat darkens her dress under her arms and in a long stripe down her back. Your mother's tools are called *savory, relish,* and *sage;* your aunt's are *rhythm* and a roll of her eyes. Your aunt gives you the high-heeled shoes to try on; your mother holds out the spoon. They are hunters: Your aunt's war paint is the red on her mouth; your mother's is a dusting of flour. They have the same smell, the smell of desire, the smell of cooking meat. The trap is set: the sprightly meal, the spicy dance. Afterward, your father pats his stomach. A man on the dance floor pats your aunt's hip. Your mother, your aunt, neither goes to bed alone.

IV. TRAVEL WEAR
Versatile cotton and linen separates for the girl on the go.

I've decided to take a vacation. Someplace exotic and warm and far away. The sort of place you read about in books and see in movies where the colors are supersaturated and the focus crystal clear. Impossible fairy-tale things can happen in a place like that. I want to walk through the movie screen, enter another world through the portal of the metal detector in the airport.

I board the plane behind a troop of Girl Scouts. Their uniforms are flashy as those of dictators in South American countries. Berets and sashes, tassels on their kneesocks, pins and badges and patches for campouts and cookie sales. Handbooks, bubble gum, first-aid kits. They are fully equipped. They walk in jangling pairs—the buddy system. One girl has glasses. One has her hair done up in a mass of fantastic little braids. One looks retarded, with sleepy eyes and a drooping lower lip. Her partner drags her along by the hand.

I sit down next to a puffy man with a tight collar and sweating face. The Girl Scouts troop past. People bustle about, stowing baggage in the overhead compartments. Most of the bags are made of soft meaty-looking leather.

The seats on the plane seem unusually small and close. My neighbor and I battle silently for the armrest, both of us trying to force off the other's elbow while seeming oblivious. The stewardesses recite the safety features in a familiar litany. The plane takes off. The pilot reassures us over the intercom that everything is normal—the weather is good; the sky is clear.

The man in the seat next to mine says he is a shoe salesman, just returning from a shoe convention. "You wouldn't believe," he says, "the synthetics they have now. I've seen stuff that looks like leather, smells like leather"—he raises his hands, widens his eyes—"pure synthetics. Incredible."

"Yes," I say. The stewardess approaches, trundling her beverage cart. The shoe salesman offers to buy me a drink. I say no thanks, but he requests two Bloody Marys anyway. "If you don't drink it, I will," he says.

I hear the crackle of cellophane, the crunch of peanuts all through the cabin.

"What's your address?" the shoe man says. "I'll send you some free shoes."

"No thanks," I say.

"No, really. I can send you some samples. What size do you wear?" A quick glance down. "Seven and a half, isn't that right?"

"That's right."

"You know, you have nice feet. Nice thin ankles. You know what I always say—you gotta stay away from a woman if she's got thick ankles. Even if the rest of her is thin. A woman with thick ankles is doomed. Over the years, or maybe overnight, you never know, that thickness will start creeping up her legs, puffing them up, then her thighs and hips and stomach, and eventually it reaches your neck and fats up your face. I mean, not *your* face—like I said, you have nice thin ankles, so there's nothing to worry about." The back of his hand brushes my arm.

"Thank God," I say.

The plane suddenly swerves and plunges sickeningly; there is a confusion of running figures, a struggle, raised voices, a stewardess shriek. Three figures stand in the front of the cabin, hoods covering their faces. Each holds a gun so ridiculously large, it doesn't look real. The plane veers over an edge into a realm of impossibility, of bad movies, tasteless jokes, the evening news.

The tallest one says, "This plane is being hijacked. Please stay seated and remain calm."

Instantly all the passengers stand up and move into the aisles. Voices rise to a shrill pitch. People fumble about, push at one another. It seems they are not trying to escape; instead, they are all trying to retrieve their carry-on luggage. Then they sink into their seats, clutching their suitcases for comfort. Some, I think, are sucking their thumbs.

My head is ringing. I am in denial. I am thinking, No, this can't be happening; this sort of thing never happens to me; it is some kind of joke, a silly dream. I look out the window, and I'm aware, as never before, of the emptiness of the sky, and our incredible distance from the earth. The shoe salesman tries to rise; he bucks and kicks, panting, nearly weeping, before he remembers to unfasten his seat belt. He finds his case of shoe samples and cradles it in his lap. He remembers the Bloody Marys and gulps them down.

The tallest hijacker retreats to the cockpit, to talk to the pilot (or perhaps he *is* the pilot? Their voices seem suspiciously similar), while the other two watch the cabin as the hubbub subsides. Then the shortest hijacker gestures to one of the stewardesses with his gun. It is the blond stewardess, naturally. He leads her into the lavatory in the front of the plane. The cabin grows silent; we listen to the thuds and screams as he ravishes her, in the tiny room hardly large enough for one. They soon emerge, the stewardess rumpled and weeping, the hijacker, in spite of the hood, undeniably smiling.

Now it is the middle-sized hijacker's turn. He looks over the stewardesses, then begins walking up the aisle, eyeing passengers. It is silent except for the humming of engines, the sound of his slow steps. He approaches; I watch his scuffed boots. He is almost past me when I remember the Girl Scouts sitting near the back of the plane. Pretty braids, skinny legs. Lips scented with cherry lip gloss. The retarded one. I raise my hand like a schoolgirl, then undo my seat belt. It slides down my thighs and I stand up. He turns his head and gives me a nod.

We walk together down the aisle. He in his black executioner's hood, I in my white linen suit crumpled from sitting. We walk with a slow, measured step. I stare at the passengers as I pass, but the women look away, breathing small guilty sighs of relief.

To the back of the plane we go, then through a secret door and down a ladder into the baggage hold. It is dark here; the suitcases are stacked up in hulking, uneven piles. I can see a narrow path winding mazelike among the mounds.

The hijacker removes his hood and his black leather gloves. He comes close and grabs my arm, his breath hot and heavy with peanuts. His sweat is rank like the sewers of a foreign country. Without a word, he licks my face and starts to tear at my clothes.

I begin to form a fantastic plan.

I push him away—gently. I give him a big smile and take off my jacket, dropping it on the floor. The shoes go next. He watches suspiciously. I start to unbutton the blouse, retreating into the luggage. I drop it on the floor and walk farther into the darkness. He begins to understand the game, and follows the trail.

He finds my skirt next, then my bra. This he holds in his hands a minute, trying to judge its size. The light is dim; we can barely see each other in the narrow passageway, a dark tunnel in the middle of the sky.

I leave my slip next; he fingers it, rubs it against his face. I pull off my stockings. The next bread crumb is a glittering pile of jewelry. I can hear him breathing harder now, getting excited as he imagines my bare body waiting just ahead.

Next I drop a girdle in his path. This confuses him; it takes him a moment to figure out what it is. He holds it in his hands, trying to remember how I looked in the lighted cabin. He squints now, trying to see me. He is wondering if perhaps this woman he is following is older than he thought. Perhaps she is not what she seemed.

Next he finds the panties, and these reassure him somewhat. They are skimpy, silky; they have a certain smell. He walks faster now, perspiring with desire, eager to reach the naked perfect woman waiting just around the bend, splayed out on a garment bag.

I have not yet laid myself completely bare. I now leave for him: false nails, a dental plate, corn pads, contact lenses. A tampon. He slips and skids on this litter. It disturbs him, and his mental picture begins to crumble. Yet he doggedly pushes onward, still hopeful that his goal will be curvy and intact.

But I have only begun to strip down; I am peeling myself like a complicated fruit and leaving the husks in his path. So many layers: scrapings of makeup, blobs of cellulite, breast implants like two clear disks of Jell-O. Scars, tattoos, an IUD.

Now I begin to pluck out the deeper things, which grate against my bones and aggravate my stomach. The things that fester in my cramping brain. Barbed memories, secret thoughts, hairy hands, thickened skin, dirty secrets whispered drunk late at night. Abortions, braces, blood tests. I am plucking these things out with tweezers; I am throwing them down in a flood of tears and mucus and menstrual blood. Here I am: This is my pure center, the fruit's core, the inner nugget.

Down here in the luggage hold, I am unloading my own personal baggage and strewing it at his feet. And he—at the sight of this blinding nakedness, this shocking intimacy—flees, howling.

He races away, and I chase after him, scratching at his back with rough-bitten nails. He tosses the gun aside and vaults up the ladder. I follow after him, wild and cackling.

We dash through the cabin, past rows of surprised faces. The hijacker is raising his hands in surrender. I run faster; I am nearly upon him.

Then the shoe salesman leaps to his feet. He sticks his foot into the aisle and trips up the hijacker, who falls flat. I am running too fast to stop. I plow straight into the shoe man, who catches me in his arms. The passengers applaud wildly. He pushes me aside and plants a foot on the hijacker's rump.

I look down and see that I am no longer naked. I am as I was before—sheathed, concealed; only bits of my clothing are missing. Passengers crowd around. The heroic shoe man nods and beams, accepting high fives and slaps on the back. The captain awards him an airline pin. Children beg for autographs.

I twist about, trapped in the crush. My blouse pops open and men are staring at my breasts. The stewardesses are passing out free cocktails. People are dancing around with oxygen masks on their heads for party hats, the elastic straps beneath their chins. The plane dives and loops; people raise their hands and whoop as if they're on a roller coaster. The in-flight movie begins. I'm blinded by dancing colors. "You're blocking the screen!" somebody yells. The passengers cheer as the opening credits scroll across my chest.

Framed in the window is a sunset, with the words *The End* sketched across the sky.

And then suddenly there is a *whooosh*, a great blast of air as the hatch is opened. Everyone turns to stare. The twelve Girl Scouts, fully equipped with parachutes and helmets, spring out into the air. They're looking ahead, squinting, sunlight glinting on their braces. They float down two by two, holding hands. Sailing free and brave in the wide-open sky.

DIRECTIONS

This is a city of many faces. It folds itself into dark corners. It stretches out its fingers of neon signs and asphalt. It unrolls itself like a magic carpet. It changes from day to day. It had a heart that beats in the center, though no one knows where the center is. This is a city of paths and destinations. A hundred thousand people make their way through the maze. Their paths meet and cross; they leave their trails of broken hearts and bread crumbs behind them. They think their ways are secret, their desires unknown. But they are like the ants in an ant farm: Anyone watching from above can see exactly where they are going and where they have been.

Mr. and Mrs. Clark stand on a street corner. They are looking for the Theater District. They are visiting their daughter here in the city for the first time. They are to meet her for an evening show. She had offered to make arrangements for them, but Mr. Clark said, "What? Do you think we're senior citizens already? We can take care of ourselves, thank you." But now they are lost; they have wandered far from their hotel and the streets are unfamiliar. The boys playing on the sidewalk speak in foreign tongues. Some have no shirts; some have no shoes. Mr. Clark has a thick red neck. He is perspiring a bit. Mrs. Clark clutches his arm, not because she loves him but because her new shoes are too tight. Now Mr. Clark looks for a cab, then tries to make sense of the street signs. Mrs. Clark tries to ask directions of the boys. They laugh and call her "fat lady" in their own language, but she understands anyway. She turns away from them, lips trembling, and says, "We're going to miss it, aren't we? We're going to miss the show."

You're lost. Or you're looking for something. You're trying to find your way. You turn a corner, then another—no, that's not it. The streets all look the same, but they change their stripes as soon as you turn your back. You need a guide; you need a map. You walk with your collar turned up and your chin sunk in. The sun's going down, the streets are empty, and it's getting later and later. The something that you're looking for is waiting for you to find it, but it won't wait forever.

Gordon sits on the examining table in his underwear and a paper robe. His feet are very, very cold. "I'm sorry," says the doctor. "I have some bad news." "Yes," says Gordon. The doctor shows him shadowy pictures of his insides. The doctor points to this dark splotch and that one, and tells him a long, dull story about the microscopic things in his blood. "I see," says Gordon. "I'm sorry," says the doctor. Gordon says, "How long do I have?" "According to the statistics, you have about five to ten years. But they could be wrong." "Five years. Five years," says Gordon. "Five years or fifty thousand miles, is that it? Is that my warranty?" The doctor has no sense of humor. He is a bald man, all business. Gordon looks with envy at the doctor's bald head. Then he puts on his clothes and leaves. Outside, the receptionist tells him that his fly is undone. She is white-haired and wrinkled. Gordon looks covetously at the wrinkles in her face, the soft folds of her neck, and her twisted fingers.

This city wakes and stretches itself like a cat. New neighborhoods spring up overnight like tropical jungles. Old neighborhoods die majestically, slowly sinking to their knees in the muck like dying dinosaurs. The old theaters are the last to go, the gilded palaces filled with ghosts of music. They groan and settle and expire with a wheeze, and then there is only dust.

Natalie is a practical girl. Not about money or everyday things. She is practical with her heart. When she loves, she does it efficiently and well. Her heart is reliable. She has two arms and two legs and her hair is red. Just yesterday she lost something. She lost it to a man she thought she loved, and then afterward he put his hand on her thigh in a proprietary way and told her about his wife. Most girls would have slapped and cried, to have lost what she did, to a man like that. But not Natalie. She is a practical girl. She put on her shoes and she put on her coat, and she went out into the street and started walking. And she's still walking today. She's searching. She's a practical girl— she lost something and now she's going to get it back. "I'll find it," she says, "I'll find what he took from me."

You're still looking. You'll never find it. You know it's here somewhere, but this city keeps teasing and changing in the corner of your eye. You're about to give up—but then you look up from the sidewalk and there it is—the map shop, wedged in between the skyscrapers. It's there waiting for you. Low, sagging, with a mansard roof like a hat pulled low on the brow. MAPS—GUIDEBOOKS—DIRECTIONS reads the sign. What a coincidence, you say to yourself, that it should be right here, right when I need it.

"Five years or fifty thousand miles," says Gordon as he walks the streets with his hands in his pockets and stubble on his face. He passes the lit windows of shops: stuffed animals, grapefruits, shiny dresses on mannequins that gaze at him longingly. What should I do now, what should I do? he sings in his head. Quit my job? Spend my savings? Do I have time to love a beautiful woman, start a family, star in a movie, study Zen? Is there time to do anything before the time's up? Maybe, he thinks, if I don't have much of anything, it will be easier to give it all up. Maybe I should keep walking and walking, use up my miles as fast as possible, get it over with. Then I'll never have to know what I'm missing.

You're looking at the sign, peering in the windows. They're coated with dust, broken, patched with cardboard. What a coincidence, you say. But it's not a coincidence at all. It's simply practical. People who know where they are don't need maps; those who are lost do. So naturally, the mapmaker has situated his shop in the place where people are lost, the place where demand is greatest. The mapmaker and his shop are waiting here for you. He saw you coming; he put himself in your path. The map shop is here especially for you, like the gingerbread house in the heart of the deep dark forest.

"Look—maps," says Mr. Clark. He's hurrying up the sidewalk, mopping his neck with a handkerchief. Mrs. Clark wobbles after. "Surely they can at least give us directions," he says. The place looks deserted, some of the windows broken. He reaches for the doorknob. It is shaped like a fish and slithers in his hand. They push their way inside. And inside—maps. Rolls and rolls of them, on shelves, pinned to the walls, lying crumbling in corners. Blurred splotches of color. Thin tangles of line that trail into nothing. "This isn't what we need," Mrs. Clark clucks. "Can I help you?" says the man behind the counter. "We're lost," says Mr. Clark. "I see," says the man. "Theater District," says Mrs. Clark, and stumbles against Mr. Clark in her tight shoes. "Sorry, lost my balance," she gasps. "One thing at a time," says the mapmaker.

*　　*　　*

Two men, in a booth, in a bar. Slouching before two glasses of beer. Victor has black greasy hair like Elvis. Nick has Elvis's soft, pouty mouth. "Here's the deal. It's simple," says Victor. "Yeah," says Nick. Victor says, "We got the tools; we know the codes. It's a cinch once we get in there. We can take it all." Nick says, "Right." Victor: "But we're gonna need a way in. There's got to be a way." Nick: "Yeah." Victor: "Yeah, maybe through the basements? Underneath? You think?" Nick: "Yeah. Sure." Victor: "Maybe a garbage chute? The subway carries garbage; some buildings have a tunnel going straight down there." Nick: "Yeah." Victor: "Can't you say anything useful?" Nick thinks for a while and says: "Yeah." Victor grabs him by the hair and knocks his head against the table twice, spills the beer, and laughs.

Natalie walks the streets. She looks for what she lost. She looks in grocery stores and in alleys. She looks on park benches. She wanders through hotel hallways, watching the maids airing out the rooms and killing last night's sweaty ghosts. She watches the people leaving the movie houses with their eyes glazed and dreamy, full of distant cities and music and imagined touches. She asks prostitutes and drag queens if they have seen it—the thing she lost. "Sorry, honey," they say, "everybody knows once you lost *that*, you don't ever get it back." She knows that in a way they are right. But in a way they are not.

You go inside the map shop. Inside it is like a church gone to seed. High ceiling, stained-glass windows, a holy hush, the pews replaced by shelves. You almost wish it was a church. You would like that sort of guidance. Here are maps. Hundreds of maps in curling piles. Fantastic faded colors. Delicate lines across the paper like a lover's hair on the pillowcase. Street maps as intricate as the designs on a computer chip. Continents cramped into strange new shapes: a dog begging, a charm bracelet of islands, a centaur, a toilet seat. Maps in which sea monsters, mermaids, and watery gods are drawn where the oceans spread into the unknown. The best parts, you think, are these unknown regions.

DIRECTIONS

The wife says I should take a vacation. She says to me, "You should close up the shop, take some days off." I tell her I can't, but she doesn't understand. "Your back," she says, "you're straining your eyes, and your arthritis. You're old; you should retire." "This is my job," I tell her. "These people need me. What can I do?" "Let's take a trip," she begs. "Let's go to another city. You draw maps of a new place if you want." I tell her a new place wouldn't make any difference, but she doesn't understand.

The map shop finds Gordon. It seems to spring up out of the ground in front of him. He has been walking for days, nonstop, and he bumps his nose on the wall before he sees it. "Maps," he says. "Hmmm." He scratches the stubble on his face. He pushes open the door and steps inside. "Can I help you?" says the mapmaker. "Maybe," says Gordon. "I'm looking," he says. He looks at the mapmaker, who has wrinkles grooved deep in his face, marking his age like the rings in a tree. Gordon sighs. "I'm looking for something. A place I can go to. A destination. A reason to keep going. Do you have anything like that?"

"A simple street map," says Mr. Clark, "of the neighborhood. A subway map even. Don't you have anything like that?" Mrs. Clark says, "The Theater District. *Everybody* knows where that is!" The mapmaker looks at them blankly. "I'll do my best," he says, and sharpens his pencil. "We're going to be late," mutters Mr. Clark. Mrs. Clark moans, "She'll think we're getting senile."

Natalie goes to the map shop. She makes a beeline for it; she knows it is there. She's a sensible girl. As she goes inside, the bell on the door tinkles. She goes to the counter and explains what she is looking for. "I see," says the mapmaker. He looks at the gooseflesh on her bare legs and the blisters on her heels. "I have something for you," he says, and hands her a roll of paper. She studies it. "I don't see anything," she says. "You will," he says. "Well, thank you." She is as polite as ever, gives him everything in her pocket—a bus token and $3.45. He takes it with a gallant bow.

You ask the mapmaker if he has a map for you. He looks at your face and then takes your hand and studies the whorls and lines of your fingertips. His hair is white; his eyes are deep; his skin is dry and paper-thin. "I might have something," he says.

"There is a map for you," says the mapmaker, "but I don't have it. It's a map you have to find yourself." "Then can you give me a map to find *that* map?" says Gordon. "Sorry," says the mapmaker. "I see," says Gordon sadly. He turns and leaves, and the bell on the door rings softly after him.

"I need a map," says Victor, who has found the map shop even though it tried to hide from him. He says, "I need a map of the underground." "The underground?" says the mapmaker. "Yeah," says Nick. Victor says, "You know, a map of the subways and basements and things in the city. Infrastructure. Don't you have anything like that?" The map-maker says, "The underground? Is that like the underworld?" Nick says, "Yeah." Victor says, "Yeah, I guess. You got anything like that? Something for the neighborhood around the First National?" The mapmaker smiles and says, "I do."

Natalie steps outside and studies her map. Now she sees a line on it, starting in the middle and snaking to the right. So she turns to her right and begins walking. At the corner she stops and consults the map. The line has hooked to the left and now she can see it moving, bleeding across the paper in a decisive way. She turns left and follows it.

The mapmaker knows you. Some people say he can follow you every-where. Your shadow is like the ink spot the mapmaker traces to draw your path. Some say he has your future and fate drawn out in the lines on his map, indelible as the lines on your hand, and as he watches you walk the paths of your life, he is proud of his handiwork. You don't know what to think, but you look into his piercing hawk eyes and feel his talon grip on your wrist, and you are suddenly not sure you want to see the map he has for you.

"The Theater District," says Mrs. Clark, as if it will help the mapmaker understand. She leans against her husband. Mr. Clark clears his throat in annoyance. The mapmaker bends over his work.

Gordon wanders the streets, not looking for anything. He tries to remember his mother's face, the laugh of a friend, the dog that was a childhood companion, his toy soldiers. They are all gone, all lost. The streets are cold underfoot. He will not stop walking.

Victor and Nick wear dark clothes and leather gloves. They have made arrangements. They carry their tools and heavy metal things and ski masks. They follow the map, the map that the mapmaker gave them. They follow it down streets, down some stairs, down below the subway, through hidden passages, down and down and down. Past pipes and rats and blasts of steam, down into the underbelly of the city. "This map is incredible," says Victor.

Natalie follows her map. She follows the line as it wanders over the page, bending, turning, twisting back on itself like a restless sleeper. She's determined; she will reach the end. Her feet hurt terribly.

You take the map he gives you. You fold it in your hands and go out to the street. You decide you'll look at it later. But you wonder if he has, back in his shop, a master map with every person's life drawn out neat and indelible, all the paths that cross and join and separate, all the lives that run parallel and never meet at all. You wonder if he is laughing as he draws the thoughts you are thinking right now, to amuse himself.

*   *   *

Gordon stops walking. The world stops flowing past him. It holds still so he can look. He looks up at the buildings, so high that they nearly meet over his head. He looks at the neat lines and squares beneath his feet. The children playing on the corner speak another language. He is lost, and there is no map shop.

"What's this?" says Mr. Clark as the mapmaker hands him a piece of paper. "That will take you where you want to go," the mapmaker says. "I can't read it," Mr. Clark says. "Let me see," says Mrs. Clark, and snatches it from him. The shop is dim; she takes it to the door to read it in the twilight from outside. "I can't—" she says as the door bangs open with a gust of wind, and the paper is swept out of her hand.

Natalie is near the end; she can feel it.

Down stairs and ladders, through passages where the rats look up, surprised at being disturbed. Moisture drips down the walls. "This is terrific," says Victor. "We should be getting there soon." Nick says, "It's really hot down here."

Natalie's map has ceased to move. She folds it and puts it in her pocket and looks up. She sees a man sitting on a stoop, watching her. "Hello," she says. He says, "Hello. I'm so tired." He has a grizzled face and kind eyes. She says, "I am, too." She sits beside him. He opens his mouth and so does she and they talk for hours, gazing at each other and at the little section of starry sky visible between the buildings.

Mr. Clark chases the bit of paper as it blows down the street. "Damn it!" he cries, and runs after it, panting. "Wait!" cries Mrs. Clark. She takes off her shoes and flies after him, her breasts bouncing, her shoes in hand. She runs like a gazelle, in leaps and bounds, chasing her husband as he chases the paper. Mrs. Clark has found her balance.

Victor and Nick reach a metal platform surrounded by a railing. They lean over and stare into a chasm. Nick wipes his forehead. "It's so hot in here. Very, very hot," he says. "Shut up," says Victor. "We have to go on." "Down there?" says Nick. Victor says, "That's what the map says. Do you see a ladder?" And then a fiery breath heaves out of the chasm, bringing with it a hot burning smell and shrill screaming echoes. "Did you hear that?" says Nick. "It's the subway, jerk," says Victor. And the two of them make their way down.

Gordon stands and asks her to come home with him. She consults her map and finds that this is the right thing to do. She knows it is, but she is a practical girl and wants to make sure. They walk to Gordon's apartment. She takes off her coat and she takes off her shoes. And then he sees it—the curves and shapes and colors. He puts his finger on her arm, on a thin blue vein that bends and branches like a river. He explores the texture of her skin, the shape of her coastline, her temperate regions, the mountains and valleys that poets write about. She is warm and wet and dry and large and small all at once. She is a country he can live in. Here is a place he can be.

Natalie is a practical girl. She knows she has not found the thing she lost. But she has found something else, something better.

The paper blows, dancing on the wind, and Mr. Clark follows, cursing and sweating, Mrs. Clark skipping with her newfound lightness, and the paper leads them in a fluttering, flailing dance all the way to the Theater District.

You can't resist. You look at the map he gave you. You see wondrous colors and dancing shapes; everything you want is spread out on the paper, waiting for you. It is just what you wanted. And so you go on your way, feeling secure that now everything will be all right; the mapmaker has said so.

Back in his shop, the mapmaker sits over his master map, watching the paths converge. He smiles at your thoughts, and then he leans his head on his hand. He sleeps. He sleeps, and dreams of dandelions and tiger lilies that roar in foreign lands. In his sleep he reaches out to stroke them, and he knocks over his pot of ink, and it spills all over the map, and all your lives take a glorious, disastrous, unexpected turn.

G O T   S P I R I T

Question number 2: *What is your favorite extracurricular activity? Please describe how it has affected your life.*

Cheerleading, for the true believer, is no extracurricular activity. It is a vocation, a calling. I myself received the call when I was a mere novice, a member of the junior varsity drill team. It was the first football game of the season, third quarter. The score was tied and the tension mounting. Our boys were looking haggard. The spectators murmured softly in their seats. Someone in the stands tossed a ciga-rette onto the field and it sparked the dry grass on the sidelines. I watched the blaze, and that was when the vision came to me. I stared into those flames, and I heard a voice. It sounded like the voice of the announcer who called the plays over the loudspeakers, but I *swear* to you it was not. It was the voice of the Spirit. School Spirit. It called my name. It told me to take up the pompoms and megaphone and bring my message to the people. I was filled with ecstasy. The manager's assistant doused the fire with Gatorade and the game continued. But I knew what I had to do.

I immediately turned in my drill team uniform and tried out for the varsity cheerleading squad. My ascension was swift. I acquired the short skirts, the tight sweaters. I visited a tanning salon three days a week, I had my teeth bleached. I began at the bottom of the ranks but progressed quickly. Soon I was elevated to the second, and then the third tier of the pyramid formations. I learned the jumps, the cheers, the ritual of the pep rally.

During that first season, I came to know the thrill of leading the masses. We regularly incited a stadium full of fans to madness and hysteria. "Let's go, Westside, let's go!" we would chant, and they would repeat the mantra in one voice. I experienced the euphoria of victory, felt my heart catch at the sight of the blazing scoreboard; and I knew, too, the despair of defeat. After our losses my sister cheerleaders and I wept on one another's shoulders with mascara running down our faces. We tried to console our bruised brothers as they spit out their mouthguards and swore.

I gracefully accepted my new social responsibilities. I confined myself to dating varsity players with scholarship prospects. I bonded with my sisters. We had our own table in the school cafeteria. We held bathroom conferences, skipped class to watch soap operas, waxed one another's legs, raided our fathers' liquor cabinets at slumber parties, slept with one another's boyfriends. We spent our summers at cheerleading camp, practicing back handsprings, whip-backs, and slingshots (in both tucked and pike position). During our quieter moments we composed new cheers, heartfelt little haikus full of tender sentiments, which we would later screech at the tops of our lungs to the enthusiastic masses.

Those were the heady, early days of my cheerleading career. I felt invincible. My life had purpose and meaning. My skin was clear. The seasons passed. I became first lieutenant of the squad, second only to our intrepid captain, Bunny Beckman. I had a boyfriend with a car.

Then I got my own car. Then I dated college boys with trust funds, who wore chinos and loafers with no socks.

The squad became tighter than ever. Bunny and I maintained a strict discipline. We practiced two hours a day, followed by an hour of step aerobics or the *Buns of Steel* video. Our stunts were flawless. Our united voices could set off car alarms. I could feel the great Spirit walking among us.

Then came the fall.

Things started to unravel in September. Right at the start of the new football season we lost three cheerleaders in a stunt gone bad. None of us knew what really went wrong. No one on the squad is a genius at physics. Suffice it to say that at the first game of the season, we were doing a three-level "Eiffel Tower" human pyramid and there was a weakness somewhere in the structure. No one pointed fingers, but we all had our suspicions. I myself thought Staci looked a bit wiggy that day. School spirit was no match for the forces of gravity. The pyramid fell, bodies tumbled and rolled; several uniforms were irreparably damaged. We lost Bibi and Gwennie and Cat that night.

But the boys on the field kept playing, so we, too, had to smile and carry on with mates missing from our ranks. We bravely cheered through to the end of the game, but our hearts weren't really in it— we couldn't erase their memory from our minds, or the stains from the field. We maintained our composure, and our boys won the game 21–7.

It was a tragedy, certainly, but we couldn't afford to linger over it; we had to think about the future. We did not want to lose our momentum. We needed replacements immediately. We were forced to hold emergency tryouts. Plenty of eager hopefuls showed up, but our standards were very exacting, and we feared none of the girls would measure up.

Sadly, we were right.

One of the girls who tried out was a member the U.S. national gymnastics team. Corrie could do a great tumbling routine, of course, but her problem was that she just wasn't *happy* enough. She was a solemn girl with big circles under her eyes. When she performed the classic cheer "I've got spirit, yes I do, I've got spirit, how 'bout you?" none of us felt for a second that she *really* had spirit.

We'd all seen Corrie on television during the Olympics, sobbing because she won the silver medal instead of the gold. This was a double liability. First of all, we didn't want anyone on the squad who would *cry* on national TV; didn't she have any *dignity?* we asked one another. Second of all, there was the matter of that silver medal. Why not the gold? She'd really let down her team. Let down the whole country. We didn't want a loser like that on *our* squad. For God's sake.

Corrie looked terrified all during the tryouts, and she recited the cheers in a squeaky, strangled voice, as if her gymnastics coaches had snipped her vocal cords to make her neck a little more flexible. And her body was wrong. She was definitely thin enough, but she had no chest at all. You need something there, it's what people like to see. A little jiggle. You can't hold their attention otherwise.

When Bunny and I tried to explain these shortcomings to her, Corrie started to cry more of those big Olympic-sized tears and said that she couldn't help it. We told her she should have considered implants; lots of girls do it before tryouts. There's no shame in it. As long as you don't tell anyone. If word does get out, your social life is finished. We told her we were sorry.

We had high hopes for another prospect. Her name was Mei-li and she almost passed muster. Nice legs, great smile, good straight teeth. Excellent posture. She seemed to have the spirit in her. We were preparing to take her when it came to our attention that she was *not a natural blonde*. When confronted, Mei-li tried to defend herself by saying she was Korean. That's no excuse, we told her. There are rules.

It was unfortunate; we would have accepted her if we hadn't noticed the telltale dark roots. Even then, some of us were willing to let it slide, but Bunny declared Mei-li unacceptable. No bottle-blondes, that was the rule. Bunny was a real stickler; it could cause difficulties at times, but we all had to admire her fervor.

We were very excited about a third applicant, LaShonda. LaShonda had *style*. She had the moves. She had grace and panache. She looked fantastic in the uniform. She was unexpectedly strong; we were eager to use her as the base of our human pyramids. She said she was dating a twenty-six-year-old, which pleased us; it meant we wouldn't have to worry about her stealing our boyfriends. You can imagine our disappointment, then, when we discovered that LaShonda was really Sean, and had until recently been the star kicker on the football team. We questioned LaShonda, who burst into tears and swore she was on a waiting list for an operation. We hugged her, some of us cried, too, but we had to tell her no.

"Oh my God, my life is over," LaShonda told us, sobbing into her hands. But Bunny was firm. We had standards to uphold, after all. If we started making compromises, exceptions, then *everything* would fall apart. Without rules, society would quickly disintegrate and soon we'd all be living in the wilderness, eating rats and beetles, peeing on the ground and wearing stripes with plaids. At least this was Bunny's reasoning, and it seemed sound to the rest of us.

So when we learned of LaShonda's suicide a short time later, none of us felt particularly responsible. Some of us rationalized it as a sacrifice of the one for the sake of many. I admit I felt a bit sad at the time, and considered dedicating a cheer to her at the next game, but I had so much on my mind that I forgot all about it.

We eventually accepted three girls who managed to meet all our qualifications. Nikki, Sherri, and Tonya were thrilled. We put them through the usual initiation procedures (beer, branding, sensory deprivation) and then began an intense workout program to whip them into shape for the next big game.

We thought our troubles were over. We hoped the Spirit would return, now that our squad was complete.

But scandal returned to haunt us. We soon discovered that meek little Corrie had a vengeful soul. Or, rather, her mother did. Several days after the tryouts, Corrie's mother cornered Sherri's mother in the Lord and Taylor's parking lot. Instead of complimenting her on

Sherri's fine accomplishment, Corrie's mother shot her in the stomach, then quickly drove off to an appointment with her hairdresser. Sherri's mother spent the ensuing weeks in the hospital, in critical condition.

Sherri continued to cheer with us, but she was not half as perky and pert as before. Bunny forbade her to miss any practices or games. "The squad needs you, the school needs you! Where's your spirit?" Bunny said. We often caught Sherri hiding her face in her pompoms, or trying to disguise teary eyes with a thick layer of makeup. And when we lost a heartbreakingly close game to Briarcliff High, Sherri cried even more enthusiastically than the rest of us.

At first we tried to sympathize with her. "That Corrie," we'd say, "what a sore loser. Not very sportsmanlike, is she?" But soon Bunny ordered us to stop mentioning the affair. Sherri was bringing down the whole squad. "She's being awfully selfish, isn't she?" Bunny said to me privately. "Only thinking about herself, instead of the squad. She'd better start putting on a smile, or I'm going to put it on for her." Soon Sherri had to be relegated to the back row, where her gloomy face would be less likely to distract the spectators. We had to scream louder than ever to drown out her Eeyore sighs.

One night after practice Sherri begged me to go with her to visit her mother at the hospital. I went, against my better judgment, hoping Bunny would not find out. Sherri's mother lay flat on her back in the stark white room, hooked up to several monitors and IV bags. She did not look at us when we walked in. In fact, she did not do anything at all. It was extremely boring. Her hair was all flattened on the pillow, and she had no makeup on (and she needed it), and she was wearing a really unflattering gray nightgown. Sherri put her head down on her mother's thigh and sobbed. I wanted to tell her to save her tears for more important moments, like rained-out games.

Around this time we started to notice the change in Staci. She seemed to have put on quite a bit of weight, which is a definite no-no in the squad. She was having trouble getting off the ground; her Russians and split leaps and back tucks were beginning to look sloppy.

There was a puffiness to her face. She had changed in other ways, too. She no longer participated in the obligatory girl-bonding sessions on the weekends; she developed a habit of pressing her side and holding her breath.

Bunny decided to say something before the matter got out of hand. One day after practice she approached Staci and said kindly, "Do you feel okay? You look a little sick. Do you think you need to throw up?"

"No," Staci said.

"Well, I think you do," Bunny said. They looked at each other. "I think you do," Bunny repeated, "so why don't you waddle off and—"

Staci finally walked away.

Bunny turned to the rest of us and said, "I'm doing this for you all, you know. For the squad. We don't want her dragging us down. Or dragging herself down. Do we?"

We all agreed that we did not want that. Then we held hands in a circle and said the Mighty Westside Pep Chant five times, slowly and with feeling. Then we hugged one another and went home to weigh ourselves.

Things came to a head at the Halloween dance. Bunny came dressed as Pamela Lee in *Baywatch*. I came as Julia Roberts in *Pretty Woman*; I had these fabulous thigh-high boots. Lori showed up and told us we were both totally passé. *She* was dressed as Demi Moore in *Striptease*. Bunny and I told her she looked like a slut. We all had brought vodka in contact-lens solution bottles, and Lori had some of her father's coke hidden in her G-string, so every fifteen minutes or so we went to the bathroom for a squirt or a snort.

Sometime after midnight, during one of our bathroom trips, we heard moans, and peeking into one of the stalls, we discovered Lori's boyfriend (dressed as Dennis Rodman) having sex with Nikki (dressed as Madonna in the cone-bra phase). Lori and Nikki screamed and went at each other with their fingernails, and half the student body crowded into the bathroom to watch, and soon people were cheering and placing bets. There was so much commotion, with all the shrieks and moans and cheers echoing around the bathroom, that no one noticed how in another stall Staci (also dressed as Madonna) was busy giving birth to a seven-pound baby boy.

She put the baby in the trash, fixed her hair, pushed her way out of the bathroom, and went back to the dance floor. No one noticed the little body at first; later people said they thought the blood and gore were part of the Halloween decorations. It was much later that the police finally came and broke up the catfight and took Staci away for medical treatment and questioning. After they left, Lori and Nikki hugged each other, and cried, and tried to piece their costumes back together, and we all trouped back out to the dance floor and requested "Papa Don't Preach" by Madonna and danced until dawn.

So we had lost Staci. At first we hoped that after all the courtroom nonsense was over she'd be able to come back on the squad, but then we found out that the probable father of her baby was Bunny's boy-friend. That finished Staci. We no longer mentioned her name. We burned her pompoms and megaphone, and did our best to ignore all the hoopla surrounding her case.

Bunny referred to Staci as the evil in our midst, the source of all our problems. With her gone, the Spirit would return to us.

I wanted to believe Bunny, but I couldn't. Weeks passed, and Bunny insisted that she could feel the Spirit, flowing through us and lifting us during our chants and stunts. Some of my sister cheerleaders nodded their heads, their eyes filled with rapture. But I couldn't feel it. School Spirit seemed farther from me than ever.

It was the beginning of a great split. Bunny swore that the Spirit had returned, that our trials had brought us to a higher spiritual level, that the squad should prepare for a loftier mission. I argued that the Spirit had not returned, that we were deluding ourselves with false hopes. I thought that we should simply practice, return to the old cheers, and try to heal ourselves. Perhaps even hold a bake sale.

The rest of the squad refused to take sides; they wanted unity at all costs: team spirit, cooperation, squad solidarity.

By November I could sense Bunny distancing herself from me. She returned my angora sweater and my Spice Girls CD before I asked for them back. She lost four pounds without telling me. I realized she would soon try to sleep with my boyfriend; I immediately broke up with him to avert that betrayal.

To make matters worse, the football team was having its best season of the past twenty-five years. The team was expected to advance to the state playoffs, and possibly even win the championship. This cemented Bunny's position; she swore it was proof that the Spirit was with us.

Bunny's fanaticism was infectious. The rest of the squad followed her every move. When she jumped, they jumped. When she screamed, they screamed. When she flung herself into a round-off back-handspring double-tuck with a split landing, they did the same. During pregame pep rallies she whipped the entire student body into a frenzy. With her fist in the air, eyes ablaze, legs flawless, she led the crowds in chanting "West-side! West-side! West-side!" for twenty minutes at a time.

It seemed I was the only one not affected. I took part in the cheers, the jumps, the victory dances, but in my heart I longed for the purity of the old days, the ecstasy of my first vision.

During this time, too, Bunny began her campaign to change the school's mascot. She had chosen the phoenix as our new symbol and filled the school hallways with banners and posters depicting the mythic bird. Her reasons were vague; everyone assumed she was simply caught up in the thrill of the winning season. The local television stations began broadcasting our games; Bunny smiled fiercely for the cameras, light glaring off her teeth.

I sensed I was being excluded from something; my sisters whispered behind my back. I tried to attribute my uneasiness to the season: It was late autumn, cool and crisp, the dusk began at four o'clock and seemed to last for hours, a mysterious time with the trees like black silhouettes in the dying light; then a purple sky, a prickle of stars, and the voluptuous sighing of mourning doves.

Homecoming approached. The evening before the Homecoming

game we held the annual bonfire on the playing field behind the school. The football team set up a huge pyre of old railroad ties and newspapers, then lit it.

It was twilight, that electric, dusky time. Darkness crept around the edges of the field as the flames shot upward. Nearly all of the students and teachers were there. They stood with dazed looks on their faces, hushed and awed by the blaze. The band blared out the school anthem, repeating the chorus over and over. My sisters and I turned cartwheels, and I was filled with hope and serenity. All those people, united in a common purpose. And they were watching *me*. I felt the old thrill. I had veered away from the others. I turned another cartwheel, then another cartwheel, and another, and then I stopped and faced the fire.

I heard a piercing noise and spun around to look. It was the squad. The cheerleaders. My sister cheerleaders. They were cheering. *Without me.* They were dousing themselves in gasoline, marching into the fire in their flammable polyester uniforms. They were screaming for the Westside Phoenixes, ghastly smiles on their faces as their hairspray ignited; they lifted their arms in final salutes, windmills, Russians, whip-kicks. "We got spirit!" I heard, and "Victory tonight!" and "Let's go, Westside!" And then they were gone.

Afterward everyone asked me why I didn't join them. The truth is that I hadn't heard the call. Maybe I wasn't ready yet. But most people wouldn't understand that, so I just told them I'd pulled a tendon doing that last cartwheel, and I couldn't make it to the fire in time.

The team won the Homecoming game and went on to win the state championship. At first I tried to lead cheers at the games, alone, but somehow it just didn't feel right.

Westside never did officially change its mascot as Bunny had wanted. We kept the same mascot we've always had. The lemming.

I got back together with my boyfriend. "I hope you're not going to get fat now that you're not doing the cheerleading," he said. But he seems happy enough to have me. After all, I'm the only pretty girl left in the school.

Also I've been spending a lot of time talking to my dad. He's been encouraging me to apply to colleges. I think this is mainly because he wants to get me out of the house as soon as possible. I seem to make him nervous, for some reason.

"There are plenty of colleges out there for a girl like you," he told me. "Take your pick."

I said, "I'm glad the other girls are gone; now I won't have to compete with them for the best collegiate cheerleading programs."

My dad patted my knee. He laughed, and then he shook his head and said, "Sweetie, you are living proof that ruthlessness and stupidity are not mutually exclusive."

I'm not sure what he meant by that. But I have ways of making him tell me.

ART LESSON

A massive woman lounges, naked, in the middle of the room.

"Draw her," barks Andre.

So we do.

These figure-drawing classes are given twice a week in a classroom in the basement of the museum. Andre is the teacher. He wears tinted glasses and pants that shimmer. They cling to him as he walks, like the coat of a golden retriever in a dog-food commercial.

"Draw," he says as he walks the perimeter of the room, his heels clicking. "And think about weight. And volume. Draw all those curves. Look at the way the flesh hangs. Do you see?" He springs to the center of the room, lifts her arm, and gives it a shake. Her eyes narrow. We all nod attentively. It is the first class.

"I want to be able to look at your drawing and *feel* what's going on," he says, rubbing his hands together. "Know what I mean?"

The woman is not voluptuous. She is monstrous. She quivers and rumbles. Chins cascade down her throat. I sit near her feet. Her body is foreshortened so that all I see is the soles of her feet and then the thighs and hips and stomach rising in a series of bulges like a mountain range.

The man sitting next to me wears overalls and bowling shoes. He has yellow crust on his eyelashes. He mashes his charcoal to dust between his fingers. The woman on my other side makes practice strokes across the paper without leaving a mark.

We begin drawing gingerly, as if we are afraid that when we draw the parts of her body, she will feel a ghost of a touch on her skin in that place. I trace the shape of her breast. She shivers and draws herself in.

"Hold still," Andre orders.

Her body ripples as she draws in an angry breath.

"Change poses now," he says after a moment. "Don't just lie there. You're not on a beach. Pose."

We all look down at our hands. She heaves herself up and then kneels, her back to me. Her heels dig deep into her buttocks. There is hair under her arms.

After a moment she says, "I'm cold."

"No talking," Andre snaps.

"I'm cold," she says again.

His mouth is a thin, tight line. He drags a lamp to the platform where she kneels. He plugs it in and turns it on so that the light and heat fall on her body. The texture of her skin is sharply illuminated: It is all ripples and dips, like the surface of water. I can see the two dimples on her lower back where the fat does not ever collect.

"What is *that?*" Andre says from somewhere behind me. I drop the sheet of paper to the floor and begin again.

Her face begins to shine. She is sweating. Her hair is dark and bushy. It grows down low on her forehead like a wig that has slipped forward. Sweat glistens in the creases around her nose.

Drawing her is drawing gravity. No matter how she poses, the floor seems to pull at her. The earth pulls at her flesh even as her bones struggle to stand up against it. How can you draw that?

Only her hair escapes the struggle. It floats heavenward, and east and west, with a life of its own.

After an hour Andre tells us to take a break. We leave our easels and benches and file out of the room. The woman remains, sprawled unmoving on the platform in the center of the room. Her eyes are closed. Is she dead? None of us would ever want to put an ear to her chest, between the massive drooping breasts, to find out.

We scuttle down to the end of the hall, where there are bathrooms and a Coke machine. We can hear overhead the slow meandering steps of the museumgoers. We all have charcoal-blackened fingers. Some of us have Ash Wednesday smudges on our foreheads from brushing away loose hair.

We borrow cigarettes from one another and laugh in the strange, embarrassed intimacy that the naked woman has forced upon us, making us all feel exposed. We make jokes about the circus and Jenny Craig and the Rubens paintings in the rooms above our heads. One man tells a story about his girlfriend, how she can't have sex unless her cat is in the bed with them. Another man announces that Andre is cute. The woman who sat next to me says that she recently had a tumor removed from her breasts and when she showed her friends the scars, they laughed and accused her of getting implants. "They're gruesome scars, too," she says, as if daring anyone to contradict her.

We troop back to the classroom. We are ready, almost eager, to jab at the sad sagging flesh with our eyes and charcoal.

But there is someone new on the platform: a young man, a boy almost. Skinny, dark eyes in a sharp, pointed face. Pale, sickly skin and a smooth, hairless chest. He stands sullenly, hands on his hips, one bony hip stuck out.

"Draw," Andre calls. In a far corner of the room slumps a thick dark shape. It is our original model, swathed in a black dotted dress with red canvas sneakers on her feet. She is reading a magazine, her lower lip tucked between her teeth.

"Draw," Andre says again.

Every bone, every sinew shows, the boy is so thin. His body is pathetic, like a UNICEF child, like a concentration camp inmate. Dark scraggles of hair hang in his eyes. He glares at us defiantly. His nostrils twitch.

He stands perfectly still. Doesn't blink, doesn't seem to breathe. The only thing that moves is the pulse at the base of his throat, above his collarbone. The skin there flutters; it flickers like a candle.

He keeps changing poses, every five or seven minutes: raising his arms, twisting and bending, shifting his weight from one hip to the other. He keeps his eyes on the clock on the wall and his nostrils pointed at us.

His legs are hairy, almost furry. His ears are pointed. He looks like a faun.

He looks like the runaways I see in the park, those little-boy faces with world-weary looks, pierced ears and lips, smell of dirty underwear.

He has heavy scars on his knees. Scars on top of scars, as if he kept bashing himself in the same place. I try to draw them.

We draw him, pages and pages of him, dark figures twisting and writhing against the sheets of paper like restless sleepers. We are reproducing him, over and over.

After an hour he breaks pose. He stretches. He breathes deeply. It is very quiet.

None of us noticed Andre leaving, but he is gone. That is why it is so quiet.

Our model hops off the platform, his bare feet slapping the floor. He strides around the room, peering over our shoulders at our drawings. We shy away from him. We would rather not see him up so close. He is like a savage among civilized peoples. There are pimples on his back. He smells unclean, as I imagined.

We are embarrassed of our drawings and shield them with our bodies. We try to hide the deformities that our mistakes have given him.

He snorts disdainfully, arms folded across his chest. "Okay, now it's our turn," he says. His voice is a shock. Deep, grinding, not a boy's voice at all. We stare at him blankly.

"It's our turn," he says again. "Now me and Regina get to draw you. Right?"

The room is silent. The fat woman lowers her magazine and nods. She rises. Her folding chair collapses with a clatter. The noise dies. The silence aches.

Someone's stomach growls.

"Go ahead. Get on the platform," he says. He stands there, skinny and naked and unmovable. The woman lumbers up and taps the shoulder of the nearest student. He jumps up quickly at her touch, and she seats herself on his stool, before his easel.

"We can draw real good," the model says. "We've had practice. Now go on, get up there."

I look at the man beside me, then we both look at the woman on my other side, who crosses her legs. Crazy. But then, why not? We are artists, aren't we? We're supposed to take chances, shock people, be outrageous. We are liberal and open-minded. We're not afraid to expose ourselves and make a statement. Isn't that what art is all about?

What's there to be afraid of?

The thin man and the fat woman wait. They don't think we will do this.

One of the men is the first to take the dare. He pulls off his shirt and unzips his pants. The woman next to me unzips her dress and lets it pool around her ankles. Then we all follow. No one wants to be the chicken. No one wants to appear repressed or prudish.

The room is warm enough. The door is closed. We will experience art. We will prove ourselves. We unlace shoes, pull off socks, unbutton jackets and shirts and sweaters, then draw off the underwear in one quick swoop, like a leap into a cold pool of water. No going back now.

We approach the platform gingerly. We try not to stare at one another. The strong light makes some of us look shrunken, others flabby. We try not to touch one another, but that is impossible. It is too crowded on the platform. We rub skin as we arrange ourselves, our knees pulled up and our arms wrapped around ourselves.

The room is filled with our heavy breathing, like cows in a stable.

There is a buzzing in my head, a numbness, and I look up to see the man slipping into some too-big overalls, wrapping himself in a jacket that looks like mine. He gathers up the clothes and purses scattered about the room and then scampers out the door, the fat woman behind him.

The door slams behind them before we realize what is happening.

So here we sit, silent, still, wondering what happens now. The harsh light teases our eyes. We listen to the footsteps of museumgoers above our heads. We imagine leaving this room and walking there among the dignified, cultured, clothed people.

We don't move.

We glance at one another, hoping for a volunteer.

We wonder, Where is Andre? Was he a part of this? Has he even now joined the other two in rifling through our wallets and trying on our clothes?

Or is he on his innocent way back to the classroom right now? Will he laugh? Will he sneer? Will he walk in and tell us not to move, not to speak, to think about weight and volume?

How long will we sit?

How long before someone breaks away and escapes the room at a scampering run? Will we trust him to send help, or will we follow him down the cold winding hallways?

Or will we wait here until we are discovered? By a janitor, perhaps, come in to sweep up long after the museum has closed and the people have left. We will not, perhaps, be ashamed before a janitor.

We sit, our arms wrapped around ourselves, the platform rough against our skin, watching one another breathe, listening to the *thud-thuddud* of hearts. We will sit, perhaps, until morning, glassy-eyed and unmoving, surrounded by the debris of our drawings and attempts, until the door rattles and swings open and some early visitors meander in to gawk and marvel at the latest exhibit.

YELLVILLE

On Tuesday night Linda got out the tablecloth, the good silver, the good china. Her daughter was bringing a new boyfriend home to dinner.

Earlier that afternoon Charlene had said, "You won't like him. You guys don't understand about anything. Parents are so close-minded."

Linda had said, "You've hardly told us anything about him. All I know is that he doesn't go to your high school. I already checked your yearbook. You're not hiding anything about him from us, are you?"

"No, Mom," Charlene replied sullenly.

Linda persisted. "Charlene, he's not"—she tried to put it delicately—"differently *pigmented*, or anything, is he?"

"Pigmented? Well, sort of," said Charlene, and headed up to her room.

Linda gasped inwardly, and for the rest of the afternoon she kept reminding herself and her husband, Kurt, to be "tolerant and open-minded people."

So when the doorbell rang that evening, she opened the door, bracing herself for a black boy or possibly a Chinese one. She was so startled by what she saw that she blurted, "You must be Russell— you're not what we expected."

He was very tall and bleached-out-looking. Thinnish, and pink, as if sunburned. His hair was longish, unevenly hacked, and so blond, it looked white. He offered her a bouquet of flowers, the grocery-store kind, and asked, "What did you expect, Mrs. Harden?" He had large teeth, like a toothpaste ad, and pale, barely blue eyes with white lashes.

"Oh, you look older than I thought," she said quickly, and led him inside. She smiled brightly, her Realtor's smile. His hand when she shook it was strong and clung to hers longer than necessary. He was wearing a white shirt and dark pants and sharp-pointed, high-heeled cowboy boots with metal tips. Snakeskin maybe, or lizard. She shuddered.

"I guess it's the hair," Russell said as Kurt walked in. "Don't worry, I'm not going white already. It's just that I'm part albino. You know, missing some pigments."

Kurt laughed. "You can't be *part* albino," he said. "Either you are or you aren't."

Russell turned to face him. "Some people are part French or part Eskimo. I guess you can be part albino, too, if you want."

Kurt squinted up at him. "It's a medical condition, son. Either you have it or you don't."

"Well, I guess I'm the exception," Russell said cheerfully, and held out his hand. Kurt smiled a tight little smile. His wife jumped in.

"Dear, this is Russell Adams. And Russell, this is Charlene's dad, Kurt Harden."

They shook hands mechanically. "Great to meet you, sir," Russell said. Kurt's face was flushed. Linda guessed he was sucking in his stomach.

Charlene came clattering down the stairs. Lately she'd been sulky and slouchy, had taken to wearing raveling sweaters and chewing on her hair. But tonight she seemed happy, almost excited. She smiled at Russell, who bent down and kissed her on the top of her head, where her hair parted. Kurt glared. Savannah minced in slowly, keeping her back and head perfectly still, as if she was balancing a tray on her head. "Why don't we all sit down?" Linda said, renewing her smile. She could feel her teeth drying out.

Kurt sat at one end of the dining room table, his wife at the other. Charlene and Russell sat on one side, facing Savannah. The table was a long one and they had to get up and walk to pass around the butter and the salt. The prisms on the chandelier tinkled when anyone took a step.

As soon as he sat down, Russell peered around the candlesticks at Savannah. "Hey, over there. Who are you? How old are ya?" he said.

"I'm Savannah," she said. "And I'm eight."

"Are you a dancer?" he asked. "You look like a dancer." She was wearing a leotard and had all her hair strained back in a bun.

"I'm in training," she replied coldly.

"She takes ballet lessons once a week," Linda broke in, "but she wears that leotard and puts her hair up like that every single day."

"I'm learning self-discipline," Savannah said with dignity. She was sitting ramrod-straight, not allowing her back to touch her chair. She held her head up and her neck stretched out so that it looked as if there were a string attached to her head, pulling her toward the ceiling. "You wouldn't understand," she added.

Russell's smile faded.

Silence around the table. Kurt attacked his meat.

"Tell us about yourself, Russell," Linda chirped after a long moment. "Anything. Anything at all. Where are you from?"

"I'm from Yellville, Arkansas, ma'am," said Russell.

Linda, down at the foot of the table, nodded at him encouragingly over her water glass. Kurt sawed at his meat, his knife screeching against the plate. Savannah stared across the table, a milk mustache on her upper lip. Charlene bent her head to her plate as if she was saying grace. The silence stretched out like queen-size panty hose.

Abruptly Kurt put down his knife and fork. "*What* did you just say?" he asked, squinting.

"Yellville, Arkansas," Charlene repeated.

Kurt leaned back in his chair and laughed. "Come on now. There's no such place."

"There used to be, sir. There sure enough used to be," Russell said solemnly. He tinkered around on his plate.

"Tell us about it, Russell. What was it like?" Linda said, trying to glare at her husband and smile at Russell at the same time.

"Well, Mrs. Harden, Yellville was a real small town. A close-knit family kind of place. We didn't mix up in outside affairs. You know how that is?"

Linda was fiddling with an earring. "Why, yes, yes, of course, of course I do," she said.

"It was real small. Downtown was just one road with Dairy Queen and International House of Pancakes and a twenty-four-hour combination gas station/convenience store and a combination pizzeria/video store/tanning salon and a beauty parlor/antique store and a bingo hall/discotheque and—"

"A beauty parlor and antiques?" Linda said incredulously. "What do they have to do with each other?"

"Well, people had to make ends meet. If they couldn't survive running just one business, they'd add another. I thought it was pretty convenient for dates. You could get a tan and pick up pizza and a movie all at once."

"How could you get a tan if you're an albino?" Kurt broke in, waving his fork.

"We had a fire station," Russell continued, as if he hadn't heard, "and a miniature golf course/karaoke bar, and a graveyard, and the Hanging Tree—"

"Hanging Tree!" cried Linda. "How morbid. It must be a historic site. Was someone famous hanged there?"

Russell thought. After a moment he said, "No, no one I can think of. They only hung regular criminals, nobody famous."

Kurt leaned over the table. "You don't mean it's still in use?"

Russell blinked at him. "Why, sure. Why have a hanging tree unless you're going to use it? There's nothing like a good hanging to liven up a dull week. When I was a kid, they used to let us out of school early so we could watch. Everybody went, old people, mammas with babies in strollers, and couples came holding hands and sat in the back and necked like it was a drive-in movie or something. It was great—the band playing, balloons everywhere and flowers in the springtime, and people flocking to the Hanging Tree, the little kids dancing around it like it was a maypole or something. Better than a ball game. . . .

"Then when I got older, they started having hangings regularly, once a week. The novelty wore off. It wasn't fun anymore. It was like: blah, blah, another Tuesday, another hanging, and people just went about their work. It's sad, in a way. Best memories I have from being a little kid is going to those hangings. There's nothing like it."

"You think you're pretty funny, don't you, boy?" Kurt began.

Linda gasped, "Those people! All those people being hanged! Who were they? Where did you get so many people?"

Russell turned and looked at her pale, rapt face. "Unfortunately, Mrs. Harden," he said sadly, "there's no shortage of evil in this world. There's always a need for another hanging." Charlene patted his hand reassuringly.

Kurt wiped his mouth with his napkin. "Linda, the boy's telling whoppers. Russell, do me a favor and apologize to my wife for these lies you've been telling. Otherwise, she won't be able to sleep at night for worrying about the souls of a hundred hanged people."

Russell turned to Mr. Harden with a blank look in his pale eyes and his mouth half open.

"What's that on your neck?" Savannah asked, pointing.

"Here. I'll show you," Russell said, and began to unbutton his shirt. A small gasp escaped Linda. Russell said, "Don't worry, I'll just give her a little peek." He loosened his shirt enough to reveal that the mark on his neck that Savannah had spotted was part of a tattoo, and more tattoos swarmed over his shoulders and back. He was richly coated with dragon-headed ladies and fire-breathing winged horses and two-headed mermaids with tattoos of their own. From a distance they looked like a complicated paisley pattern, and they covered him as smoothly and uniformly as wallpaper.

Charlene smiled proudly at him.

"Got 'em all when I was pretty small. Everyone back in Yellville had a full set," Russell said as he buttoned up his shirt.

Linda leaned back in her chair to put more distance between herself and Russell. "What does your mother think of *those?*" she asked.

"Oh, my mother picked them."

"Oh, come on now," Kurt began, but Russell continued.

"I got them when I was just a baby. Everyone back home got them that way. It was cheaper. You see, Tyler, the Yellville tattoo artist, he charged by the square inch. So everyone got their tattoos as babies, and then as they grew, their skin stretched and the tattoos grew, too. It was quite a bargain really, what with inflation and all."

"How could your mother do that to you?" Linda said, aghast.

"She thought it was for the best. She figured if I didn't get them early, I'd go sneaking out to get them later, and I might end up going to some cheap, sleazy place where they used dirty needles, and then I'd pick up diseases. Or bad manners. She did it for my own good really."

"Son, you're going to regret those one day. When you're trying to get a job and wanting to look respectable. And when you're my age, won't you feel a bit ridiculous?" Kurt grunted.

"Well, frankly, by the time I'm so old as to be embarrassed of tattoos, I'll also have a potbelly and hair on my back. So I won't be wanting to take my shirt off in public anyway."

Kurt wasn't sure if he'd been insulted or not. "You think you're pretty tough, don't you, with those things all over your back?"

"Why no, Mr. Harden, I don't think I am. I don't know about around here, but back in Yellville, the older you got, the tougher you got. Like an old piece of steak. The old folks were the toughest people around. My grandmother used to do her grocery shopping on a motorcycle. She used to get into brawls over bridge games. And the retirement community apartments—you don't want to go there after dark. The women all wore leather miniskirts and spike heels."

Savannah giggled.

"Oh be serious, son. How can you say these things with a straight face?" Kurt barked.

Russell turned an earnest face to him. "I'm completely serious. Wouldn't you do the same if you were going to die any day now? Wouldn't you want to live it up a little?"

"I suppose so," Linda said quickly, trying to make peace. But she was drowned out by her husband, who asked loudly, "So who was keeping order while these grannies were beating each other up? Where were the police?"

"There weren't any police. Whenever there was a problem, people just called the Dammits."

"Excuse me?"

"That's not table talk," Linda said primly, giving Russell an accusing look. Savannah giggled and snorted into her milk glass.

"That was their name," Russell said innocently. "The Dammit family. Mr. and Mrs. and six or seven kids. They could fix anything. Washers, dryers, VCRs, matrimonial disputes, broken bones, broken hearts. Whatever. They could patch it up. All you had to do was, if something broke or you banged yourself or there was some problem, all you had to do was yell for the Dammits—"

"Dammit! Dammit!" Savannah cried joyfully.

"Savannah, hush! You know better than that!" her mother hissed.

Russell grinned at her and said, "Yes, exactly like that. And when you called, no matter where you were, one of the Dammits would come running to help."

Linda took a deep breath and asked brightly, "But surely, Russell, they couldn't fix *everything*. That's impossible. You're joking."

"Well, ma'am, I got to admit you're right. I can think of a few times when they couldn't fix things no matter how hard they tried. One time the brakes on the Perkinses' truck gave out, and none of the Dammits could make 'em work again. It turned out all right, though. Whenever the Perkinses went out in the truck after that, they kept a couple of their kids in the back, and when they needed to stop, the kids would jump out and run in front of the truck and push against it. It worked real well."

"But that's terribly dangerous! They could get killed doing that!" Linda gasped again.

"It wasn't really. Mr. and Mrs. Perkins always wore seat belts, and they had air bags put in just in case. But the kids were real good about easing it to a stop, not at all jerky. Even in rain and snow."

Kurt let out a long, low, exasperated sigh. He glanced down the length of the table at his wife and raised his eyebrows at her. She mouthed, "Tolerant and open-minded people." Kurt snorted and then looked at his daughter. Charlene wouldn't meet his eyes. She looked only at Russell. She's probably ashamed to look at us, Kurt thought. I guess we should humor him for her sake.

Russell kept talking, oblivious to the glances being exchanged. "The other thing the Dammits couldn't ever do anything about were the Adams brothers, Karl and Jarvis. They lived together in an old house down by the swamp, and they were both kleptomaniacs. You know, itchy-finger disease. They'd take anything as long as it didn't belong to 'em. And the harder the thing was to steal, the bigger the challenge, the more they'd want to steal it. You have Karl and Jarvis over for dinner, and then after they left you might find your dishwasher missing, or your dining room table, or the moose head that had been mounted on the wall. Once we found the Hanging Tree in their backyard, and we had to dig it up and take it back to the center of town. Karl and Jarvis just sat on their front porch pretending like they didn't notice what was going on, like they had no idea how that tree ended up in their yard next to their stolen outhouse. . . .

"Not the Dammits nor anybody else could cure them of it, and after a while no one would have them in their house. So they were stuck all the time in their old shack by the swamp, and they started stealing from each other. It was like a sickness, you see; they couldn't help themselves. First Jarvis would steal things from Karl's end of the house, then Karl would take stuff from Jarvis's side. Underwear, spoons, bits of string, floorboards—anything. But the house was built on the swamp, see, so it was real unsteady, so when one of the brothers stole too much, his end of the house would start to sink. Then the other one just *had* to steal, in order to keep the house steady. So they went back and forth like that, the house rocking like a seesaw."

The food on the table had grown cold and gummy. Kurt rolled his eyes. *Liar, liar, pants on fire,* he sang inside his head. Linda twisted her beaded necklace around her finger. Stop it; you'll break it, she told herself. But she half-hoped it would break; she wanted to see the beads fall from her fingers, bounce and clatter on the table and the floor, roll into the corners of the room like drops of mercury.

In the silence Russell cleared his throat. "I . . . I forgot to tell you about Bassala. The Dammits couldn't help him, either. He was Yellville's champion arm wrestler. He was missing his left arm."

"How awful!" Linda couldn't resist saying.

"Well, he also had no legs. He was also missing one ear and most of his teeth, and he had no sense of smell and no sense of humor. He had no tact, and he didn't have a way with women. But it was to his advantage really. Because all that strength and power that would normally go into his legs and those other things was concentrated instead in this one massive arm. He was unstoppable. He and his arm were a team. Until the day came when the arm decided to go out on its own to seek its fortune in Hollywood. The Dammits tried to drag the arm back, but it was too strong for them. They tried to entice it back with money and promises, but the lure of fame was too strong. That arm was gone for good.

"Poor Bassala was a broken man after the arm left. I remember him weeping: 'We were a team, the two of us. I can't make it without him. He was my best friend. I feel like I've lost my right arm.' " Russell gazed sadly at the ceiling. Charlene sighed sympathetically.

There was dead silence around the table. Was that a punch line? Linda wondered. Are we supposed to laugh?

"It's just an expression, you know, saying you lost your right arm. Haven't you heard it before?" Russell asked. Kurt growled into his napkin.

"Only for him it was true," Russell added.

Kurt growled louder. It was the sound a grizzly bear's stomach might make after several years of hibernation. Linda stood up. "Why don't you all talk about . . . school or something while I bring out the dessert?" she suggested.

Silence around the table.

"Did you have to go to school *there?*" Savannah said, looking at Russell expectantly.

"I sure did. I went to Hellgate High," Russell said. Kurt sucked in his breath but said nothing. "Well, actually it used to be called Yell Gate High School, after the man who founded the town. But after the Howie Kingfish incident, people started calling it Hellgate."

"What was that?" Savannah wanted to know.

"Well, Howie Kingfish was the school janitor, and one day he must've gotten real drunk, or maybe just went crazy or something, and he decided he was the Grim Reaper. So he put on an old bathrobe and bought a scythe at the hardware store. Then he came to school and went after the kids who were smoking cigarettes under the stands next to the football field. The sinners, as he saw it. He went after them, swinging that scythe, but he was swinging it pretty low, as if he was mowing hay, and most of the kids were able to dodge him just by moving their feet out of the way. And those who weren't quick enough . . . well, they're all right, they can still get around on the stumps. As for Howie Kingfish, after he sobered up he still liked the Grim Reaper act, so he quit being a janitor and left Yellville. I hear he travels all over and finds work in horror movies and at antinuke rallies."

"You mean there were kids at your school without *feet?*" asked Savannah incredulously.

"Son," Kurt said tiredly, "That's disgusting, and it's not fit talk for my home. Mutilation is not a laughing matter."

"Oh, no, sir, don't misunderstand. It was taken seriously," Russell piped up as Linda returned and passed around dishes of peach cobbler and ice cream. "*Everything* at Hellgate High was taken very seriously. Even laughing. You know, they've discovered that when you laugh your brain produces this chemical, this enzyme or something that prevents cancer. Our school was real progressive, and right away they instituted a Laugh Period, twenty minutes when we had to sit there and laugh.

"The principal loved it. He'd wander around the school during Laugh Period and he'd check the bathrooms and chase out any kids who were hiding in there sobbing, and then he'd walk all through the school, with the halls just ringing with laughter and sunlight streaming through the windows, and he'd raise his arms and say, 'This is the happiest school in America!' and then he'd wipe away a tear of pure joy. A few kids died of asphyxiation every year, but no one ever came down with cancer, so they decided it was worth it. Do you have a Laugh Period at your school?" he asked, turning to Savannah.

"No. But we have an ant farm," Savannah said. "It's cool. I want one."

"I'll tell you what's better than an ant farm," Russell announced, leaning over the table. "Back in Yellville, our next-door neighbor Don-Don used to do research on his cows to find out how they worked. He had windows installed in their stomachs so he could observe the digestion. These clear plastic windows in the sides of their bellies. Watching that food slide around, from one chamber to the next, back and forth and around and around, always changing shape—it was way more fun than watching a few ants push around some dirt. You know what the real fun of an ant farm is, don't you? It's that feeling that you're spying on those little guys—you know, you feel like you're peeking right into their private lives and they don't even know you're there. Like climbing a tree one night and peeking in a window where they forgot to draw the shade and seeing all of somebody's secrets. You know?"

Savannah nodded. Charlene gazed at him dreamily.

"Well, imagine looking straight into someone's *insides*. It's ten times better. It was like you could see what Don-Don's cows were thinking. The stuff moved around among their four stomachs as regular as sand in an hourglass. You could tell time by those cows.

"Don-Don did years of research on them. He thought he'd discovered a cure for indigestion, and he wrote it all up to send to the National Institutes of Health. He explained to me once that all we need to do basically is chew our cud more slowly and eat standing up, and our digestive problems would be solved. Then someone happened to tell him that humans have one stomach, not four like cows. Don-Don sent in his research anyway. The National Institutes of Health never wrote back. Last time I talked to him, he was thinking of putting a window in his own stomach."

Kurt and Linda and Savannah looked at the ice cream melting untouched on their plates. Linda dabbed her spotless lips with her napkin. It was the same perfunctory dab she might give to her eye at the funeral of someone she didn't like very much.

Kurt leaned back in his chair. He grasped the edge of the table as if he might throw it over. He turned to Russell and said heavily, "Son, what is it you want out of life? Do you care about a decent job, raising a family? Don't you have any goals, any heroes?"

"My heroes?" Russell blinked. There was a creamy coating of ice cream on his lower lip. "Well, did you know there's this particular kind of crab that lives on the bottom of the Atlantic Ocean and he spends his whole life running? I saw it on *National Geographic*. He lives deep, deep, deep down on the very bottom, and all he does is run back and forth, New York to South Africa and back again without ever stopping. He's so far down, nothing else lives down there except some kind of invisible eel. He doesn't go sideways like other crabs; he runs head-on. He's blind and deaf, but it doesn't matter. There's no day or night and he never sleeps, just keeps running. All alone in the dark. And it's not a part of some weird mating pattern, either, because there aren't any females waiting at either end. The only way he can mate is if he happens to bump into another crab in the darkness. He can't stop. No time to eat. He's twelve feet across when he's born and gradually he just digests himself away, getting smaller and smaller. He lives forty years or longer. And he just runs and runs forever. Isn't that beautiful?"

Kurt rubbed his eyes and sighed.

"You asked about my heroes, sir. I guess that crab is sort of a hero to me, in a way."

Kurt sighed again. "Young man, have you finished high school?"

"Why no, I didn't. You see, when I left Yellville, I hadn't finished yet. And I don't have the heart to go to any school but Hellgate High."

Kurt leaned over the table, thrust his sweating face into Russell's, and spoke through clenched teeth. "If you liked your Yellville so much, then *why'd you ever leave?*"

Russell sat quietly, blinking his innocent blue eyes.

"Dad!" Charlene cried.

Russell gazed at him a long moment. He looked over at Savannah and then at Linda, who sat with both hands to her mouth. "There is no Yellville," he said sadly, boweing his head.

"Finally!" Kurt barked, and sank back into his chair. "Thank you, thank you for finally ending that little charade. Charlene, did you put him up to this? I can't believe we sat through all that bullshit—"

"There is no more Yellville," Russell broke in mournfully. "They tore it all down to make room for a new superhighway. We never knew they were planning it, because, like I said, we kept to ourselves and didn't mess in outside affairs. They tore down the buildings, bulldozed up the Hanging Tree. That's the only reason I came out here. Everyone's gone who knows where. The Perkins family, and the Dammits, and Tyler from the tattoo place, and Howie Kingfish, and Bassala—they're all scattered. They could be anywhere, anywhere by now." He gazed sadly at the ceiling. "If only we'd listened. If only we'd paid attention, we might have been able to do something before it was too late."

Silence around the table. Kurt stood up slowly. "I've heard enough," he said. "Charlene, why don't you see your friend to the door," he added, then strode thunderously into the kitchen.

"It's been nice to meet you, Russell," Linda said hastily. "Very interesting. Here, Savannah, help me clear the table."

"Thank you so much, Mrs. Harden. Your cooking's wonderful. And it was nice to meet you. You and your husband seem like real nice people. Just like your daughter." He grinned hugely, flung one arm around Charlene's shoulders, and held the other out to Linda. She shrank from his hand, murmured, "Good-bye now, Russell," and hurried into the kitchen with a stack of plates. Savannah glided after her with a dish in each hand and a third balanced perfectly on her head.

"I can't believe I listened to all that crap. Lying to me, in my house! Eating my food!" Kurt stormed at his wife. She washed dishes. He paced the floor.

"He made a fool of himself and he made fools of us, and he embarrassed our daughter so much, she couldn't talk!" he went on. Then, picking up a dirty plate, he said, "Look! Look at this. He didn't eat a thing, he was so busy talking bullshit. All he did was play with it." They both looked. Russell had mashed the peas and potatoes and meat into paste and spread it all over the plate. "Disgusting kid," Kurt muttered.

His wife held the plate and looked closer and saw that it was a map of the world, in global projection, with all the oceans and continents in perfect proportion, and the land in different shades of green and brown according to the altitudes. She tried to rub her eyes with the back of her hand, and as she did, the plate slipped into the dishwater.

"I think he could be emotionally disturbed. A compulsive liar," she offered. "Maybe he doesn't know what he was doing."

"Oh, he knew what he was doing all right. He's probably laughing all the way home, thinking he pulled one over on us."

"Maybe, like you said, Charlene put him up to it. Maybe she was afraid we wouldn't like him as he really is, so she told him to do something to impress us."

Kurt said, "I kept thinking she'd brought him over as a joke, and any minute she was going to throw him out and bring the real boyfriend out of the wings, and he'd seem wonderful compared to that jerk."

"I'm not sure I want Charlene seeing him anymore. He may be on drugs or something," Linda said, squinting at each plate before she scraped it.

"Where is she, anyway?" he asked. "Let's get her down here."

"I heard her run up to her room after Russell left. Why don't you go have a talk with her?"

Charlene was not in her room. Kurt looked at the half-open, half-empty drawers and the curtains dancing around the open window. He sank down on the unmade bed. Charlene's stuffed animals stared at him stupidly.

Then he found the letter, scrawled on a piece of paper torn out of a notebook.

He read:

> *Dear Mom and Dad—sorry I have to leave like this, but it is the only way. I am in love. Russell is a kleptomaniac like his brothers Karl and Jarvis, and he has stolen my heart away. You don't understand true love; you don't understand the truth when it is told straight to your face. So I am leaving with Russell to search for bluer skies, greener pastures, and another place like Yellville. Good-bye. Love, Charlene.*

Mr. Harden let out such a roar that Savannah, who was doing pliés in her room, fell over backward and Mrs. Harden dropped a dish to the floor, where it smashed into a million pieces, and fifteen miles away on a motorcycle heading west, Russell and Charlene felt a tremor in their bones like the buzzing of a bee.

In the kitchen, Linda looked at the shattered pieces on the floor. She looked at the stack of dirty dishes waiting in the sink. Why should I wash them all? she thought. She took another dish and held it over the floor speculatively.

Savannah sat on the floor in her room, inspecting the blue-veined insides of her feet. Soon she would be ready for toe shoes. And then she would dance and dance and travel the world and be famous. She saw it all stretching out before her sure and shining, like the Yellow Brick Road in the movie. She heard her father shouting, "Dammit! Dammit! Damn him!" not as if he was angry, but as if he was crying for help.

AVERAGE JOE

So I got this phone call last week. Monday night, I'd just gotten home from work. I was settling down in front of the TV, got my cold beer and reheated macaroni and cheese, got my feet up on the coffee table and my dog, Sheena, walking back and forth in the space under my legs like it's a fascinating game. I was waiting for my show to come on. I was watching the commercials. They're not bad these days—all those bright colors, so cheery and upbeat, fast cars and gorgeous glistening food in close-up. There's a happy ending every thirty seconds.

And then the phone rang. I considered not answering. I'm having dinner, I told myself. I should just let it ring. But in the end I got up to answer it. That's the kind of person I am—I can't stand to let it ring, always afraid I'll miss out on some big news.

So I found the phone and said hello, and this woman said, "Good evening."

"Hi."

"Mr. Morris? Joe Morris? I was wondering if you could spare a few minutes. I have a few questions I'd like to ask you." She had a bossy schoolteacher voice.

"I guess."

So she asked me where I bought my groceries, and what kind of car I drove, and how much television I watched. I could hear the clicking of a keyboard as she typed my answers into a computer.

"What kind of toothpaste do you use?"

"Um, I don't remember. I guess I don't brush much."

She sucked in her breath. Apparently this was the wrong answer. "But don't you buy toothpaste? Don't you have it in the house? Surely you've bought some in the last six months?"

"I guess so, yes, I did. Once I bought some of that baking-soda toothpaste—you know, the kind that's sort of salty and sort of grainy? I think I bought it because it reminded me of my grandmother; she used to make me brush with baking soda when I visited. She used to give me cookies and then make me brush till my gums were bleeding. Jeez, I kind of miss her."

"Do you remember what brand you bought?"

"No, not really. I think it's the kind that has a TV commercial with a little cartoon swirl of toothpaste chasing away the green cartoon germs."

"Don't you have the tube somewhere? Couldn't you go check?"

"Do I have to?" I said. "My show's about to start." I wasn't lying, either; the bouncy theme song was just beginning, and Sheena stopped her pacing to watch.

"It's terribly important," the woman said. "We really need to know."

"Why?" I said.

"Your opinions are very important to us," she said. "Your answers to these questions will influence a great number of marketing decisions worldwide. . . ."

"That's bullshit," I said. I don't usually speak to women that way, but this one was getting on my nerves. "You don't care about my opinion. If I hadn't answered the phone, you would have called some-one else, and he would have been just as good."

"Oh no, Joe, I called you in *particular*. Your opinion is *extremely* important." Her voice had dropped; she was sort of purring into the phone.

"Oh yeah? Why do you care so much what I think?"

"Because, Joe, according to the statistics, the very latest statistics, you are the most average man in the United States. At this moment, according to the most up-to-the-minute research, *you* are the absolute mean. By every method of measurement, you fall in the exact middle of the road. You have no distinguishing attributes or defects. You are the epitome of the ordinary, the mainstream, the pedestrian. You are the quintessential common man. According to the statistics, your every opinion is shared by millions of people all over the country. You speak for all mankind. Thus, your opinion is very important. Do you think you can recall the brand of your toothpaste now?"

I didn't really grasp what she'd said. She'd said it so quickly, all in one breath. I wasn't sure whether I'd been complimented or insulted. "So you're saying I'm special?" I asked.

"You're absolutely average," she said.

"Does this mean I've won something? I can't wait to tell my ma; I've never won anything in my life."

"No, you haven't won anything," she said impatiently. "If you *did* win—say, the lottery—then that would be quite unusual and you wouldn't be completely average anymore. Don't you see?"

"Yes," I said, though of course I didn't, but her voice had that tone that meant she was tired of explaining and wanted to move on to something else. A tone I've been hearing all my life.

"Now, the toothpaste—" she said.

"I just remembered," I said. "I have no teeth. I eat everything through a straw. Good night." As I was hanging up the phone I heard her screech, "Really?" and then a strange sort of roar, like hundreds of peo-ple shouting in amazement, before I placed the phone in its cradle.

My macaroni had congealed in a gluey brick, and on my show a fat man was gesturing at the blond secretary character and the studio audience was laughing uproariously. I'd missed the beginning, so now I'd never catch on to what was happening.

But as it turned out, it didn't matter, because the phone rang again. This time it was a man who wanted to ask me about my long-distance phone company. And then another woman called to ask me about tires and gas station chains. A third woman wanted to know about oven cleaners, and a fourth questioned me about fast-food places. I talked to the fast-food lady for quite a while, maybe because I was so hungry by that point.

"What kind of toppings do you get on a hamburger?" she asked.

I said, "You know, the truth is, whatever I get, I never open it up and look. I just bolt it down, and it always tastes okay. They could slip me some kangaroo with motor oil and I'd never know the difference."

"Hmmm," she said. "That's what we thought."

A lady called to talk about TV. At first when she asked me which shows I watched, I sort of blanked out. There were so many, I couldn't think of them all offhand. But she was very patient, and helped me think about it day by day.

"I still watch Saturday-morning cartoons," I told her. "If I'm away Saturday mornings, I tape them on the VCR."

"Is that so?" she said. "Maybe our Saturday-morning advertising has been targeting the wrong audience."

"Maybe," I told her helpfully.

After that I was exhausted. All the questions reminded me of being back in school. Except in school I worried about giving the wrong answers, and now it seemed I was always right, and these people listened very carefully to every word I said.

The phone rang again. I thought about unplugging the phone. But then I figured, These people need me, I can't turn my back on them. I am the only one who can give them the answers. "Hello," I said.

It was my friend Bob. He asked if I wanted to go out bowling. "I'll bring Nancy along," he said. Nancy was some cousin of his; he had fixed me up with her a few times. He thought we were perfect for each other. But she had such a dull, uninteresting face that every time she changed her hair or clothes, I failed to recognize her and asked to be introduced.

"Not tonight," I said. "I'm kind of busy." I wanted to tell Bob about all the calls—maybe I wanted to brag a little, I admit it—but it was all too complicated to explain.

"Man, you're so boring," Bob said. "You never want to do anything."

"Sure I do," I said.

"Then what? You wanna shoot some pool? Get some beers at Mickey's? What?"

"Nah, not that. I don't know what I want."

"That's what I mean. Well, I'll see you tomorrow at work."

"Yeah."

After that I finally unplugged the phone. I didn't feel like answering questions anymore. I turned off the TV. I was thinking. What do I want? What does anyone want?

Sheena pressed her cold nose against my leg. I'd taken off my pants when I came home from work; I like to sit around in my boxers to relax. I looked at my body. My stomach had grown lately; I had to remember to suck it in sometimes. But why should I, I thought, if everybody has a stomach just like it? What am I ashamed of?

If I suck it in, I reminded myself, that means most people in the country must suck it in, too. I thought about that for a bit, and I started laughing, thinking about all the skinny actresses and fashion models sucking in their gut when the cameras were rolling, and then once they're safe in their dressing rooms they let their breath out and suddenly have huge beer bellies bursting out of their clothes.

I thought about that, and I laughed and laughed. Sheena raised her ears and looked at me quizzically; usually I don't laugh at all unless the TV is on.

I laughed some more. Sometimes I'm the funniest guy I know. I turned the TV on and didn't think anymore. Around midnight I got up and brushed my teeth, just for the hell of it. Then I went to bed.

The next morning I plugged the phone back in, and it started ringing almost immediately. So I unhooked it again. I didn't want it ringing all day when I wasn't home. It would drive Sheena nuts.

I made some coffee and ate a bowl of cereal. Then I rushed to shave and get dressed, and I nicked my face twice and had to put tissue on it, so I looked like your regular nerd character in a movie—you know, the kind with crooked glasses and pieces of tissue on his face and maybe some toilet paper stuck to his shoe.

So I went to work, and the funny thing was, nobody treated me any differently. My boss even yelled at me. "You haven't been filling out the proper forms when you make a sale," he said. "Why haven't you been doing the paperwork? What, do you think you're better than the rest of us or something?"

"Why should I fill them out when no one ever looks at them?" I said. "I used to spend half the day filling them out, and then I put them in a folder in the filing cabinet and no one ever looks at them again, I might as well put them in the trash. What's the point?"

But he wasn't interested in my opinion.

Bob said, "We had a good time last night. You should've come." I think he was still a little sore at me.

I went home. This was Tuesday night. Sheena was glad to see me. I took off my pants before she could drool on them. I made two peanut butter and bologna sandwiches. I got a beer, put my feet up on the coffee table, and turned on the TV.

Then Roderick showed up.

This is what happened. I had just gotten settled when there was a knock at the door. Not a timid "Can I borrow your hedge trimmer?" knock. More of an FBI-type knock.

I got up and opened the door. On my front steps stood an army of men. They were all different sizes, but they all wore black suits and black turtlenecks and sunglasses, and they all had their hair slicked back with wet-looking gel stuff. Behind them I could see a black limousine and several foreign cars parked at the curb.

"Roderick McCabe would like a word with you," one of the suits said.

"Okay, I guess. Come on in," I said, but they were already swarming past me. They walked rapidly; some carried briefcases, others carried shiny metal boxes, and they all bristled with importance. I followed them back to the living room.

I sat down on the couch. The suits stood around the room with folded arms, shifting impatiently. One of them turned off the TV. "Which one of you is Roderick McCabe? And who is he, anyway?" I said.

At that moment all the pairs of sunglasses turned toward the door. I turned and looked, too. In the doorway stood a tall, pudgy man with shaggy hair and the beginnings of a beard. He wore glasses and a V-neck sweater and baggy tan pants, the kind that have pockets all over, even in places where there is absolutely no need for pockets. He was wearing Velcro sneakers, the kind that went out of style maybe fifteen years ago.

"Hi, Joe," he said. He had an aura of power about him; all the suits seemed to cringe away as he shuffled across the room.

"Hi," I said. He had a ballpoint pen hooked in the V of his sweater. He unclipped it and started clicking the point in and out. "Do you want a beer?" I said.

"No thanks," he said. One of the suits sprang forward wordlessly and handed him a bottle of spring water. He took a swig of that and then wiped his mouth with his hand. He looked like my dad, only sadder.

"Joe," he said, "do you know who I am?"

"Nope," I said.

He looked at me sadly. "I'm a movie producer," he said. "I've produced fourteen blockbusters in the past ten years. Each one was an incredible commercial success." He named some movies.

"Hey, I've seen those," I said.

"Of course you have."

"Except the third one you mentioned. That one, I rented for the VCR. I *wish* I'd seen it in a theater, though."

"Of course you do," he said. "I've been extremely successful. I've made more money than you can possibly imagine."

"Oh, I could probably imagine it," I said.

He was looking at me very intently. I half-expected him to tell me to stick out my tongue and say aah. "Joe," he said, "my problem is this. My last two movies, the most recent ones, were flops. They were terrible. No one went to see them."

The suits hung their heads, perhaps in shame.

"I'm afraid I've lost my touch," Roderick said to me. "I'm afraid I don't know what people want anymore."

I felt like giving him a pat on the back or something, but I didn't want to give him the wrong idea.

"I don't care about being artistic or political. I just want mass appeal; I want another commercial smash."

All the men in the room were staring at me. I remembered I was sitting there in my underwear.

"Joe," Roderick said softly, "I need your help. You've got to tell me what you want—what everybody wants. You're the only one who really knows. Tell me what sort of movie to make."

The suits leaned closer to listen.

"What kind of movies do you like, Joe?" he pressed.

"Oh, I don't know . . . the good ones."

"But what's good about them? Is it the adventure? Sex? Violence?"

"Violence, I guess."

"So what kind of violence do you like?" he asked eagerly. "Shootings, or fistfights, or stabbings?"

"Stabbings, I think, and disfigurement, fingers getting cut off and things like that, and also stranglings, when they're done really well—you know, with the person making those really gut-wrenching noises. I love that."

"You like blood, then."

"Yeah," I said. "I don't know, it just seems more personal than seeing a car blown up, you know?"

"Right," he said. "And what about nudity?"

"Oh, I like naked people. Only when it's tastefully done, though. I like a movie where you can look at a naked woman without feeling guilty about it. Like that old *Romeo and Juliet* movie, where Juliet's gorgeous, and she takes off her clothes, but it's okay because it's Shakespeare—it's poetry and educational and all that."

"Go on," he said. He was taking notes. Half the men in suits were taking notes. Roderick asked more questions and I answered as best I could. It was difficult because I'd never thought about movies before, I simply sat through them and then tried not to step in gum or spilled soda on the way out.

And I never got around to telling him the main reason I go to movies, which is that everyone else goes to them, and I feel like if I don't, then I'll miss out on something the rest of the world knows. I get that feeling a lot.

"Do you like small children in movies?" Roderick asked.

"No, they point at the screen and ask questions, and then get scared," I said.

"I mean *in* the film. Child actors."

"I guess so."

"How about animals?"

"Oh yes. Dogs, horses, dolphins, whatever. Especially dogs."

"What about them do you like?"

"I don't know exactly. But they always get to me. Especially when they die. That's the only time I ever want to cry in movies, when an animal dies."

"You cry when you see an animal die?"

"I said it makes me *want* to cry."

"Did you cry when Bambi's mother died?"

"Well, sure, but that's different. I was a *kid* when I saw that movie."

"What if you saw lots of animals dying? Like a whole herd? A whole *species*? Would you cry then?"

"Maybe," I said. "If I cared about them enough."

"But you wouldn't cry if you saw a whole crowd of people gunned down?"

"Probably not," I said.

Roderick was writing down every word. "Good, good," he kept saying.

The next day, Wednesday, I was pretty groggy at work because I'd spent most of the previous night answering Roderick's questions. I would have kicked him out sooner if I hadn't felt sorry for him; he seemed to really need me.

My boss stopped by to say, "I don't pay you to sleep."

"I'm not sleeping. I'm absorbing information through the skin of my forehead," I said. I can be pretty witty even when I'm tired.

"You'd better get on the ball. I could replace you in a second," he said.

Later, Bob said, "Want to grab some beers after work?"

"I've got to get home. I'm expecting visitors," I said.

"Who?"

"I don't know yet," I said. Bob walked off, looking pissed.

When I drove home, I noticed a number of nondescript gray cars parked or cruising around the neighborhood. I parked in my driveway, and as I walked up to the door I noticed men with guns in camouflaged jumpsuits lurking in my shrubbery. My shrubs were very unhealthy, so it was easy to see them. And then, before I could get my keys out, four more guys approached me. These were middle-aged, with hard, leathery faces, gray suits, sunglasses, and gun bulges under their jackets.

"Would you mind coming this way, Mr. Morris?" they said.

"Okay."

A black limousine with tinted windows pulled up. A door popped open. I slid inside, and found myself face-to-face with the President.

"Hi, Joe," he said.

"Hi," I said. He was a big man. I never realized just how big he was, since I'd only seen him inside the box of my television set. He had a puffy, friendly pink face, like a high school football coach. And sad eyes, with bags. He gave off this powerful chemical smell, aftershave or cologne, or deodorant maybe.

"You know who I am, I hope?" he said as the limo started to move.

"Sure."

"Joe," he said, sighing and shifting around on the squishy leather seats, "I need your help."

"Are you making a movie, too?"

"No," he said, surprised. "Should I?"

"I don't think so."

"Joe," he said, "I need your advice. You represent the masses. You speak for the entire nation. So tell me, Joe, what do the people want?"

"What? You're asking *me* to tell *you* what to do?"

"Yes, Joe."

"Now?"

"Please."

"Jeez, I don't know. You're the President. *You're* supposed to tell *me*."

"I don't think you understand," he said, "the kind of power you hold in your hands right now. I'll do whatever you say, Joe. What do you want from the government?"

"I don't know. . . . It's a tough question."

"I don't trust polls and surveys," he said. "I'm tired of listening to Congress. I want to hear from the common people. That's you."

"I don't know. I never follow politics much."

"But isn't there anything you want to change?"

"Nothing comes to mind."

That's when the President lost his temper. It was something fine to see. He slammed his big meaty fist into the leather seat right next to my leg. "Damn it, Joe!" he said, "Everyone is dissatisfied with the government."

"I think people just like to complain," I said. "I think it's just human nature."

He slumped back in his seat.

"I don't think there are any problems," I said. "At least none that people know or care about."

He said nothing.

"It's easy to complain. But it takes too much effort to actually make a decision and act on it. No one wants that kind of responsibility."

The President's head hung down like an exhausted bull's. "Do you mean to say," he asked, "that we are basically a spineless, apathetic nation?" He raised his eyes and gave me a piercing look.

"Yes . . . no . . . I don't know . . . I guess so."

On Thursday I went for a walk during my lunch hour. It was an unusually hot day; my shirt was sticking to my back. I passed old ladies with shopping carts, young women with babies in strollers, kids in nylon jackets skipping school, ancient men with canes who walked as if their bones were made of glass. I avoided meeting their eyes; I didn't want to answer any more questions.

There was a comic strip I read in the paper sometimes, the one about prehistoric people. Sometimes in this comic strip the characters climbed a big mountain and at the top lived an old wise man who could answer all their questions. The old man was called the Great Guru.

I was beginning to feel like the Great Guru. Except that I could never think of wise and witty answers, the way he did.

As I walked along I began to imagine myself with a long white beard. I thought about living alone on the top of a mountain. I would take Sheena along. It wouldn't be so bad.

I stopped to look at a beautiful Harley-Davidson parked in the street. I cleared my sinuses and spat into the gutter. I pulled at my shirt where it stuck to me. I adjusted my pants.

Just at that moment a black limousine screeched to a halt next to me. Two tall, stunning women stepped out. They both had long necks like ballet dancers and wore sunglasses and high heels. They watched me adjusting myself.

One wrinkled her nose. "Ugh. Typical," she said.

"This is definitely the man we're looking for," said the other.

"Come on, Joe," they said. They pulled me into the limousine and whisked me off to a meeting of the Grand High Council of the Secret Sisterhood of All Women.

I was not terribly surprised to find out about the Sisterhood. I had always suspected such a thing existed. I've noticed the way women have secret conferences in the bathrooms of restaurants. I've seen women whispering into their makeup compacts: I'm sure they have tiny cellular phones hidden there. They have their own language, their own signals. Their magazines are full of sinister-sounding code words like *exfoliate* and *chartreuse*.

All women baffle me. Even my mother is a mystery. Even Nancy. So I was not at all surprised to discover their conspiracy.

My two escorts brought me to the secret meeting place of the Sisterhood. It was a cavernous dark room filled with tiers of seats, like a basketball arena. I sat before the seven women of the Grand High Council. The councilwomen were all different ages, shapes, and colors, but they all looked equally beautiful and equally fierce. My escorts sat on either side, occasionally snickering at me, or pricking me with their nails when I did not answer quickly enough.

"So this is the quintessential man," said one councilwoman.

"He doesn't look like anything special," said another.

"Joe, we need your help," they said.

"What now?"

"Joe, we want you to tell us what men want."

"What do you mean?"

"What do you men want from women? We don't understand you, you don't understand us. We've all suffered through centuries of beastly misunderstandings. Why don't you clear it all up and tell us what it is you men want?"

"How should *I* know what all men want?"

"According to the latest statistics, you represent—" they began.

"But—"

"Why don't you just tell us what *you* want," they said.

"I don't—"

"What do you look for in a woman, Joe?"

"Love?" I said hopefully.

They all laughed derisively. "Oh come on, Joe. Be honest. Don't just tell us what you think we want to hear."

"But I don't know what you want to hear. That's *my* problem."

"Come on, Joe, tell us—why can't women and men get along?"

"Because men are afraid of you," I told them.

They scoffed at this but seemed secretly pleased.

"Keep going, Joe," they said. "Tell us what you like."

"Um, long hair," I said. "Brown eyes. Faithfulness. A wet nose."

They were writing in their notebooks. "A wet nose? Are you sure?"

"Unconditional love. A brisk walk in the morning. A warm body to keep your feet warm at night."

"Keep your *feet* warm?" they said.

"Definitely."

They seemed dissatisfied. "Let's talk fashion," they said. "Do you like a woman in furs?"

"Oh yes."

"Where do you like a skirt hemline," they asked, "above or below the knee?"

"Oh, I like knees," I said. "In fact, why bother wearing skirts at all?"

They scribbled furiously in their notebooks. All seven leaned close to me; my hair moved in their tropical breaths. They said, "Do you like a woman to be more intelligent than you, or less? Should she be taller or shorter? Stronger or weaker? Older or younger? More or less experienced? Are you a leg man or a breast man? Do you go to strip clubs? Do you have fantasies about old elementary school teachers? Do you have fantasies about schoolgirls? Do you want to marry someone just like your mother? Do you fold your own laundry? Do you keep dirty magazines in the cabinet beneath the sink? Do you ever dream about water? Rapids or ponds? Do you dream about movie stars? Naked or clothed? Do you wake up most often alone, wishing you were not, or *not* alone, wishing you were? Do you prefer starch in your sheets? Ketchup on your eggs? Sex on the beach? What about kids? Do you have an embarrassing tendency to stutter during intense high-pressure situations?"

"Yes," I said. "Yes. Yes. *Yes.*"

The next day was Friday. I stayed home from work.

That morning God came to me. No fuss, no fanfare, no limo, no cohorts in sunglasses. He came to me as I lay in bed. Sheena lay with me, though officially she wasn't allowed on the furniture. The sun fell in warm bright stripes on my legs. My alarm clock buzzed for the tenth time and I knocked it to the floor.

"Joe," said God.

"Here I am," I said quickly. I knew immediately who it was. "Come on in," I said. I wasn't scared at all. I felt curiously calm and relaxed, and at the same time intensely alert, the way I felt the times I smoked weed in high school.

"Joe," said God.

"I'm here, Lord," I said.

"Joe, I need your advice," God said. He sighed and put his head in his hands. I mean, he *would* have, if he'd had a head and hands and was built that way. That's how despondent he was.

"I don't really think I'm qualified to advise you," I said. I was trying to be humble; the Bible says God likes that.

"I think you can, Joe," he said. "I need you to speak for the people. Tell me, Joe, what ails them? Why are their spirits weak? Why don't they believe in me any longer?"

"It's complicated," I said.

"They don't come to me with their problems anymore," he said.

"They go to their therapists, they read self-help books. They get acupuncture. They take antidepressants," I explained.

"Perhaps if I performed some miracles, it would revive their faith," he said.

"I doubt it," I said. "Miracles are commonplace now. Doctors put baboon hearts in babies. Machines fly through the air. Virgins give birth. Bald men grow hair. People are jaded now; there is very little you could do to awe them."

God thought for a minute. "Perhaps," he said hopefully, "if I sent a prophet or angel to bring my word to the people—"

"I doubt it would work. Unless he was a rock star or software designer," I told him.

"When did this happen? When did they start to lose their faith?"

"Probably it's all the wars, and disasters and diseases and things. People figured you'd forsaken them."

"I gave man a beautiful planet, and I gave him free will. And now look what he's done with it all."

"We do our damnedest."

"I thought you could help me," he said sadly. "But I'm beginning to think you're a lost race."

He started to leave. "Hey, where are you going?" I said. "You can't just give up on us! We need you down here! Don't be a quitter! What are you going to do, go start up something new on Mars?"

I tried to grab God's sleeve, but he slammed the doors of heaven in my face.

Saturday morning, I watched cartoons but I didn't enjoy them as much as usual. I felt like talking to someone, anyone, so I plugged in the phone.

It didn't ring.

It didn't ring for hours. I sat and watched it. Every now and then I picked up the receiver and listened for a dial tone to make sure it was working.

I couldn't believe no one had any questions for me.

No one called. No one knocked at the door. Still I waited. I felt as if it was my responsibility to be there, in case anyone needed me. No one did.

Around five o'clock the phone finally rang. I snatched it up.

"Hi, Joe," the woman said.

"Hi," I said. I recognized her voice right away: It was the toothpaste lady.

"You were kidding about using a straw, weren't you?" she said.

"Yes."

"Have you remembered the name of your toothpaste yet?"

"Yeah," I said, and told her.

"Thanks," she said, "I always like to follow up. Although it doesn't really matter that much now."

"What do you mean?"

"Well, you see, the newest statistics show that you're no longer the most average man in the country."

"How can that be?"

"Lots of things happen in a week, Joe. People are born, people die. Populations shift. People change their minds. The tiniest things cause major fluctuations in trends. Say one day it rains, so people eat more soup; kids catch more colds; women yell at their husbands; the water table rises. Everything's changing, all the time. *You're* changing."

"Oh."

"Now the most average person is a guy named Jimmy Cho in St. Louis. I've been trying to reach him all day, but I can't get through."

"Oh."

"Actually, the average person normally changes every few hours. It's quite unusual for someone to be the average for as long as you were. You were quite an *exceptional* average."

"Thanks."

"Well, have a good evening."

So I hung up the phone, and now I'm sitting here, the same old Joe once more.

I've got peace and quiet; I've got the Saturday-night programs to look forward to; I've got a case of beer in the fridge. I've got Sheena. I've got my health.

I ought to be perfectly happy.

F L I G H T

There was a time when the women jumped off buildings regularly. They wore hoopskirts then and carried parasols. They fell gently, their skirts filling with air, their legs dangling in long lace knickers. Men were gentlemen then; they did not look up and snigger when a lady fell.

Now the women wear blue jeans and spandex. They have sleek haircuts. They slip too fast through the air; you can't get a grip on them. No place to fall to—there are too many busy streets, too many antennas and telephone wires ready to slice off a finger or snag on an earring. Now when a woman jumps, everybody looks. They have no manners.

It makes Kanisa sad sometimes.

Kanisa took the leap the first time when she was five. She jumped from the front stoop. Her sandals made a *wop* sound when they landed, and she rocked forward on her hands. That was all.

Now she is so much older and so much heavier, she needs to jump off higher things. Thirty stories at least, she thinks, to get any feeling of flight.

She thinks about it often.

In the time before, women had reason to jump. An incriminating letter, a misplaced glove and your life could change forever. They jumped with necks outstretched, swanlike, tears in their eyes and the sun sliding a burning path down the sky. Gauzy scarves trailed after them, and impassioned speeches, and perhaps a lacy handkerchief fluttering down late, like the last leaf off the tree in autumn.

Now women like to get where they are going as fast as they can. No time for a journey. It must be done as soon as they think of it. That's the way Kanisa's mother did it. She took the leap headfirst on a cloudy day in the middle of rush hour, didn't bother to wait for the dramatic sunset. Her mother splattered neatly next to the curb. It was street-cleaning day: lucky coincidence.

And then her aunt, who was in such a hurry that she leapt before even she was ready, and had to finish her coffee and pull up her panty hose midflight. Not that it mattered; no one had time to look up.

Back then the woman leapt off cliffs. It was a beautiful thing. Songs and poems were written about them. People wept for them. Lovers leapt after them. They fell neatly into rivers that carried them along and away to the sea, to the dark, dark deep, where the mermaids braided their hair and sung them to sleep.

Now it is the police report, the juicy mess, the spot on the evening news. The bums check the street for loose change and the landlord looks for another tenant.

Kanisa stands at the window in their apartment on the seventeenth floor. Not high enough. It must be the thirtieth floor at least. There is a gull from off the bay perching on the building opposite. He shrieks for company. Behind her the baby screams and screams for a fallen toy.

What if someone tipped the high chair, she thinks, and the baby spills out and thunks his tender head on the floor and doesn't move? What then? Why, then she will burst through the window, like a tropical fish bursting through the glass of the aquarium with a crash and a splash, gasping and flapping its fins like it might fly.

But the baby's still in the chair, sucking his fingers. The gull flies away. A tropical fish, if it's lucky, will be scooped into a saucepan of tap water while someone sweeps up the pieces of broken glass and sops up the mess.

Kanisa trips over the baby's fallen toy. It's a woman, hard and smooth and egg-shaped, and weighted on the bottom so she always rolls upright. Her body clings to the earth like a magnet.

Dennis said once that most people who jump have heart attacks and die before they even reach the ground. "It's not fear of falling," he said; "it's *landing* they're afraid of." He said that and laughed, his teeth caulked with mashed potatoes. Soon after, he left for good.

What did he know about it anyway? He was a trucker, accustomed to moving in horizontals, not verticals, she thinks as she takes the elevator.

Now Kanisa stands on the roof of the building. The iron railing comes only to her waist. She leans way out. Someone could tip her over. She looks out across the stunted forest of chimneys and TV antennas. She looks down into the hot wind barreling up from the street. The wind carries with it the smell of subway and pretzel stands and a small, thin wailing—her baby wants his toy. The yellow cabs slide past one another on the street like pieces on a game board.

Long ago, Kanisa thinks, the villains were easy to pick out. They wore black clothes, cape, and gloves, and had pencil-thin mustaches. They carried swords and made women swoon. These days they are much harder to spot.

She thinks, The terror of falling is not the earth rushing up, smiling and effusive, to embrace you like an old friend you had hoped never to see again. Nor is it the fear of impact, the teeth-rattling jolt, like the violent thrust you close your eyes and brace yourself for in the night.

It is the sense of betrayal, as you arch earthward like a shooting star and look down to see no one there waiting to catch you.

C O M P O S E R

You see in the paper how the composer died today.

He was a young man still. He had the dark haunted eyes, the requisite long tangled hair. He looked like a regular maestro. But with him it was slovenliness, not affectation.

They say he was born with six fingers on his left hand. Don't believe a word of it.

He was a virtuoso pianist, but he could play all kinds of instruments. He would play the saxophone with his toes, at parties, for a laugh.

He never laughed himself.

He died by sheer act of will, they say. He just crumpled inside like paper on fire and couldn't go on anymore. He got tired of himself. He willed his heart to stop beating. Got annoyed by its ceaseless rhythm. Imagine that—a will like his mother on a diet, increased a hundredfold. His puny heart didn't have a chance against a will like that.

She was his inspiration. Don't laugh. It's true, you can see it in his works. The big pieces, the symphonies he wrote in those years his mother was huge. In the years she dieted and beat the weight down, he composed string quartets, piano trios, solo pieces for flute and violin. Even the sound was different: During the fat years the sound was like wedding cakes stacked on top of one another, thick, rich, ornamental, crushing. In the thin years the sound was a dime tossed into a dark pool, sparkling and flickering a bright path in the darkness all the way down, or else a sound like a single tight-strung wire vibrating with a distant earthquake.

He loved his mother. In his way.

They used to live together in that old brownstone with the drapes drawn. Old books, old dust. Old piano, seldom played. In that house they dodged each other for days, then met, tangled their words, and parted again in a smooth graceful way as if it had all been rehearsed before. He loved her, he lived for her, he lived in terror of her all at once. He was fascinated by her changes.

She had two wardrobes. One for the fat years, one for the thin ones. In the obese years she wore dresses in vibrant shades. Oriental silks. They enveloped her in clouds. They trailed on the floor. Ropes of pearls around her neck. Hair dyed copper, gold, blue-black. Scarves and gloves and fantastic hats. Her reasoning must have been: If you can't hide it, then monumentalize it. In these clothes she didn't walk, she sailed. She was stately. She was magnificent. Her son the great composer dwindled next to her.

And he loved her like that. When she came to his concerts, she created a stir, and he loved it. People were forced to get up from their seats and move aside to allow her to reach hers. Even after she was seated, she created a bustle. People craned their necks to stare: *That's the composer's mother, in the peacock blue.* Those behind her had to shift and stretch to see over her lofty coiffure. She always created such a sensation that the composer himself was overlooked. This he relished.

The mother's other wardrobe was the one she wore in the years she dieted, or went to spas, or *underwent surgery,* it was whispered though no one knew for sure. These dresses were simple, severe, and always black. They had decorative buttons and hidden zippers, so it was impossible to tell how she got into them. She wore shoes with precarious heels. In these dresses she was small-voiced and reserved, yet full of a sort of ringing tension that made her eyes overbright. She walked rapidly, wore sunglasses on the street, and held her son's arm at public gatherings. He did not like her at these times. She lingered in his shadow or out of sight, and he in turn felt huge, ungainly, and awkward, like a coltish child.

Without her he had to answer questions. He had to smile so that his face could be processed into a hundred thousand dots printed on a hundred thousand newspapers that he would see for days on newsstands or blowing about in the street. It was a secret satisfaction to him that he never truly smiled for these pictures, he merely turned up the corners of his mouth mechanically, so that no one would ever see his real smile. No one but her.

She seesawed like this, back and forth, for years, and he echoed her. Sometimes she was huge, regal; she dominated him, ordered him about. Other times she was slim, almost attractive, and her attention turned to herself and her occasional admirers. Then the composer languished for her affection. She seemed like a stranger to him. He wandered the house, alone, betrayed, stayed up all night drinking coffee and writing thin watercolor melodies that wept along and then died with a quiver.

He read comic books in which everything turned out all right while his mother dated widowers and aging millionaires. He waited up for her the nights she went out. When she came home, she made him tea or hot milk, which didn't satisfy. He stayed awake until dawn writing music to her.

People wondered about his childhood. Only the few people closest to him knew anything about it. Once there had been a father in the house. An excitable, energetic man who juggled stocks and toyed with companies. He played piano, not well but with a passion that made his wife laugh aloud, or cry, depending on the music. The composer could remember them laughing together; he remembered the softness of his mother's lap, her cheek pressed against his head, and the sunlight coming through the tall windows and falling in long golden paths on the floor.

When the composer was still very small, his father fell ill. He lay in bed slowly dying, the sickness working its way through his body. The house fell silent. The curtains were drawn. After he died, his wife went to her room and would not come out for weeks. She grew thin and angular. The composer wandered through the house alone, dragging the furniture around and stamping his feet to disturb the silence.

Again and again during the long days he went to his mother's room. She locked the door against him or warned him away in a dull voice.

One day he found the door open, and when he went in she offered no resistance. He went to where she sat in a chair by the window. She did not look at him. He tried to climb into her lap. She did not stop him, did not help him. He sat on her thighs; she was as stiff and unmoving as a cane chair. He called to her and she looked past him. She let out a soft feathery sigh. He thought she might break under his weight.

He slid off her lap and went downstairs in the heavy silence. He went from room to room until he saw the piano hulking in a corner. He thought of his father's flashing fingers, the noise, the sunlight streaming in the windows, his mother's laugh. He pulled himself up on the bench. He could barely see the keys. He raised his hands and began to play.

Most likely, all that came out were the meaningless sounds of his small fingers pounding the keys. But the composer remembered it as the most beautiful music in the world because as he played he heard a shifting upstairs, then footsteps. His mother flew down the stairs, put her arms around him, and pressed her cheek against his head.

Perhaps he was a genius. Perhaps she wanted another piano player in the house.

Whatever the reason, she sent him to the best schools, found him the best instructors. He read about Mozart and began composing when he was fourteen. She was proud of him, sometimes fascinated by him. But as she grew older she touched him less and less, paid attention to her own affairs. The composer continued to write, always struggling to recapture the days of sunlight and mother's laughter.

He didn't have to live like that. He could have moved out of that house with its mercurial climate. He had plenty of money. He acquired fame early. He had plenty of friends, actors and writers and hangers-on; they liked him because he was such a hoot at parties—what a riot! Dirty jokes, party tricks, anything he did was funny, though he never laughed himself.

And not an ugly man, either. There were women who said, Leave that house, why don't you; come stay with me and *be* with me. Maybe not in those words, but that was what they meant.

He looked as if he had never really grown up; he had a secretive child's face. Yet he had the fiery glow of the genius about him, too. It drew people to him, they basked in it. His face came alive when he spoke, his hands made frenetic gestures, his forehead shone. You could see the delicate blue veins on the insides of his wrists when his sleeves slid up. Like rivers on a map, leading into unknown regions. Where did they go? There were women who longed to touch those veins, trace them up the pale underside of his arm, follow them up and up to wherever they might lead. Women wanted to touch the heart of him and be his muse.

But no woman wanted to follow him home to the dusty dark where his mother waited. And the composer was never tempted, never enticed to spend the night in another place.

He said he could not leave his mother alone.

If you asked him about his mother, you would see his lips tighten, and he would answer you in a perfunctory way: her health, her latest vacation. He might invent something: a pet chow with digestive troubles, a new pair of Italian shoes, a Brazilian admirer.

If you asked him about himself, he would stare blankly, as if you had mentioned a distant acquaintance he hadn't spoken to in years.

He approached thirty. Their struggle escalated. Every time he celebrated his mother's bulk with a symphony, she returned to diets and pills and self-improvement courses. He wanted to write a huge, enormous thing—an opera!—to make her love him and love herself as much as he wanted her to.

But she died before he could. She was old enough, it was not unusual. They say the death was to be expected: All that weight being lost and gained, it puts a strain on the body. Those dieting pills, they ought to be outlawed, they say.

He did not cry at the funeral. The casket was closed. He did not want anyone to see her as she had been in the end. The funeral was held in a great church, and hundreds of people came, out of respect for him, but also in the hope that they would hear him speak and hear some of his music. But he requested a requiem by Bach. During the service he hovered in the shadows where no one could see him. Afterward he approached the casket and touched it, then brought his hand to his chest. When someone touched his shoulder, he shuddered and turned away.

He refused to listen to his own music after her death.

He shut himself in the house and said he would not write again now that his inspiration had departed. His hair grew longer and hung in tangles because he did not comb it. He seldom answered the phone. He played loud rock music in his bedroom late at night like a teenager. He said the noise drowned out his thoughts. He said no one would ever know the secrets of his heart the way his mother had. He did not want to share himself with anyone else.

Only my mother loves me, he said. But he was wrong.

No one knew what went on inside that house. People wondered. His patrons waited. The newspapers tried and failed to get an interview, so they ran old pictures of him instead.

Often friends came to the door and knocked, but he would not see them. People called, but he let the phone ring, enjoying the noise. He saw no one, let no one in.

He changed, grew fury-frozen and wild. He had said he would write no more music, yet his thoughts were still filled with it, clamoring to be written down. He tried to empty his head by writing, then burning it, but it didn't matter. Every morning he woke with fresh stanzas ringing in his ears. He tried not to sleep, to keep his mind from working without him. But the music slipped in through the chinks, note by note. He heard it. In everything: the leaking faucet, the plane overhead, the children outside on the street, the rhythm of his breathing.

Nothing could distract him. The drinks and drugs and pleasures that distracted other men left him cold. He sat or paced, day after day, hands to his temples. Nothing moved him. An admirer visited but could not rouse him. He ignored her long sun-colored hair splayed across his chest, the fingers probing his unknown places, the whisper in his ear. Even when she put on his mother's gaudy, glowing clothes and pranced and preened before him, he did not stir. Did not shout in anger, did not snatch the clothes away, did not cry or laugh. The woman left, saying she could not compete with ghosts.

The composer stood before a mirror holding one of his mother's dresses against him. The dress moved and shimmered in a draft. He stared at his features and searched for traces of hers.

He spoke aloud, ranted, as if his mother could hear. He asked her if she was with God now, enjoying the heavenly choirs. He said he was jealous of God. If there was no God, then he was jealous of the worms instead.

He was angry at her for leaving him. As if she had run off with the milkman.

He said the music would not cease. It sloshed and crashed in his head. He refused to open the floodgates to let it out. A flock of violins, like seagulls. Kettle drums thunder-rumbling. His heart beat a rhythm like dance music. Music! For dancing! His own traitorous heart!

He directed his anger against it, as if his heart were the enemy. He cried out that if he had the means, he would stop it. He said he could not stand to go on any longer. He did not care about anything but her.

His own voice began to grate on him, for in it he heard the cadences and pauses of the music that swarmed within him, seeking an outlet. He clamped his lips, chewed his tongue. He wrapped himself in a furious silence.

He was found some time later, his face strangely bloated, a hand to his throat as if choking. And yet his throat was clear.

The papers all said things like: what a young man he was, and what a genius, and how he was only at the start of a glorious career, cut short, such a tragedy, a great loss to all of us, a loss to mankind, a genius now silent, no one will ever know the secret of such genius, a secret only his mother knew.

We can only wonder.

The men summoned to perform the autopsy were skilled doctors, ignorant of music. The composer's body lay on a table, a cold bundle that had once writhed and sweated and sighed in passion. The doctors opened the chest cavity and were startled to find an engorged, en-larged heart, coated with plaque, the muscles gone weak and flabby. It was the heart of someone much older, much heavier. The doctors continued to explore the secrets of his body with their clinical hands. As they worked they heard a faint faltering sound, like a tune escaping a music box opened after years of disuse, and beneath the table they tapped their feet to an unconscious rhythm, the rhythm of a beat beat beating heart.

PARK BENCH

This is the park bench where I fell in love with Denise. It looks the same: wood slats, chipped green paint, somebody's initials (not ours) carved on the back. It was autumn when it happened, and the trees were like traffic lights, going from green to yellow and red. The air was crisp and smelled of burning leaves.

This is also the park bench where I saw Denise for the last time. It was autumn that time, too, same details: chipped paint, initials, burning smell.

It happened like this. I was crossing through the park during lunch hour, scuffling through the leaves and holding a bag with a sandwich and a bottle of pop in one hand while trying to loosen my tie with the other, when I saw Denise sitting there. Only I didn't know her name was Denise then.

She was sitting there reading a book. It was a big thick book, I remember, with tiny print, and she was almost done with it. She sat with her ankles together and her knees together, kind of hunching forward, as if she wanted to dive in and blast through the last pages.

I sat down on the bench next to her, but not too close. Her hair was cut short, but it looked good on her; she had the right sort of head for it. I waited for her to look up. I rattled my bag around, cleared my throat. She turned the page and her eyes flew back and forth over it.

"Hi," I said.

She looked up and blinked. Her eyes were like swirled marbles, gray and green mixed. "Hi," she said.

"Jack," I said, introducing myself.

"Denise," she said, and that's when I knew, seeing her lips hissing out the end of her name; I knew she was a home run, a keeper, a real thing, a long-term plan, something worth hanging on to forever, or for at least a month and a half. I can't explain how I knew. Call it intuition. Call it fate.

"So . . ." I said, trying to get started. I crossed one ankle over the other knee. I stretched my arms out along the back of the bench. "So, what's a nice girl like you doing in a place like this?"

She laughed a polite, mechanical little laugh and went back to her book. We sat there a few minutes. She read. I stretched out and stared at the sky. We were quite companionable really. I mean, some people have to be talking all the time; it's rare to find someone you can just be quiet with—you know, not need to say anything because you already understand each other. She was quite comfortable with me already, like she'd known me a long time. I could tell this by the way she wasn't at all self-conscious in front of me; she even picked at her nose a little as she read, as if she knew I liked her enough not to care.

It was good like that. But we needed to move on. We were neither of us getting any younger. The leaves were turning, turning. "Denise," I said, and "Denise . . ." I said again, my voice choked with longing, and she turned to me, and we locked eyes. We looked deep into each other's souls and knew each other, truly, deeply, and in that split second we smashed down all the barriers of gender and class and politics and age and sex that people write books and advice columns about. One brilliant flash, I swear to God it can happen even in this shabby old world, brilliant flashes, true communion. That's what I felt as I sat on that park bench and squashed my sandwich under my thigh in my excitement.

She gazed long and longingly at me and didn't say anything. There was nothing left to say. I took her in my arms and kissed her, a deep, probing kiss that plumbed her very depths; deliciously delirious, I nudged the base of her brain and tickled the backs of her eyeballs with my tongue. I didn't stop until I knew her insides the way a blind man knows the face of a loved one beneath his fingertips.

She pulled away, blushing, suddenly shy. She drew back to her end of the bench. She crossed her legs and laid her book on her lap. But in spite of her demurrings, I knew she was as inflamed as I. This thing that had sprouted between us was growing unchecked. We could not resist it; we could only follow along.

I took off my jacket and tossed it over the back of the bench. I took off my tie. I bent to unlace my shoes and pull them off. I took off my socks. She was watching me.

"So you're staying, then," she said. Her voice was cool.

I straightened up. "I thought you wanted me to," I said.

"It looks like you're planning to stay whether I want you to or not," she said, getting all defensive, like she was afraid to trust me.

"I'm only trying to do what you want—what we both want," I said. "I won't stay on your bench if you don't want me to." And I stood up.

"Yes, yes, I want you to. Please stay with me," she said after a moment, holding herself as if she was cold.

So I stayed and we made love on the bench as only two people who are truly in love can make love, and we leapt and swooped and flew in a fantastic oneness surrounded by fireworks in slow motion and Vivaldi violins, and with love like that, who notices the hardness of the boards, or the splinters?

Afterward she cried and said I would leave her, like they always did. She held me fast by a belt loop and prepared for a struggle. But I had no intention of leaving.

We set up a home there, on the park bench, and we started out the way all good idealistic unions begin: with lots of love and hope and few material possessions. We had all we needed: The ventilation was good, the facilities adequate, the provisions only slightly squashed.

We thought our love would sustain us, but unforeseen difficulties arose. She adored me. She was attentive—too attentive. She hovered over me constantly, tending to my clothes and the maintenance of my body. I am self-sufficient by nature. She was suffocating me. And she was dissatisfied with the place; she wanted to move. She thought a higher elevation would be healthier for the children, when they arrived.

Our lovemaking was still a glorious tumbling union through space, but I began to feel the roughness of the bench, where I had not before. Her short hair tickled my nose, making me sneeze.

"I wish you wouldn't throw your clothes around," she said. "You know I hate it when you do that." She folded up my jacket, rolled the tie into a neat ball.

"And I hate it when you nag," I growled. She leaned over and untied my shoelace so that she could retie it in a neater knot. "Quit it," I said, jerking my foot away.

She turned away and sulked and opened her book. I had to coax and plead with the back of her neck to get her to turn around.

Our lovemaking grew less and less like gymnastics in zero gravity; it was becoming slow and ponderous, like sumo wrestling.

I liked to sit still and watch the world go by. But she could not sit still. I watched the leaves fall in slow spirals; she fidgeted and stroked the hair at my temple. "Oh, look," she said. "A gray hair." I felt a ping of pain in my scalp as she pulled it out. Her fingers moved again, stopped again. "Oooh, here's another."

I slapped her hand away. "Pick, pick, pick. Nag, nag, nag. That's all you ever do. You're worse than your mother."

"You've never even met my mother."

"But I know what she's like, and I bet you're even worse than she is."

"You leave my mother out of this!" she screamed.

"You know she's just an old bag, a lonely old bag who does nothing but nag and pick the clothes up off the floor, and—"

"Stop it, stop it, stop it!" she screamed.

"And one day you'll be just like her!" I finished. She beat at me with her fists. Boy, I'd really struck a nerve with the mother thing. But I couldn't stop myself; it was as if I could see her turning into her mother before my eyes, I could see her growing old long before I did, and suddenly I was terrified of our future together.

"You don't know anything about it! What do you know! Insensitive clod!" she cried. She snatched up my clothes and things and flung them off her bench. "Get out! Get out! Get out!"

I stood up. "Don't worry, I'm leaving, and I'm not coming back. You'll be the one to regret this one day, not me. One day when you're all lonely and old, dragging around, you'll remember Jack. You'll re-member the one who got down on his hands and knees and offered you true love and you just threw it away."

I was rather proud of that last part, about the hands and knees. I made it up on the spot. I stood there and tried to remember our happy times together, our immediate intimacy, but all that was gone. Sud-denly I didn't know her at all, and all I could think of was the way she'd nagged and smothered and held me down on that bench for so long. Resentment curdled the air between us.

That was that. I gathered up my clothes, and the sandwich in the paper bag, and the soda pop. I left her exactly the way I'd found her, with her legs tight together and her head bent. Only this time, she was weeping with fury and (I'm sure) regret. She looked up and screamed, "Get out! Get *out*, I said!" So I did.

I was only a little late getting back to the office. I got right back to work on the accounts I'd begun earlier. I lost myself once again in the columns of numbers, and soon I felt like I had never left.

But I didn't forget Denise. I still haven't; she's stayed in my head all this time. I mean, here it is already Friday, and still I'm thinking about her. That's why I'm back at the park, looking at the same old bench, with this foolish kind of hope that maybe, just maybe, she'll still be here.

Of course she isn't. I sit on the bench gingerly and watch the leaves fall. I think of all the time I spent with her. Then I think of all the ways I might have used that time instead: golfing, learning Spanish, traveling the world, loving another woman.

But I think the time was well spent. These days, it's hard to keep track of time once it's past and done and gone. Sure, some people take pictures, write it all down. But it's just paper; it doesn't mean anything. All you can do is try to hang on to those significant moments.

And that's what it was with Denise—the brilliant flash, the moment of communion. *That* moment I'll hang on to. And I can make it as long or as short as I want it. It is safe in the past, just as I want it to be; no one can prove it is otherwise.

So this is how it will be: Denise and I sit on a park bench, eyes locked, lost in the brilliant flash, whirling in the celestial dance and squashed sandwiches, giving off sparks, knowing each other to the deepest and fullest, completely naked to each other—no, beyond naked, *skinned*, maybe, metaphorically of course, our inner working exposed to each other, incredible intimacy, our insides dissected, centrifuged, laid out on microscope slides, numbered and labeled down to the last chromosome. *That's* how thoroughly we know and understand each other and ourselves, and everything is clear and right in this one glorious melding moment that lasts a hundred thousand years.

HUNDRED-POUND BABY

There's a hundred-pound baby in the house, whom no one's talking about.

I can hear it thumping around. It's just a baby, too young to walk; it's crawling, its belly sliding across the linoleum. *Sssssssth. Sssssssth.*

I've tried to tell my mother. She says, "Baby? The baby's right here. Kay, stop it. Don't eat that."

Kay is my sister. She won't eat anything you feed her on a spoon, but she'll eat anything she finds on the ground. She is red most of the time from screaming.

"Not Kay, the other baby," I tell my mother. But she doesn't want to talk about it.

My mother got really big before Kay was born. Then she went to the hospital and we went to visit her, me and my dad. And we went to the room with the glass wall and the rows of babies and Kay was in there somewhere, and my dad said, "Isn't she a beauty?" and I said yeah, though I couldn't tell which one she was.

Then my mother came home, and she was still big. She stayed in bed, with the pillows heaped around her and one under her knees. She had dark circles under her eyes, like she'd been hit on the head.

She'd yell for me sometimes: "Nick! Nicky! *Nicholas!*" When I came in, the shades would be down and the bed unmade and my mother puddled in the middle of it. "Nick, would you turn on the TV," she'd say. "I can't seem to rouse myself."

She was right. She was too heavy to get up. So I would turn on the little TV on her dresser and flip channels till she said stop, and I'd fiddle with the volume and the antenna until she was satisfied. Then she'd say, "Bring me the *TV Guide*, will you?" I would take it over to her, and up close her mouth had an unbrushed smell and her hair had a mousy smell.

If she saw dirt on my face, she'd lick her finger and try to rub it off. I hated that. I'd try to get out of her room as fast as I could. "Could you come back in an hour and change it to Channel Seven?" she'd yell after me.

"Okay, okay," I'd say, and run down the stairs and go outside. I think the sky was always gray then, and heavy and low and not a breath of air stirring. The air was thick, humid; it made me want to pant like a dog. The sparkly summer insects and the moths and grasshoppers were all gone by then. All that was left were those black gnats like bits of dirt that liked to fly in your eyes.

My dad bought me this kite with ninja warriors painted on it. It was supposed to do loops and tricks in the air, but I could never get it off the ground. I had my friend Newt hold the string and I held the kite and we ran across the field behind the swimming pool. Again and again, back and forth. The air was too heavy and brooding to lift it. Once I lost my grip, but Newt kept running. And I ran after, yelling, "Stop, stop!" I kept trying to grab it, but it was dragging along just beyond my fingers, catching and tearing on the dry grass.

Newt was not really my friend.

My mother kept Kay in a crib in the storage room off of their bedroom. One morning she yelled, "Come here." I went and found her shuffling around Kay's room in her slippers. Her nightgown was unbuttoned more than it should have been.

Kay was lying there wiggling around. So pink all over, and her arms and legs were so fat, they had creases in them. Her eyes stayed closed most of the time, and with her bald head and scrunched-up face, she looked like a little old man.

"I want to show you something," my mother said. She leaned into the crib and I saw her breasts swinging loose. She lifted Kay up, carried her to the changing table, and changed her diaper.

"Now you do it," she told me. "Take this one off and put on a new one."

Kay squalled. She didn't like going through it all again. Her body felt soft and trembly and loose. It felt like my face, my chin. She was so light. I could have picked her up by the ankles and swung her around and around over my head.

I tried to do it quickly and it was like wrapping up raw meat, like chicken. It was not too hard because she was already clean. My mother looked satisfied as she went back to sink down in her hollow on the bed.

Afterward my mother asked me to change Kay again and again. I started to wish I hadn't done such a good job that first time.

I stayed out of the house. It was so hot, but the sun wouldn't shine. It was so humid that it made sweat break out on your forehead and drip down your back. There was a creek near our house and I went there with Newt. It was down in a deep ravine and none of the kids in the neighborhood were supposed to go there. So we all did. Someone had tied a rope up in one of the trees and if you swung hard enough and jumped at the right moment, you would land on the other side of the ravine. If you missed, you'd go slipping and sliding on the loose dirt down the steep slopes and land in the creek. The creek was only a foot deep, but so murky that it must have been full of tropical diseases.

My mother had said some kid broke his leg or back or head swinging on that thing, and I wasn't supposed to go there. I wondered why no one had cut down the rope, then. I figured some of the parents went there secretly sometimes to swing on it. They liked to keep the secrets to themselves.

It was a wonderful swing, a wonderful flight feeling to swing out and see the creek fifteen feet below, feel the dip and sway as the tree branch bent with the weight, the soft floating moment after leaving the rope and before meeting the ground. Then the earth leapt upward with a knee-buckling crash landing on the other side.

Sometimes we went wading to catch crawdads or the little orange lizards that were named after Newt. People said there were leeches there. I didn't mind leeches, but I thought of the African worms I saw on TV that could bore into your foot and work their way into your stomach and get longer and longer inside you.

One day when I came home, I found my mother sitting on the edge of the bed with her feet on the floor. Her hair was matted up. Her nightgown was unbuttoned again and slipping off one shoulder. "I can't stand up and I can't lie down," she said. "I can't seem to get my feet off the ground."

It almost sounded like a song I had heard somewhere.

"Would you go check on Kay, honey?" she said. She'd never called me honey before.

My dad was not around much.

My dad was an accountant and that meant lots of papers and wearing suits and getting migraine headaches. His hair was receding on the sides, but not as fast in the middle. His hair was dark, and when he didn't shave for a day, the stubble gave his face a gray shadow.

He and my mother used to touch each other a lot, even at the dinner table. He liked to run his fingers through her hair and she would laugh and stroke his smooth forehead. Then they would lean over the table and kiss, and afterward I would have to check my plate for stray hairs.

He was happy that day in the hospital when he said, "Isn't she a beauty?" He said it the way he talked about cars or boats in magazines: hushed. "Isn't she something?"

But soon after, he changed. He stayed at his office later and when he came home, he spent a long time drinking coffee and reading newspapers with very small print. My mother would not go out, so he started buying the groceries: peanut butter and microwavable TV dinners. He started sleeping downstairs on the living room sofa. So Kay's crying wouldn't disturb him, he said. He was very busy and he needed his sleep, he told me.

I think it was my mother who disturbed him.

I know my dad bought me things like the kite to fill in the spaces. It didn't fly.

Then they started fighting. It started small and soft and then grew. My dad would sneak into the bedroom to get something from his closet and my mother would call from the bed, "Steven, could you change the baby?"

And he said, "Why can't you?"

"I'm tired," she said. "I was up all night with her."

And he said, "I have to go to work, remember, and I'm trying to run this house and take care of the kid, and now you're asking me to change diapers? And what do you do besides lie around all day?"

She said, "Is it so hard to change your own daughter's diapers?"

"Why can't *you?*" he growled back.

She curled back herself in tighter and said, "You, you don't understand."

"You're right," he shouted. "I *don't understand how you can lay a guilt trip on me when you're the one who's such a goddamn lazy—"*

"Don't talk like that in front of Nick," my mother said.

"I didn't know the kid was here," my dad said. "Nick, get out of here."

"Wait, Nick. Could you go check on Kay?" my mother said.

Kay was sort of whimpering and kicking her legs like she was swimming, but she wasn't getting anywhere. She was very wet. She reminded me of my mother.

My father didn't like to see my mother lying in that dim room day after day in the same flowered nightgown, her face hanging slack. I didn't, either. I went to the creek. Dad stayed later at the office, then he started going out for a drink with some of the other men.

"Where have you been?" my mother shrieked the first time.

"Just stopped for a drink on the way home," he said, very cold.

The next time she said, "Where were you?" And then: "There's someone, isn't there?"

Then my dad closed the door and I heard only the ups and downs of their voices. I got out of bed and went downstairs. It was dark and everything looked blue in the moonlight. I kept holding my breath, listening for something, something, something, and it seemed something was holding its breath, listening to me.

Soon after that my dad moved out. He said, "Look Nick, it's not permanent. Just until we sort some things out, okay? I'll still come visit, lots, and you can come see my apartment, and maybe I'll be back home when we work this out. Okay?"

That's what Newt's dad told him last year. Now his mother works at the Quiki-Mart and she dates an old man with white hair and an accent and a glass eye. That's what happens.

"Will you watch out for your sister? Your mom and your sister?" my dad said.

"Okay, okay, okay," I said.

After that my mother really got big. She'd never gone back to normal size after Kay, and now she was growing like crazy. It was cooler outside and leaves were changing and shriveling and the sky was still gray, but now it was crisp and anxious. Inside, my mother swelled like bread rising. Twice a day and sometimes more she'd yell to me, and when I came, she'd give me some money from her purse and tell me to run to the store down the street. She asked for very particular things. Sometimes she was in a sweet mood, sometimes a salty one.

Now that my dad was gone, she had groceries and Pampers delivered from the supermarket. I helped the delivery guy carry the bags in. "Thanks, sport," he said. He had a big smile and a gold tooth. When we finished, he hovered in the door for a while. "Didn't you say your mother was home?" he asked after a while, gazing up the stairs.

"Yeah, but she won't come down," I told him.

His smile went away. "It figures," he muttered as he let the screen door slam behind him.

My mother still sent me on daily trips because she wanted the plastic-wrapped artificially sweet things you can only get at a place like the Quiki-Mart. Sometimes she asked for things neither I nor the man at the store had heard of. She must have eaten them when she was a kid.

My mother told me I could get some junk if I wanted. But I couldn't stomach anything after seeing her plunge her fists into a bag, seeing her face all greasy with crumbs and powdered sugar and slow sweat.

What I liked to do was stick my finger in the peanut butter jar and lick it off, and then do it again. I liked to think of everyone eating my germs and not knowing it.

School started up again, and third grade was worse than second grade. We had to run laps during recess. They didn't let us put number lines on our desks to help with subtraction anymore. Someone kept stealing my lunch money out of my desk. I went straight to the creek after school. I stayed at the creek for hours, looking at the water so dark and thick and decayed-smelling.

My mother was huge and I noticed it all of a sudden one day. I had given her a bag with some pretzels and Twinkies and the change, and she looked at my face and said, "Oh, honey," and hugged me. And my face pressed into her breast or her neck or her shoulder or her upper arm—I couldn't even tell; she was all one quivering, smothery mass. She gulped little sobs deep inside. I couldn't wait to get out.

She'd gotten big before Kay was born. And back then she'd been sort of tired and grouchy and she'd cried sometimes. And she'd asked for strange things to eat.

Looked like she was going to have another baby—a big one.

My dad wasn't around, so I thought I would have to act as a kind of father. I wasn't sure what I had to do. I wasn't sure I'd be able to pick the baby out from a roomful of babies the way my dad did.

I probably could. It would be the biggest baby in the room.

Aunt Sandra showed up then.

She was my mother's sister. She lived a ways away. We visited there last summer; it took us a day to drive. She had a big house and a husband who was a dentist and laughed a fake ho-ho-ho laugh. Aunt Sandra wore big rings and high heels and was fluttery like a bird. Her laugh was sharp and real, like a sneeze.

She came in without knocking, calling, "Helloo, Helloo, anybody hooome?" I came running down the stairs, and she said, "Nick! Nick! Where's your mother? Is she all right?"

"She's upstairs," I said. "She's okay."

"I haven't talked to her for weeks. I was so worried—I had to come out. Every time I called, you told me she couldn't come to the phone," Aunt Sandra said, glancing around.

"Yeah," I said. "She told me to say that to everyone who called, even my dad."

"Your dad? . . ." she said, and then clicked up the stairs in her high heels. I heard her go into the bedroom, heard her say, "Helen? Helen? Oh Hel . . ." and then the door closed and there was muffled talking and crying and the bed creaking beneath them.

Much, much later Aunt Sandra came out and tapped at my door. "Nick?" she said. "Nick, I think your mother needs a vacation. I'm going to take her away for a while."

"Where?" I said.

"We'll go to my friend's lake house up in New Hampshire. It's beautiful, and she can relax there. . . . Nick, someone needs to stay here with you and your sister. Do you want me to ask your dad, or should I find a sitter?"

"A sitter," I said.

So that's what they did. Aunt Sandra had to buy my mother a new dress; her old ones didn't fit. My mother lumbered out of the house, not looking up, Aunt Sandra's arm around her shoulder. She was huge;

Aunt Sandra was child-size next to her. They drove off under the gray sky and it was raining—so light that you couldn't see it, but you could feel it tingling.

Mrs. Moore came to stay with us. Kay didn't like her. Neither did I. Kay didn't like her new formula; she kept spitting it up on Mrs. Moore's shoulder. Mrs. Moore had stiff gray hair and big glasses and perfect posture. At night she snored. I walked around downstairs and nothing was there, but the snores and Kay's cries filled the darkness, so it was not empty.

They were gone three weeks.

My mother came back changed. Her eyes were steadier. She laughed, and her laugh was short and sharp. Her hair was smooth and shiny, and when she hugged me, I could tell her neck from her shoulder from her arm again. She was smaller and harder. Her stomach had gone down some.

She'd had the baby.

"Look at your mother. Doesn't she look great?" said Aunt Sandra.

"You've lost about a hundred pounds," I said.

My mother laughed at that. She had Kay in her arms. Kay looked like she might spit up any minute. Or maybe she was smiling.

They were all so happy-looking, I didn't want to ask about the new baby right then.

I know it's here. I can hear it. No one wants to talk about it.

How can they ignore a hundred-pound baby?

My mother drinks diet milk shakes. When I ask her if I can have one, she says, "No. We grown-ups get all the good stuff. Those are the rules."

When we are downstairs, the baby is upstairs. When we are in Kay's room, I hear it crawling on the kitchen floor. *Ssssssssth. Ssssssssth.*

"Baby? Here's the baby, right here," my mother says, thrusting Kay at me. Kay smiles for real. She has a head full of hair and spit bubbles on her smile.

"Not Kay," I say. "The other one. The big one you had."

"Don't tell me you want another baby. One in the house is enough," my mother says.

My mother takes classes at night now, and Mrs. Moore returns to sit. She sits straight upright, as if something has startled her.

My father used to stop by once a week. Now he doesn't come at all.

My mother is busy all the time. She rushes around; she changes all the diapers. She stays out of bed. Her feet are never still. She is too happy. Her smile is strained. There is tension heavy in the house, phone conversations buzzing behind closed doors; something is waiting to happen.

It's that baby. Babies don't like to be ignored. He must be wet by now; someone should change him. I'd do it if he would stay still and let me find him.

My mother smiles hard at me but does not tell me anything. She calls me honey now and then. She knows about the baby and she won't tell me. She must be the one feeding it and changing it, changing the big hundred-pound diapers. She talks on the phone to Aunt Sandra lots, but she won't talk to me. All secretive. The parents keep all the good things for themselves. Isn't a hundred-pound baby a good thing? All babies are good things, so a really big one must be even better.

He's like a turtle, with the big head waving around and the big stomach holding him down and baby hands swimming in the air. I worry about him being hungry, so I pour some of Kay's formula into three bowls and leave them in different places around the house.

The next day my mother says, "What's that smell? Nick? Did you do this?"

I hear my mother talking on the phone: ". . . I don't want him in this house anymore. . . . Get rid of him as soon as possible. . . . I don't want him seeing Nick, either. . . ."

So she is hiding the baby from me. But she doesn't want him herself. No wonder he stays so quiet, never cries. He knows he'll get thrown out.

My mother takes long, hot showers. She buys new clothes and high heels like Aunt Sandra. I see her dusting with a rag torn from the flowered nightgown. She is always busy, in and out, on the phone. The hundred-pound baby dodges her. So do I.

I hear her on the phone again, saying, "I need to tell him. . . . He needs to know. . . ."

She's going to break the news to the baby. He can't hide forever.

One afternoon in November my mother comes to me all serious and stern. "Nick," she says, "your father and I are getting a divorce. Do you know what that means?"

I say, "Yeah."

"We both love you, Nick. And we still like each other. We're still friends. But we need to spend less time together. Do you understand that? It's . . . it's like your friend Newt. He's your friend, isn't he, but I haven't seen him come over here for a long time. But he's still your friend, isn't he? Sometimes friends need to be apart. Don't they?"

I think of Newt dragging the new kite through the weeds and brush. I remember it sliding along jaggedly right in front of me, just out of reach. It is shredded and broken; it will never fly.

"Nick, I want you to think about something. Do you want to live here with me and your sister, or would you like to live with your dad? I want you here and Kay wants you here. Do you want to stay?"

My mother has two lines between her eyebrows.

I don't want to talk about that. I try to turn away, but she grabs my arm.

"Okay, okay," I say, twisting away from her. It is not hard to say; I decided that a long time ago. Okay.

The hundred-pound baby comes to me that night. I can't see him—it's too dark—but I can hear his breathing like soft hiccups. He whimpers beside the bed; he thumps against it, shaking me. He's saying, Me, me, me, what about me? Can I stay? What about me?

He doesn't say it, but that's what he means. I can tell. I have learned from reading Kay.

I reach down to touch him, give him a pat maybe, but he is already lumping away. I can see his shadow cross the hall. He's crying, crying, crying; his tears leave a wet path behind him like a snail's trail.

After things get all settled and arranged, my dad comes back to get the rest of his things: the tennis rackets in the basement, the encyclopedias he won as a prize in high school. He's growing a beard now, a grayish brown scruff all over his face. All you can see are his eyes.

I help him put books in boxes and carry them to his car. I remember the delivery guy with the gold tooth who called me sport. I remember his face.

"I'll miss you, Nick," my dad says in between trips.

"You can still visit if you want," I say, and shrug. "It's okay with me."

"I'm moving to Chicago, Nick," my dad says. "But I can still call. I'll want to talk to you. You can come visit on vacations. It'll be fun."

"Well, it's good I decided not to live with you," I say, "because I wouldn't want to switch schools and all that."

"You decided? But I never asked for custod—" he said, then caught himself. "I mean . . . Nick, I meant that I . . . Christ, Nick, that's not what I meant. . . ."

That is all. While he's inside saying good-bye to my mother, I slip one of Kay's dirty diapers into an open box in his trunk. Then he comes out and puts his hand on the back of my neck and gives it a squeeze and a shake. That's good-bye.

He drives off with his car coughing and growling. I go down to the ravine.

The rope swing is still there. The sun comes through the trees in sudden jabs and splotches. Down below, way down there, a million miles down, is the creek. *Trickle-drip-drip*, wet rocks and tropical diseases. That's where it all goes. Down. Can't get my feet off the ground. Can't change the channel. Can't get up. My mother was right.

I yank on the rope. The branch bends. It creaks like bedsprings. Nothing holds up. You can't fight gravity. You can't ever fly.

I jump up anyway.

I jump and the swing holds; it holds together. I swing back and forth, higher and higher, and my feet aren't touching the ground. Higher and higher, until I can make it across the gap. The creek will not get me and now is the time to let go for the floating, swimming feeling before the slamming crash landing.

Kay would like it. I will show her one day.

When I go home, it feels like a hundred-pound weight has lifted. That baby is gone.

"Where's the baby?" I ask my mother.

"Right here," says my mother. "Look, Kay, there's Nicky."

Kay looks up at me and gives me a smile, a big gummy one. She is getting better and better at smiling. So is my mother.

I think the baby must have slipped into my dad's car when no one was looking.

Won't he be surprised, halfway to Chicago, to find a hundred-pound baby in the backseat.

WHAT HAPPENED

Things happen sometimes in a way you don't expect. The katydids stop singing, all of them at the same time for no reason. Or else the roads are always clear and then suddenly for one week there's a roadkill epidemic, squirrels and possums every few hundred yards along the highway. Or else there's an immaculate conception and an exodus right in your neighborhood and everyone pretends it didn't happen. But it did.

It happens like this.

It happens two summers ago. July. It happens in a town in South Carolina. Shiny new McDonald's and long, low strip malls and the orange roof of the Howard Johnson motel for the Yankee tourists on their way down to Disney World. But the rest of the town looks weathered and gray like driftwood, though the sea is miles away. The houses are hidden in the trees, tall swaying pine trees that whoosh and whisper like the ocean roar.

It is July and Leah is seventeen. She is a skinny string-beany kind of girl, speckled with freckles on her face and forearms and even her ears. Years ago her mother refused to let her get her ears pierced, but Leah went and did it anyway. Her mother didn't notice, not for months; the holes just blended in with all those other dots.

Now Leah's thinking about a tattoo. "Right here," she says, pulling down the waistband of her skirt and pointing to her hip. "A fish maybe, a rainbow trout with real rainbows on it, or a dragonfly. Mom would never see it." Ellie just nods. She is Leah's sister, thirteen, and wears glasses. They both have the same hair, sort of hair-colored hair, not really blond, not really brown. But Ellie's grows forward and hangs in her eyes and Leah's falls back, so you see the freckles on her forehead.

It's July and it's hot. They sit on the swing on the front porch with its *creak-creak* chains and weathered boards. It's cooler inside, but Leah wants to sit out here and Ellie wants to be with Leah. Ellie sits stiff, her arms tight against her sides. There is hair under there all of a sudden; she would like to ask Leah about it, how to get rid of it, but Leah's mind is on exciting, important things now, like tattoos.

Ellie's a funny kid, doesn't talk much, and her eyes are always magnified by those glasses, so she seems to look everywhere at once. And once when she was younger, she came in from playing with a broken arm, wouldn't say how it happened, like she was embarrassed to admit she'd fallen down or lost her grip. Just stood in the doorway, her arm hanging bent, as if it had two elbows, while her mother ripped through her purse looking for car keys to take her to the hospital. But this story is about Leah.

Leah's not thinking about tattoos; she's thinking dark, stealthy things and she presses her hands against her stomach. She squeezes, frowns, and Ellie, watching her, thinks, *menstrual cramps*, and is envious. Leah glances at her watch and yelps and springs off the swing and rushes off late for work again. The swing rocks wildly in her wake and Ellie watches her go.

Leah works in a diner part-time for the summer. It is not picturesque or nostalgic at all—no jukebox, no old-fashioned soda fountain. There's just a counter and plastic booths and a greasy fast-food smell. Mostly old people come in for coffee and a Danish. They sit at the counter and they have trouble getting up on the high stools, and once up, they complain about their backs and the heat.

Leah pours coffee and writes down orders and passes them through the window to Raymond, who cooks things in the back. She has to wear a hateful uniform, pink and old-fashioned like a cotton-candy nurse. Everybody likes her; it's hard not to. She can hang a spoon on her nose. "Look, look," she says, and tries to juggle silverware. She can almost do it, too. She took tap-dancing lessons when she was little; now when she's bored, she taps out a little rhythm on the linoleum and the people at the counter applaud. Even Raymond sticks his head out sometimes and flashes her a grin—white teeth shiny in his handsome black face.

The old ladies wear straw hats with velvet ribbons and dried flowers, and stockings with seams up the back, even in summer. Some have violet hair, some put on too much makeup, pink circles on their cheeks and lipstick caked in the wrinkles around their mouths. But there is something refined and delicate in the way they raise their reading glasses to their eyes to read the same menu that they see every day.

They tell Leah all sorts of useful things, like the signs of diabetes—a dry palate and having to pee a lot—and they fill her in on the soap operas she misses when she is working. They talk about debutante balls and their daddies as if they were still sixteen.

One time someone snatched Mrs. Ramsey's purse and Leah chased the guy and got it back. Turned out he was only a kid, Ellie's age, and when Leah grabbed his shirt, he started to cry. So she left him alone, his nose running, and brought back the purse. On the way she looked inside the purse. Nothing there but a can of Mace. "Thank you, dear," Mrs. Ramsey whispered when Leah returned it. "I swear this place has changed so; I don't feel safe anymore. Do you know I sleep with Mr. Ramsey's pistol next to the bed?" She clutched the purse and glared suspiciously beyond Leah to where Raymond was humming and chopping up lettuce with a big cleaver.

Mostly nothing happens in the diner; the purse theft was so exciting, the old ladies are still talking about it weeks later, still talking about it this particular day in July when Leah is distracted—her green cat eyes narrowed, squinting at nothing, and her hands on her stomach again. The other waitress is on the phone. Someone wants more coffee. Something sticky spills over the counter and a fly buzzes furiously as the ceiling fan stirs it around in the air, but still Leah stands thoughtful, at a standstill. No tricks today.

Her face is a puzzle. If you could play connect the dots with the freckles, what would you find? Then she sighs; she nods at no one. She rubs her eyes and tunes herself back in, to the empty coffee cup and the fly and the spilled bloody ketchup and Mrs. Ramsey's voice saying, ". . . snatched my purse, just *ripped* it right out of my hands. He was huge, over six feet tall and arms like an ape, horrible. . . ."

Leah is back; she pours the coffee, but her smile is strained, like a hammock stretched too tight.

Leah comes home that day in time for dinner. Her mother makes sure they have dinner together every night to discuss things. Roast beef and mashed potatoes and a glass of milk for Ellie—she's still growing, needs calcium—and cloth napkins for everyone, blue-striped seersucker.

Leah and Ellie and Mother and Father, they sit like a football huddle around the round table. Leah's mother has a no-nonsense haircut; when she turns her head, her hair moves, then falls back into the exact same waves as before. "Leah, you should cut your hair this way, don't you like it? No? Maybe before you go to college, then," her mother says.

Her father's hair is thin and he has a reddish mustache. Years ago her father would say, "Look, look, see the elephants living in my mustache?" Leah would look closely and say, "Yes, yes, I see them," because somehow she could. And Ellie would say yes, too, only because Leah said it, because actually Ellie couldn't see much of anything at all, she was so nearsighted, but no one seemed to notice for a long time.

Now her father never talks about elephants. He works in real estate or realty, or is it retail? There is gray in his mustache.

It is a rule at the family dinner: Everyone must contribute, everyone must say something. Sometimes it is difficult to get Ellie to open her mouth. But her mother is insistent. Everyone must *share*.

It is like show-and-tell.

And Leah has something to tell, though she won't begin to show for another month or two. She takes a deep, shaky breath.

"Mom, I'm pregnant . . . I think." It ends on a high note, as if it's a question.

Her mother's face falls, the hair stays in place, impossibly perfect, but the face is pinkening to red. Leah thought it only happens in books, people's mouths falling open in surprise. But her mother's drops open. All that comes out is a little moan.

Her father is red, so red, he's bulging, he's sweating, forehead glistening. Is he furious? Or is he choking on something? Heimlich maneuver, Leah thinks irrationally. How does it go? Get behind, wrap your arms around, make a fist and wrap the other hand around it, then push in and up just below the breastbone. Leah has not touched her father for years and thinks she cannot do it now even if he's dying.

Ellie? She stares at her plate, her nose almost touching the mashed potatoes. White swirls and crags and mountains of mashed potatoes, fluffy like snow, with lakes of melted butter, think of people skiing on the slopes, swimming in the lakes, small enough to hide behind a pea. A good place, Ellie thinks.

But this is Leah's story. She sits and braces herself against the storm. Her mother is past questions and into statements. She wipes her face with a napkin sometimes and her father interjects a sound of agreement. He seems to be breathing again. Good. But he's too angry to speak; he just grunts. They are no longer asking who, who, who, because of course they know who the who is.

The who is Corey, someone Leah has been dating for a long time. Not boyfriend-girlfriend—they don't hold hands; they don't call it dating. They just *do* things together. But they did go to the prom together back in May, way back. "And that's when you *did* it, wasn't it?" says Leah's mother. "I know what goes on. I wasn't born yesterday. I know what goes on on prom night."

They all picture Corey: He looks like a lizard sunning himself—his eyes always half-closed, his mouth always half-open. Dark hair, dazed eyes, and nice in a backhand way. He wants to be a rock star. He's trying to grow his hair long. Maybe he could be one if he learned how to play an instrument. Anyway, he can sing really good. Everybody says so. Even Leah says it. She laughs when she says it, but she says it. He's going to the University of South Carolina in the fall.

Picture it: lazy lizard Corey and Leah lip-locked, legs splayed, un-ladylike pant-panting, like puppies steaming up the windshield, and sticky, because May is already hot in South Carolina, and they stick to the vinyl backseat of Corey's father's car. Leah's mother can picture it; she buries her face in blue-striped seersucker. Leah's father can picture it; he coughs into his napkin. This is not table talk. Leah doesn't picture it this way at all.

"That's not what happened at all," she says. "We didn't *do* it then. We've never done it. I've never done it, not with anyone."

Her parents both stare at her suspiciously.

"I've never done it, Mom," Leah says desperately. "Really, I never have. I don't know how it happened. It's a miracle. It's a miracle; these things really happen." Leah is laughing, crying. "Mother of God," she whispers, and doesn't even know if she says it as a curse or a joke. Her mother howls, her father roars, and all over town the katydids stop singing and there is a sudden strange silence.

Leah's mother does some research around town. She tries to be subtle. It is July. People are hot and bored and willing to talk. Yes, the high school kids say, everybody knows Corey and Leah are a thing. Yes, they are together a lot. Sure they like each other. And Don, the mechanic, says, "Yeah, I saw his car parked up there, on the back road behind the gas station on prom night. There was a whole bunch of cars; all the kids went up there, the white kids and all the black kids, too, straight after the prom."

Leah's mother has Corey and his parents over for coffee and confrontation. Corey denies it. His parents are shocked. The parents wrassle and wrangle while Leah and Corey avoid each other's eyes. Where's Ellie? Who knows? This is not for her ears anyway. Leah's mother will not stand for an abortion. They will have to get married. Lots of people get married right out of high school. Corey will have to put off school for a while and work and set up a home for Leah and the baby. The parents plan; they write numbers on pieces of paper. They will help them out, get them started, get them established.

Later, when Leah finally talks to Corey alone, she says, "Why are you going along with this?"

Corey sighs and says, "Because I want to marry you. Because it's the right thing to do. It's my baby, too, you know. I guess you were wrong—it did count that time."

Leah holds her stomach, which has not yet begun to bulge. She thinks of running away, of getting an abortion, of never coming back to this hot gray place with pine trees sighing like the sea.

But she thinks of the creation, the perfect thing inside her, and she wants it.

Picture this: prom night, Leah in a pale blue dress, long, with a little lace. She hates lace; it makes her itch. Corey in a tuxedo, rented, flower in his buttonhole. Leah's mother takes pictures and they stand with space between them and Corey tries to keep his mouth closed. The pictures come out awful. After the prom they drive up the back road behind the gas station. Yes, they park there. Yes, they lie down in the backseat. But it is not sticky and sordid. It is all right. Leah says, "Let's," and Corey says, "Okay" and reaches for his wallet. There's a condom in there, one he shoplifted years ago, and he used to be very proud of it and would show it to his friends. It's been there ever since, so long that it's made a ringworm impression in the leather. He opens the package, pulls it out, tries to put it on. It snaps.

"We could do it anyway," Leah says, "if you pull out early. Then it won't even count as the real thing."

Now the story speeds up, because that's how it feels to Leah, things whizzing past in a whirl. They get married, small ceremony, just them and their parents, and Ellie, too, and the minister. They move into an apartment, very small; it is just them. Leah misses Ellie shadowing her; she misses family-discussion dinners. They use rough paper napkins. They sleep with a space between them on the bed. They are shy with each other.

It feels as if this is not happening, but it is. The days go on and on, the summer hotness sinking, cooling, and Leah's stomach grows hard and tight and heavy. Leah doesn't go back to high school, but she keeps her job at the diner.

She doesn't feel like smiling anymore, doesn't want to do tricks, and her belly strains tighter against her pink uniform. The old ladies don't talk to her so much anymore. They don't say anything, but they look disapprovingly at the growing pink expanse. When she gets bigger and it's hard for her to bend down, Raymond comes out from the back and reaches things for her. He lifts the heavy things for her and one time he has to help her sit down; somehow, she can't do it herself. Mrs. Ramsey glares pointedly at Raymond's hand on her shoulder and hugs her purse closer.

It is cold now, wind and rain and the pines soughing and sighing, and who can remember summer porch-swing weather? Ellie reads books, fast, one after the other, without pausing for breath. At night she thinks of Leah, tries to imagine her naked—the bulging stomach, the skin stretched. Would the freckles stretch, too? And the tattoo she never got—the rainbow trout, the dragonfly.

January. The baby is born. Corey stays in the waiting room and her mother holds Leah's hand in the delivery room.

"It's a beautiful baby," Leah says.

It's a boy. His eyes are blue. His skin is dark, not pink, with funny dark patches on it. "It's nothing. Those will go away," the doctor says. The baby's hair is dark fuzz. "Like yours," Leah tells Corey. Corey is afraid to hold the baby; he pats the little head carefully.

They're naming him Stan. "Why Stan?" Ellie asks.

"I picked it," says Leah. "Stan for 'Stand by Me.' I like that song; I liked the movie, too. It's a good name."

"It's okay," says Corey. "I guess."

Now Leah spends all her time taking care of Stan. She breast-feeds him. "Don't do that. I can't stand to watch it; it freaks me out," Corey said when she started. She does it anyway. They avoid each other in the small apartment.

Something is sour. Something is not right.

Stan's eyes change as he gets older. They are dark now, brown, almost black. His skin is getting darker, too. "My, he sure is tan for February," some lady in the supermarket says to Leah. Corey does not want to touch him.

Leah hugs him close. "A beautiful baby, a beautiful baby," she says fiercely.

They cannot go on like this.

Spring is coming, poking into damp corners, making a green film on things.

Corey comes in late from work one night, walking slowly up the stairs. He is nineteen. He wanted to be a rock star once. He remembers these things as if they come from long ago. He creaks up the stairs. Can he still sing?

He enters the apartment and there is his wife, on her knees, with her back to him. And crawling toward her on the carpet is the strange dusky-skinned baby, so very, very dark.

"Leah," he says, but she does not turn around. "Leah, that's not my baby. Leah, tell me that's not my son." The words come out flat and tired and dull-thudding.

Leah turns now and looks at him. She squints up green-eyed at him for a long moment. She picks up the baby and stands without dropping her eyes. "He's a beautiful baby," she says softly, "and he's mine, not yours." For the first time in months she lets her shoulders relax. They stare at each other and in the silence there is a tiny hiss, a sigh of relief. Corey. Or maybe Leah.

Spring is migration time. Leah leaves. Picture her leaving: early-morning gray and hazy mist and the road stretching out, twisting into the pines. She takes Stan and takes a suitcase and takes a bus north. Picture her mouth a grim straight line. Her back a straight line, too. She doesn't tell anyone, not even Corey. No one sees her leave; no one knows where she's going. He never has a chance to ask her why or who or if it was some kind of miracle after all.

Corey has to tell Leah's parents that she has disappeared. They are frantic; they want to start searching for her immediately. Her mother cries, her makeup smearing. Then he tells them the rest, what she said about Stan. Her father wipes his face with a handkerchief, then folds it into neat square. Her mother stops crying. Suddenly they are not so eager to find her.

Corey wants a divorce, wants an annulment. Maybe he can go to the university in the fall. Things look good. He even buys a guitar. "Yeah, I loved her, I guess," he says when his friends ask about her. "But more like a sister. I loved her like a sister. It wasn't right."

Leah's parents and Corey's try to keep the whole thing hushed, because what would people think, what will they say, how could she, did she really? This is South Carolina, remember. This is our town, our home; these things are not supposed to happen here. But somehow the story leaks out. Leah's mother's friends begin to avoid her. There is whispered talk over coffee cups and shopping carts. The tires of Leah's father's car are slashed one night.

Someone leaves a package of Oreos in the mailbox.

"She had better not come back," Leah's father says. "She's better off wherever she is."

*   *   *

And what about Ellie? Ellie watches, listens, stays in corners. Everyone forgets her. But she thinks about her sister and wonders about the thing that no one else wonders about.

Three days after Leah's disappearance Ellie walks down to the diner after school. She's been there before, lots, with Leah. It is about three o'clock now, an in-between time, and the place is empty. She creeps back to the kitchen, and there is Raymond, humming and hacking up frozen hamburger meat.

He recognizes her right off, nods to her. No smile, no bright flash of teeth.

"I'm Leah's sister," she says. But he knows that already. "I . . . I just wanted to know—Raymond, what's your whole name?"

"Raymond Martins," he says, and slams the cleaver into the meat.

"Oh," she says, twisting her hands together. She turns to leave, then turns back again and says, "Then what's your father's name?"

Raymond pauses and looks at her hard, the cleaver in his hand. "His name was Stanley."

A few days later Raymond disappears; no one knows where. People talk; people speculate. Mrs. Ramsey and her cronies shake their heads and cluck over their coffee and hug their purses and Mace ever closer when they see a black man on the street. Leah's parents will not discuss it anymore; they don't know the whole story and they don't want to. But Ellie is happy, happy, happy because maybe Leah is not alone now, wherever she is.

Ellie thinks maybe she will see Leah again sometime, in another time, another place. And Stan, too. Maybe Ellie will go somewhere and get the tattoo Leah wanted, the dragonfly with rainbows caught in its wings painted on her hip, a beautiful, permanent, precious thing kept secret.

What about the miracle and the exodus and the immaculate conception? Did they happen like that? And what happens next? Spring happens, then summer again, the *rip-rip* sound of sweaty thighs coming off plastic furniture covers, the sighing of a sea that is not really there.

What about the katydids? Do they sing again?

Ask Ellie. This is her story, too.

Ask Ellie. She can tell you.

CHAPERONE

I heard the bell ring. I opened the door, and there stood the boy, bouncing his knees impatiently, jingling a set of keys in his hand.

"Is Claudia here?" he said.

I assumed this was Owen, Claudia's date for the evening. He was a medium-sized, sinewy boy with stringy muscles and a slouch. His skin was sickly, yellowish-tinged, and his hair was mud-colored and lay every which way on his head, as if he'd just gotten out of bed. It was seven o'clock, twilight, September; the mourning doves were calling; there was a smell of fire, of burning leaves and cigarettes.

I invited him inside. He did not introduce himself. We stood in the hall and looked at each other. He had very pale gray eyes; his blinks were slow and lazy as a cat's. There was something carnivorous about the mouth, too; the lips were swollen and a little too red. He exuded something rank and feral; he reminded me of pictures of aborigines I had seen in books. I thought he would look perfectly natural holding a spear, with a bone through his nose, wearing nothing but a little pouch for his privates.

The house seemed very quiet. Owen rested his hand on his stomach, stuck two fingers between the buttons of his shirt, and scratched.

Then we heard the clatter of footsteps on the stairs, and my niece, Claudia, appeared. I had known Claudia all of her life; she had been a beautiful child. She was still beautiful, but it seemed to me that lately she did her best to ruin it. She was wearing pants that were much too big, an orange shirt that was much too small, heavy thick-soled shoes, cheap plastic barrettes. Her hair hung limp and stringy past her shoulders; her eyes were dark-rimmed, her lips purple. She looked terrible, I thought. And she had spent hours getting herself to look like this.

"Hey, you," she said.

"Hi," he said. He smiled at her but didn't stop scratching. His teeth were ugly, crooked; some jutted out and some were twisted completely sideways. I thought most children got braces nowadays. Claudia, hands in pockets, nudged him with an elbow. They both looked at me, then at the floor. He must have been seventeen or eighteen and had started shaving; there were nicks along his jaw.

"You ready to go?" this Owen said finally.

"You've got to say hello to my mom first," Claudia said. Owen looked at me, and then down the hall, toward the back of the house. Claudia's mother appeared. We'd been watching television back there; she had asked me to answer the doorbell. She looked drawn and tired; she'd aged quickly the last few years. Branching veins decorated her legs.

I don't know where her husband was; he seemed to avoid the house whenever I paid a visit.

Claudia did cursory introductions: "This is my mom; this is Owen. Can we go now?"

Owen stopped scratching and held out his hand. "Pleased to meet you, ma'am," he said.

Claudia's mother looked at him and through him and said dryly, "Claudia needs to be home by twelve. All right? You have a good time, now, and drive careful." She waved to them. Then she looked at me and said, "Are you sure you don't mind this? Well, thanks, then."

Owen and Claudia went outside. I caught the door before it slammed and I followed them. Night was seeping into the edges of the lawn; my purse banged against my hip. I caught up with them just as they reached Owen's car, a boxy boatlike wine-colored thing.

"Wait for me," I said. I was panting a bit.

Owen turned and said, "What?" He already had his hand on the back of Claudia's neck and didn't bother to remove it.

"I'm coming with you," I told him.

"You're *what*? Who are you, anyway?" he said.

"That's Aunt Dorrie," Claudia said.

"Claudia's mother is my sister," I explained.

"Old timer," Claudia added under her breath. I ignored her. I wasn't old; I was younger than her mother. I wasn't even middle-aged really, when you consider how long people are living these days.

"Claudia's mother asked me to come along, insisted actually, to be your chaperone," I told him.

Rolling her eyes, Claudia said, "It's just for the first time."

"Claudia's mother just want to be sure your intentions are good," I said. "She wants me to make sure you are as trustworthy as you appear to be." This, of course, was a lie. I would not trust this boy to walk my dog. I would not trust him to take out my trash.

He looked at Claudia. "Jeez, why didn't you tell me? I didn't know your parents lived in, like, the Stone Age." She shrugged.

I felt a cold breath around my ankles. We were at a standstill. Some animal screamed in the bushes. The sky was clear, with a three-quarter moon. The car stood waiting to take us anywhere we wanted to go.

Owen pooched out his lips sullenly and said, "You know, I think maybe I can't do this tonight. There are things I gotta do—"

"If you back out now," I told him, "that just proves to me that you had some kind of unsavory plans for tonight. That's not the kind of impression you want to make, is it?"

He glared at me. Claudia said nothing. "I won't get in your way,"

I said. "Claudia's mother used to do the same thing for me when I had dates. She'd come along just to keep an eye on things."

"Yeah, and look at what happened," Claudia muttered.

I don't know what she meant by that. "Just pretend I'm not even here," I said. "We'll have a lovely time," I added.

He sighed. "All right, then," he said, and gave me a blinding smile. I could see incisors, canines, and most of his molars. "Let's go. Let me open the car door for you, ma'am," he said.

There are certain boys who are so well brought up that the word *ma'am* comes out of their mouths as naturally as breathing. This Owen was not one of these boys. His "ma'am" sounded as forced as an after-dinner belch.

I slid into the dark car. The vinyl of the backseat was cold against my legs. Claudia and Owen climbed in front. The car had a bench seat in front, not like these newer cars with the bucket seats. They turned on the radio and opened all the windows using automatic switches. I was prepared for this: I had sunglasses and a head scarf in my purse. I also had pepper spray, a police whistle, three hundred dollars, a map of the area, an extra set of panty hose in case of a run. I fastened my seat belt.

"Could you turn down the radio?" I said. "This isn't music, it's noise."

Owen drove with his left hand; he draped his right arm over the back of the seat and played with Claudia's hair. In the flashes of street-lights I saw Claudia's face in profile. A sly look. I wondered where her hands were.

"So," Owen said suddenly. "So, um, Mrs. Dorrie, or is it Miss? Are you married?"

"No," I said. Claudia snickered.

"So," Owen said, "Miss Dorrie, what do you do? Besides chaperone people around?"

"Just Dorrie is fine," I said. "I work for a drug company."

He said, "Sounds interesting."

Was he being sarcastic? I decided to give him the benefit of the doubt. "You'd be surprised," I said. "You should see all the lovely colors pills come in these days, such nice soothing colors. There's a certain light blue that is my favorite. I would like to find a sweater in that color. It is very satisfying to think that my work gives relief to thousands of people. I like the job. Very much. I am happy. Quite happy."

"That's good," he said. He and Claudia smirked at each other. He let his arm hang over the back of the seat. I watched his hand swing side to side in the darkness. It swung close to my knees; I tried to draw them out of his reach. I considered pricking him with the very sharp pencil I kept in my purse.

"I've never done this before," I said. "I'm doing it as a favor to Claudia's mother. She did the same for me when I was a teenager." I only repeated this because the car seemed too quiet. I heard strange, suspicious sounds, almost like the sound of a fly being unzipped. Perhaps I imagined it.

"Where are we going?" I said. "Claudia said you were planning to go to that carnival in the parking lot behind the shopping plaza."

I could tell from their expressions that they'd had no plans of doing this; it was merely an excuse.

"I love fairs," I said, enjoying the looks on their faces. "I hear they've even set up a Ferris wheel and a calliope."

"A what?"

"You'll find out when you see it," I said.

We ended up going to the fair because those two could not think of an alternative. Owen parked and we walked toward the lights, the manic carousel music, the screams of passengers as they spun in circles or whipped around corners. Owen draped his arm around Claudia's shoulders. His hand dangled near her breast. I told them to stop making a spectacle of themselves.

We rode the Ferris wheel, the three of us together in one swaying gondola. I sat facing them and all our knees touched. Claudia's two skinny knees together were the size of one of mine. I watched colored lights swoop and slide across their faces as we rose and fell, rose and fell. They stared back at me. Claudia looked sulky, exasperated, but Owen just stared his strange gray stare, scratching himself again. The gondola was cramped; one of his feet rested between mine, so I could not close my legs completely. For some reason I had the feeling that he might do something outrageous at any moment; I half-expected him to leap from the Ferris wheel when we reached the top. I thought he might try to kiss her, or try to feel her breasts again. But none of these things happened.

He would only have been disappointed, anyway. Claudia hardly had any breasts to speak of.

When we got off the Ferris wheel, Claudia looked greenish and unsteady. She left us and went to find a bathroom. Claudia had always had a sensitive stomach; she couldn't tolerate upheavals or spicy foods, couldn't handle danger, or excitement. Owen and I sat down at a picnic table next to the hot dog stand to wait for her. Our knees bumped under the table.

Owen said, "Look. Dorrie? Dorrie. Do you think you could give us some privacy? For just a little while? We just want to be alone, to talk, for a bit. Please? I'll take you wherever you want to go, and pick you up again later. How's that?"

"Owen," I said. "I wasn't born yesterday. I know exactly what you want to do, and I can't allow it."

He put his head down on the table. "Please?" he said, and looked up at me. A lock of hair fell in his face and he did not brush it away. That bit of hair annoyed me; it annoyed me very much. I was tempted to brush it away myself.

"Claudia's a silly girl; she hardly knows which way is up. Her mother doesn't want her doing something foolish that she'll regret later," I said.

"We won't do anything foolish," he groaned. "Haven't you ever been in love?"

"Of course," I snapped; I did not like the way he was looking at me, nor did I like these questions, nor did I like the way his knee was pressing and nudging against me under the table like a dog poking his nose up my skirt. But I thought I would give him the benefit of the doubt; I tried to assume he was not aware of what he was doing.

Claudia reappeared, pale and washed-out, hand over her mouth. She said she wanted to leave. She folded her arms; she insisted. I could see in her all the negative qualities of her mother: fussy, always demanding attention, always wanting to direct things, grabbing at things that didn't belong to her.

But Owen said, "I have to ride that calliope thing before we go."

Claudia said she couldn't handle any more rides, so only Owen and I rode. We sat upon the painted wooden horses with their flying wooden manes, and then the music began and the horses started to move. Up and down they went on their wooden poles. A strange thing happened: The spinning, and the rhythmic, rocking heaving of the horse, the shifting of the saddle beneath me—these things combined to give me a marvelous feeling. I became quite breathless and did not want the ride to end.

I looked over at Owen to see if he felt the same, but he looked bored. He leaned over and said, "It's not as good as those mechanical broncos in western bars." He breathed in my face; his mouth glistened wet. He rode with his hands resting on the saddle between his legs. His eyes glazed. The movement was hypnotic, like riding ocean waves. Claudia stood behind a little fence and watched.

Claudia was very quiet as we walked back to the car. She turned her face away from us, I suppose to hide her breath. "Now what?" I said brightly.

"How about some privacy?" Owen said.

"Sorry," I said.

"Let's go to the lake, then," he said.

"Fine. As long as we all go," I said.

Owen said, "Claudia?" She was standing mutely beside the car, waiting for him to unlock the door.

We drove away from the lights of the carnival and into a thicker darkness. We crossed the highway and then drove down the winding road that led to the lake. We found that the beach was closed; several logs had been laid across the entrance to the parking lot. Owen parked by the side of the road. He and Claudia got out. I got out, too. The slamming of car doors was a jagged sound in the silence. Our feet crackled and snapped on the dry pine needles.

Owen and Claudia walked ahead, but they paused every few steps to look back at me. They seemed surprised that I hadn't objected to the excursion. They stepped over the logs, and then they waited and held out their hands and helped me cross them, as well. It was so dark at first and then suddenly it was not dark at all. I could see the trees, and the three-quarter moon, the lake shining silver, surrounded by black, pretty as a postcard.

We walked down to the beach. The heels of my shoes sank in, making me stumble. We sat on the sand, which was damp and chill. I sat a little distance from them, but it was not so dark that I could not see what they were doing. The pine trees swayed and sighed, the water rippled like silk, and a high buzzing sound put a tension in the air. I don't know where it came from; it seemed to come from the moon.

I took a tissue from my purse to wipe sand from my fingers. The two teenagers looked shadowy and insubstantial. Moonlight glowed blue on their eyes and teeth; they looked like magical, sinister creatures.

"So why didn't you get married?" Owen said.

"That's not a polite question to ask someone you hardly know," I said.

"But what happened to that guy?"

"What guy?" I said.

"You said you were in love once, so what happened to that guy?"

"Someone else got him," I said shortly.

"Oh."

I could see their hands moving, like four little independent creeping animals, moving here, moving there, touching each other and themselves indeterminately.

"How did your parents meet?" he asked Claudia after a moment.

"I dunno," she said.

"Do you know?" Owen asked me. "Do you know how they met?"

I gave a dry laugh. "Oh, yes. I was there."

"How did it happen?" he asked.

I looked away from them. I looked at the moon. I took a deep breath. As I started to answer, Owen let out a Tarzan yell and the two of them raced to the water's edge, tearing off clothes as they ran. I glimpsed Owen's flashing white legs, his skinny white back before he flung himself into the water. It must have been cold—he began whooping and laughing crazily.

Claudia finished undressing. Her body was like a boy's; she looked naked and incomplete, a plucked bird. She wrapped her arms around herself and waded slowly into the water. "I'm coming, I'm coming!" she called weakly. Owen didn't seem to hear her. He was far out in the deep water, splashing and diving and hooting a strange laugh that echoed off the water.

I kicked off my shoes; I walked down to the water's edge. I knew what was going to happen, and I had to stop it somehow. "Claudia, come back," I said halfheartedly, knowing she wouldn't listen.

Owen heard, and he called out, "Claudia, come *here!*"

He called her name again and again, beckoning and splashing. I could see his sleek wet head bobbing. Claudia watched him longingly. She took another step and then stopped. Turned, swayed, looked back over her shoulder at me. She stood in waist-deep water, afraid to go any farther. She had always been afraid of the depths. But then she had always been, I thought, a shallow girl.

Owen finally understood and began swimming toward her. He swam in a straight line. I felt I could almost see this line, drawn across the water, starting at Owen's thrashing arms, ending at the point where water lapped at Claudia's navel. I had to do something to stop him; I hadn't much time. Claudia was watching him, laughing with high, excited yips like a dog.

And then I knew what I had to do. There was only one thing to do. The only way to stop Owen's attack, to preserve Claudia's precious honor, was to throw myself in his path. I would offer myself in her place.

I took off the dress, the glasses, the control-top panty nose, the underwire bra, dropped them in the sand. I floundered into the water, past the openmouthed Claudia. The water was shockingly cold; it seeped into all the corners of my body and electrified them. As the water deepened, I kicked and floated and swam, with the marvelous smooth stroke I practiced three days a week at the YMCA pool.

I swam until I was between them. We bobbed in the water, staring at one another. They were naked and beautiful. I was, too. We three were all beautiful. But then, almost anyone will look beautiful immersed in water on a dark moonlit night. Anyone, no matter how fat or graceless, becomes swanlike when placed in deep-enough water. Any face is beautiful hidden in shadow.

"I'm coming, I'm coming," Claudia called weakly. It was the whimper of a child demanding attention.

I looked at Owen; drifting closer, I could see his teeth shining. He bobbed and fluttered, like a wild bird trapped in a house, trying to find the door. He looked at Claudia, he looked at me. I saw the shine of expectation in him. I knew what to do. I knew exactly what to do.

I glided through the last few feet of water that separated us.

"What are you doing?" Owen cried in a strangling voice. "Jesus Christ!"

His body gleamed whitely through the water. He reminded me of someone I knew long ago and had forgotten, or someone from a dream: the fish that got away.

"Jesus Christ," he called again. His eyes rolled white like those of a spooked horse; he bucked and heaved.

"Jesus," he gasped, and stopped his thrashing.

"Jesus Christ! Jesus!" In a kind of horror, a kind of wonder.

Later we drove off into the night. The windows were open; wind whipped our wet hair around. I put my hand on his thigh. The road was empty and full of possibilities.

I directed him onto the highway. Owen drove in a kind of amazed stupor. Now and then he leaned over and licked my cheek. His tongue was rough as new sandpaper. It would wear down with time.

Claudia sat in the backseat. "Turn down the radio," she said. "I have a headache."

VACATION

We saw her family put her on the bus. They must have been her family: man, wife with a kid hanging on to her dress, two more kids in different sizes in the background, pummeling each other. She stood solidly among them like an obstinate piece of furniture they were trying to move.

It wasn't a real bus station. The Greyhound stopped in front of a gas station where a cluster of people were waiting. It was one of those one-traffic-light towns with almost everything closed down and boarded up except the churches and the post office and McDonald's. It had a woman's name—I forget which—La Verne or Maybell or Magnolia.

It was dull and overcast, big gray clouds lumbered around overhead. One of the churches had a sign out in front, the light-up kind with changeable plastic letters: IN SPITE OF YOURSELF JESUS LOVES YOU. That sang around in my head; it didn't quite make sense.

She stood among them with her back to the bus while other people got on. The bus shook with their footsteps, their murmurings and rustles as they settled themselves. Then the couple herded her over to the bus and boosted her up the steps. The man handed a ticket to the driver, then hopped off. She stood in the aisle, head thrust forward like a bull, solid and unmoving. The door swung shut.

I looked out the window, expecting a pretty picture: mother, father, and the kids all in a row, waving a heartfelt good-bye to Grandma, or Auntie, or whoever she was to them. Instead, I saw the father already in the car, starting the engine, and the mother's rear as she strapped a kid into a car seat, and one brother pinning the other in the dirt.

The bus pulled into the street, but the woman had not moved. She barely swayed with the motion. She stood there, arms at her sides, as if to say, I ain't taking one step until they make me.

Finally the driver yelled at her to sit down. Not really yelled, but it sounded like it, the bus was so quiet. It was half-full, and most people were asleep or in that daze brought on by stale air and the rhythmic pulse of tires.

So she plodded up the aisle, looming closer and closer. She looked so solid, so dense, yet she quivered like chocolate pudding. Her eyes were black and the whites had gone yellow with age, like piano keys. They rolled from side to side beneath half-lowered lids, searching out empty seats. There was a pair of empties across the aisle from me and Andy. I prayed that she wouldn't sit there; I didn't want her there.

She looked at me right then, as if I had spoken aloud. Then she eased up the aisle, passing several empty seats. She was so wide, she had to go sideways. She plopped down in the seats next to us, panting. She showed us a gold tooth and one damp armpit as she laid her purse on the seat beside her. She stroked it like a pet. She shook her head from side to side, saying, "Mmm . . . mm . . . mmm," as if a friend was telling her a sad story. She pulled some tissues out of her purse and let them blow out the window.

Andy was watching her, too. "Crazy," he muttered under his breath. "Crazy as a . . ." His voice trailed off. I could see a vein in his forehead standing out like a worm under the skin. I could see the big pores on his cheeks and chin where the stubble hairs were beginning to poke up. His mouth sagged as if he'd forgotten how to smile.

We had decided on the spur of the moment to take this trip to Florida. To watch the sunrise on the beach, we said. It was November; it wouldn't be crowded down there, but it would still be warm. For a weekend, just for the hell of it, we said. Andy's uncle had a house on the beach in Melbourne that we could use.

So we set out, but Andy's car broke down half an hour outside of Atlanta. I'd been driving and Andy was asleep when it happened. He wouldn't believe me when I told him about the horrible rattling sounds; he seemed to think I broke the car on purpose. We had to get it towed. Andy didn't say anything. That car was his baby; he'd worked on it since high school. He'd probably lost his virginity on the ragged backseat. He never said so, but I can tell.

Maybe we should have taken the breakdown as a bad sign, and given up. But we were determined to get to Florida, so we headed to the station and got tickets for the next bus. At least Andy was determined. He'd said once, "You aren't at all spontaneous, you know that? I can see you coming from a mile away." So I was determined to be spontaneous; I was trying as hard as I could to be spontaneous and carefree, and to not think about what was going on back home and whether I would miss a day of work and how much this would cost me.

Even Andy's spontaneity was beginning to wear thin, I thought. We'd been sitting for five hours. The bus didn't go direct; it seemed to stop in every town and crossroads in south Georgia and north Florida. At each stop a few people got on and off, so the bus never filled. Sunburned people with flat, slurry voices. There were kids somewhere on the bus. I could smell graham crackers and every fifteen minutes a small nagging voice like a conscience said, "Ma-a, I'm carsick."

I would have given anything for a magazine right then. A thick trashy one with lots of ads and articles about aerobics and orgasms. Or even a piece of paper to play ticktacktoe. We'd left our bags and things in the back of Andy's car, at the garage. Being spontaneous again. No, the truth is, we forgot. We had only the bare necessities, the things we happened to have in our hands as we left. I had my purse, with my credit cards and money, which were necessary for buying bus tickets. Andy had a two-liter bottle of Coke, which was necessary for preventing dehydration. And he had a Frisbee, which he said was absolutely necessary for the beach. And the disgusting old flannel shirt he never parted with, come hell or high water.

I couldn't talk to Andy when he was tired like that. If I tried, he wouldn't answer, like it cost too much energy to open his mouth. Or he'd talk in half sentences. He'd say, "You know me so well that you know what I'm talking about; I don't need to finish." It was true: I could usually finish his sentences for him, but that was because he talked in clichés.

Something smelled swampy and sour. It may have been Andy's breath, drifting out his half-opened mouth like his soul leaving his body. More likely it was the woman across the aisle. She was bent over, grunting, fiddling with her socks. It was difficult for her, she was so heavy. She had taken off her shoes and was pulling off the socks— pink ones with a lace ruffle around the cuff like a little girl's. Underneath was another pair, gray. And underneath, yet another pair, gym socks. She lined up all the pairs on the seat beside her. She took off a pair of men's argyle. Underneath were tan knee-high stockings, which she left on.

"Mmm . . . mm . . . mm," she grunted, sitting up. Her dark face was shiny. Her hair was mussed from when she'd pressed her head against the seat in front of her; it stuck up in a surprised way. "Mmm . . . hmm," and she studied the pairs beside her, with her middle finger pressed to her lips. She raised her eyes suddenly and caught mine. She glared, heavy lids veiling her eyes, her whole face dragging downward, with her middle finger still raised against her lips.

I turned away but watched out of the corner of my eye as she bent over again and put them back on in a new order: gym socks, pink, gray, argyle.

Andy was asleep, with his legs propped up, the bottle of Coke jammed between his feet.

The woman across the aisle was looking at her feet, muttering, "Hmm . . . hmmm . . ." and then slowly, panting, she leaned over and began to pull them off again. The new order was gym, pink, argyle, gray.

She seemed content with that; she tapped her feet and looked out the window for a while, but then she looked down and made a disgruntled sound and started all over. Pink, gray, argyle, gym this time.

As she bent forward once again, I leaned back and closed my eyes. What *I* would do, I thought, is gym socks first, then argyle, and then gray and pink. Or maybe pink, then gray.

I woke when Andy twitched beside me. His eyes were wide in a sleepy, disoriented panic. "The Coke, where's the Coke? Do you have it?" he said, checking his lap and under the seat.

I looked across the aisle. The woman had our big plastic bottle tipped up to her lips. The stuff was golden brown, the color of her skin. It flowed in; her throat pulsed with swallowing. We stared at her. She gazed back at us and kept drinking. There had been about a third of a bottle left. She finished it.

We stared at her. The socks were different again, I noticed. She wiped her lips on her sleeve and glared at us as if to say, What the hell are *you* looking at? Instead, she said, "Mmm-hmm, me, I got the jitters."

She leaned back, sank herself more solidly into the seat. "I got the jitters," she said, looking hard at us. "They send me away, 'cause of the jitters. It's the ants in the bed, the ants that sets off the jitters. Get rid of the ants. They say there aren't any ants."

She waited for an answer. "There's got to be ants in the bed," she said finally. "Why I got the jitters if there's no ants?" When we still didn't answer, she sniffed disgustedly and looked out the window. "Kids, too, giving me the jitters. Won't get rid of the kids," she muttered. "Mmmm . . . hmmm . . . mm."

In the next town the driver stopped at another McDonald's and told us we had half an hour to get something to eat. I darted off the bus and ran to use the bathroom. I could see two pairs of shoes, one big and one small, in the stall next to me. "Ma-a, I'm carsick," the little voice said. "Throw up, then," the other voice said crossly, "Here's the toilet; now you can throw up."

There was a silence. Then: "I can't throw up." "Do it now; you have to do it before you get back on the bus." "I can't, I can't, and you can't make me." I watched the feet tap-dance around, and then suddenly a pink face appeared under the partition. "Hi," she said, and stared at me like I was a freak until her mother pulled her away. I watched their feet leave.

Afterward I found Andy eating french fries with mustard, shoving them in grimly, mechanically, like he was shoveling coal into a furnace. There was a long line at the counter, and raised voices. I wandered over to see.

It was the old woman, with her purse in hand and her shoe on the counter. The chinless guy in the McDonald's visor kept throwing his hands up and shaking his head. She was trying to trade her shoe for a hamburger. "I got the jitters. I need a burger. I been on the bus all day," she said.

"Sorry, ma'am, we can't do that," the guy said impatiently. "Ma'am, you need to be moving on now." He said "ma'am" as if he was saying "damn."

I went back and told Andy. "Crazy," he said. "She's probably on her way to a home."

"She's not crazy," I said. "She wants a burger, she's hungry, and somewhere there's got to be somebody who needs a shoe. They could have worked something out."

"Oh, be serious," he said.

"I am. The world used to work that way, a long time ago before things got so complicated. She's not crazy."

Andy shrugged. He pushed my hair behind my ear with greasy fingers. "You get something to eat. Have some fries. Come on, potatoes are vegetables."

I shook my head. We had to get back on the bus then. I looked around for the old woman and there she was, lumbering along behind us, holding some saltines someone must have given her.

She changed her socks eight times during the next three hours on the bus. She kept glaring at us and muttering about her jitters. I wanted to ask her about them; I thought I might have them myself. But I didn't ask. We had almost reached Melbourne when she sat up straight and said, "Maine, I hear Maine is nice this time of year." She looked at me sternly and said, "Jesus loves you. You hear? He loves you. In spite of yourself."

I nodded.

Two weeks earlier my grandfather had died. He'd been horribly sick for a long time. He'd had all kinds of cancer and the doctors kept cutting it away, until they said if they cut any more, there wouldn't be anything left of him. It rained at the funeral. My mother held my arm the whole time, her face clenched like a fist. On the way to the cemetery I couldn't help thinking how it was the first time and maybe the last I'd ever ride in a limousine. At the cemetery, people wore bright-colored raincoats and plastic hoods. My cousins carried the casket. My cousins were all in their twenties, all tall and stooped. As I walked behind them I could see bald spots beginning on each of their heads. A lasting tribute to their grandfather.

The worst part was afterward: my grandmother hugging me, her lips so shiny red, her hair curled and sprayed up a good four inches above her head. She cried and said over and over, "I just hope I live to see your wedding day. I just hope I live that long."

"Better get busy," my cousin Lenny had said, nudging me with his elbow. Lenny was a jerk.

I hadn't seen the sun since before the funeral.

That's why Andy wanted to take the trip. He said some sun would cheer me up. I'd known Andy since high school. I'd been dating him for a few months. I'd begun to get tired of his voice on the phone, his scratchy callused hands, the way the end of his nose wiggled when he talked. I'd begun to think about breaking it off with him so I could have my weekends to myself again, but after the funeral I decided to stick it out a little longer and see if it would get better. For my grandmother's sake.

"Jesus loves you," she said again. She took off a pink sock and let it flutter out the window. Somewhere behind us I heard the screech of brakes.

Finally we reached Melbourne. When the bus stopped I stood and moved into the aisle. So did the woman. Her hip pressed against me, warm and dense and full, straining to burst out of her skirt. There was no getting past her. She heaved out ahead of me.

Andy and I walked stiffly off the bus. The woman was waiting; she followed us. I thought about what it would be like to take her with us and take her to the beach. Then I saw a tall, severe black woman take her by the arm and lead her to a car.

She looked over her shoulder to glare at us as she was driven away. She looked squashed and angry, pressed up against the window, a goldfish in a juice glass.

The evening was overcast, the sky thickly clouded like waxed paper. It blocked our sunset. There was only a gradual easing to darkness, a big sigh that ended in night.

We'll never see the sunrise, I thought. Andy looked at me and said, "Cheer up. You look like . . . like . . ."

"Like my dog just died," I supplied.

"Yeah. Something like that."

We found the house. More like a shack. Kitchen, living room, bedroom, two single beds. Musty smell and an old Trivial Pursuit board. Andy ate some more fries from another McDonald's. We walked along the streets. He held my hand. We stopped at a bar and Andy had some beers. "Thinking about your grandfather?" he said. I said no. "Work getting you down?" No. He started quoting Nietzsche. He took a philosophy class in college and now he has a handy Nietzsche quote for every occasion.

A man with a mustache drooping into his mouth asked Andy if he wanted to play a game of darts. I watched them play. Andy missed the target nearly every time. Most of his darts stuck in the wall. The man had that brown leathery skin of fishermen who are out on boats all day. His eyes were squinted up and deep-set, as if they'd seen too much already and were trying to retreat into his head. His darts clustered around the bull's-eye like hornets.

Andy wouldn't give up. After the mustached man stopped playing and sat down to his beer, Andy kept whipping the darts at the board. Fast, wild shots. He kept missing and missing. Finally the bartender told him to quit it before he broke something.

We went outside, Andy glowering and still clutching his beer glass out of spite. We walked back along the flat streets. Florida was flat as a game board. No stars. The air wasn't warm, but it was muggy and thick, a cold soup. Andy kept trying to reach for my hand, but it was as if his depth perception was off; he kept missing. I didn't feel like helping him out.

"She wanted to go to Maine," I said. "They should have sent her to Maine instead."

"Give it up already," Andy said, leaning close and hanging on to the back of my neck. "What is she to you anyway? What do you care?" I looked at his face, so close, lit white by the streetlight, lips pulled back from the teeth, and I thought how I didn't know him at all really; sleeping with someone doesn't give you a key to their head.

"Sorry," he said after a minute. We walked on with a space between us.

We went back to his uncle's house. Only one of the beds had sheets, so we thought we'd share it. Andy said he was cold and wanted to get under the covers. I kept thinking of ants in the bed and wanted to sleep on top. So we compromised, one on top and one under. All night long Andy rocked and heaved beneath the blanket under me like a stormy water bed. I thought of one-celled organisms lying against each other, separated by membranes, unable to touch.

Andy woke me at five the next morning. Rumpled, crusty-eyed, coughing, we stumbled over the dunes and down to the beach. The sky was pale and anxious with waiting.

And then it happened. Huge and orange, brand-new, it rose out of the water. I saw it move. I'd never seen the sun move before. Slow, curling up out of the water like a nuclear explosion, until the bottom edge rested on the horizon. It hung there a moment, then rose up into a regular white-hot sun in the haze.

Andy muttered, "The sun's not really moving, it's just—"

"The earth turning," I said. "I know."

It occurred to me that the longer I waited to get married, the longer my grandmother would be forced to keep herself alive.

I kicked off my shoes. I pulled off my socks and let them blow in the wind. The wind breathed up my legs. The water shone a dull gray like liquid metal. It looked as if you could walk on it and keep going all the way to the horizon and peek over the edge to see where the sun was born.

I took a step.

I waded into the water, cold water, wet jeans slapping against the water. Water so heavy and so light, water that went all the way to Maine, filling in all the empty space beneath this sky, between Florida and Africa. Far behind on the shore, Andy called out fragments that fell back against the sand like one-winged gulls.

SKIN CARE

My little sister went off to college and caught leprosy.

I remember that before she left I had warned her: Do not sit on the toilets. Do not share your drink or your lipstick with anyone; do not even share your class notes with anyone. Do not wash your underpants with anyone else's. Do not go out for fondue. Avoid deserted streets, back alleys, dark bedrooms, compromising situations. Avoid them like the plague.

I had warned her. But she never listened to me.

When she called home with the news, my mother wept and my father stormed: It's these damn liberal colleges these days, just plain irresponsible, those poorly ventilated dormitories. I'm calling the dean. . . .

My mother begged her to come home, but my sister said she wanted to stay in school, at least until the Christmas break.

My mother handed me the phone. I whispered, Jessica, how did this happen? How did you catch it? Did you . . .

No, I didn't, she cried, and now I never will; no one will touch me.

There are other things in life besides sex, I told her.

Like what? she said.

Love. I said this automatically.

Same difference, she said.

They're not the same thing at all, I said.

And how would you know?

It was true that I knew nothing about these things. Three years ago I, too, had started college, but I'd had *difficulty adjusting*; I had *problems socializing*. I came home again after a few weeks and found many things around the house that needed doing; I felt that if I did not attend to them, then no one would. I became so busy, in fact, that it became clear that I would not be able to return to school for a long, long time.

I've read books about it, I told her. I've seen talk shows.

You're not even interested. You don't care about love, or sex; all you care about is washing your bedroom windows every goddamn day! she said.

I said, They get very dirty.

Oh, fuck . . . my sister said.

Jessica, I love you, I said, but she had hung up the phone.

My sister didn't know how she caught the leprosy. It was a strange version of the disease and the doctors knew little about it. She told no one and continued to attend classes. She wore white gloves constantly so that she would not contaminate the things she touched. She did not want to pass the disease on to anyone. The white gloves gave her a genteel, aristocratic look; many young men noticed her who had not before. No one noticed the way her jeans had begun to sag around the hips, or the pale papery cast to her face, the crumbs of skin flaking at the corners of her lips. It was the gloves that caught their eye.

If I fought a duel for you, would you throw me your glove? asked the English majors who were taking the required medieval literature course. A red-haired boy at a fraternity party asked suggestively,

Would you take off your gloves for me? And a drunken senior at the same party kissed her hand and said, I glove you, I glove you.

She went back to her room that night and flung the gloves against the wall. She looked at her hands, which had the pale, bloodless look of raw fish. The ridges and whorls of her fingerprints were gradually wearing away. She shook herself, then picked up the gloves and carefully burned them and swept the ashes into a plastic bag, as she did every night, so that they would not contaminate anything.

Her bureau was filled with dozens of pairs of white gloves, a mime's treasure trove.

Every night as she tossed and turned, bits of her skin turned to dust. Each morning she woke thinking she was at the beach, because of the gritty sheets.

Every week she went to the university hospital for a checkup. Every week nurses in rubber gloves and face masks tested her blood, scraped her knees, shone bright lights in her eyes, and gingerly tested her ears and nose for signs of loosening. After this she met with a counselor for half an hour. Each week the counselor gave the same speech about hope and life and God, carpe diem, stopping to smell the roses, and taking it one day at a time. After each visit, as my sister left the examining room, she saw the cleaning crews approaching. Fourteen hospital workers would scrub, spray, disinfect, deodorize, and decontaminate the examining room, removing all traces of her.

One night in October my sister called me. It was a bad connection; her voice sounded brittle.

Come visit me, my sister said.

I'm terribly busy, I told her. I just can't.

Of course you can, she said.

I'm sorry, it's impossible, I said. Why don't you come home? Mother and Dad want you to come home.

No, she said. I won't find what I'm looking for there.

I thought I knew what she meant. I said, There's love here. Mother and Dad love you; I love you. We miss you terribly. We're worried. Please come.

You don't understand, she said. You have no idea.

What could I say to that?

Please come visit me, she said again.

But— I said. The phone clicked and then droned.

I wanted to call her back, tell her that I would come after all. But then I looked around the room and thought, How can I possibly leave? These things, these plants that need to be turned, these windows, this dresser, this carpet. The windowsills, they get so dusty. This bookcase—who will keep the books in the proper order? This bed—you see how it seems to wrinkle up, all by itself.

My sister went to the hospital. I need to see my doctor; it's an emergency, she said.

The nurse studied her. My sister's skin glittered like scales. She was hollow-cheeked and beautiful; her lips were purple and bled into her face like smeared lipstick. She left a trail of dust behind her, pale pollen. There was a smell she could not wash away.

The nurse nodded and left.

In a moment the doctor stood in the doorway. She had met him several times in the beginning, when the leprosy was first diagnosed.

How are you doing? he said. He was snapping on gloves, tying on a mask.

Please take off the mask, she said. I want to see your face.

He looked at her and let the mask hang by its strings. Well, then, what is it? he said. Are you in pain, discomfort? There are some drugs—

No.

What then?

Will I die soon? she said.

The doctor exhaled, rubbed his chin. Who can say? he said. You could get hit by a car. You could eat some undercooked chicken. You could get hit by a penny dropped by a child off a hundred-story building. You could get drunk and choke on your own vomit. You could get shot in a drug deal gone bad.

Do I look like someone who would get involved in a drug deal? she said.

He shrugged. He had a smooth, tanned face, dark eyebrows cleanly separated, perfect teeth, eyes only slightly threaded with red. His rubber-gloved hand gave her shoulder a perfunctory pat.

Make love to me, she said.

He cleared his throat. The paper on the examining table crackled beneath her.

You're my doctor, she said. You're supposed to help me.

I can't, he said finally. It's nothing personal. I'm incapable of loving anything. I've seen too much suffering, I know better than to invest my feelings in anything so transitory as a human being.

She said, You're so young. You're too young to be so bitter.

I'm not as young as you think, he said. I'm a plastic surgeon.

Again he rubbed his chin, and she saw how he touched himself, like a sculptor stroking the marble thigh of a newly carved angel. She thought she could see the seams holding him together, not puckered, but smooth, like pieces of metal welded together.

She shifted and heard the crackling sound again and realized that it was her own dry skin, cracking and spreading, a dry streambed.

Please, she said, please, I've never made love, I don't have much time. I know that you will take the proper precautions. Anyone else, I'm afraid, might make a mistake, expose themselves, I don't want to hurt anyone. Don't you see . . .

He closed the door of the examining room. He sat down on a stool and pushed himself back and forth across the room on the metal wheels. You're going about this the wrong way, he said.

What would you suggest? she asked.

He sighed, raked his fingers through his hair, looked at my sister's feet. The toes were strong; they were bumpy and scarred from her ballet-school days.

The doctor stood, sat, stood again. He said, You should know, I'm only doing this so you won't go out and infect someone else. Do you understand that?

He removed his tie, rolled up his sleeves, washed himself carefully. He sheathed himself in rubber and latex.

Are you going to make love to me now? she said.

I can't do that, he said, but I can perform genital intercourse with you. Or *fuck*, if you prefer.

That will have to do, she said.

He helped her lie down on the examining table. Now close your eyes and count to ten, and when you get to ten, it will be all over, the doctor said as if he was giving her a shot.

So they fucked, violently and without passion. Two, three, four, she said. *Clunk-clunk* went her head against the wall. Seven, eight, nine. Flakes of her skin jarred loose; bits shaped like states and continents fell on the table.

Well then, he said, and carefully removed the condom and dropped it among the hypodermic needles and bloodstained cotton swabs in a bin marked CONTAMINATED WASTE.

Are you all right? I should go, he said as he wiped his hands on the back of his pants. Then he caught sight of her face and said, No, you're not crying, are you? I'm sorry, but you asked me to, you insisted. It was what you said you wanted. I'm sorry it's not what you expected. Please, I can't stand for you to cry.

Sit then, she said, but he did not laugh. He had no sense of humor. And anyway, her eyes, she was sure, were dry.

You were right, my sister said.

Right? Right about what? I said, pressing the phone to my ear.

Love and sex, she said, they're not the same.

Oh, Jessica, I cried, you didn't. . . .

Oh yes, I did.

I told you—why didn't you listen to me?

I wanted to find out for myself, she said, not hear about it thirdhand from you.

I said, Jessica, come home, please. I'll do whatever you want. Anything at all.

Why don't you come here and visit me? Remember, when we were little, how we used to draw pictures on each other's backs with our fingers, then try to guess? Remember I used to give you dance lessons? We could do that again.

Not right now, I said, please don't ask me to leave right now. I need to stay here. Maybe next week; it's just that things are so hectic right now, the leaves are falling—

I knew if I talked long enough, she would hang up, excusing me from making any more excuses.

And soon she did.

The girl who lived next door to my sister stopped her in the dormitory hallway.

You don't look so good, the girl said. All of us are worried about you.

It's nothing, said my sister. She was careful not to stand too close.

The girl insisted: No, really, you've got such dark circles under your eyes.

I've got that flu—you know, it's going around.

No, but there's something else, something strange about you these last few days especially. I can't quite put my finger on it.

I lost my virginity, Jessica whispered.

Of course! the girl squealed. I knew it. I can always tell. That's why you have that sort of glow about you. I knew it all along. How terrific. Don't worry, I won't tell anyone—I'll tell the girls you haven't been getting much sleep lately. That's not really a lie, now, is it?

The girl, laughing, clutched my sister's arm. Fortunately, Jessica was wearing long sleeves.

Thank you, my sister said.

She went into her room and shut the door.

By now my sister's skin was flaking off so quickly that it formed a sort of constant haze around her, like a mohair sweater; her arms and legs were insubstantial and downy. Even her face was misty and in-distinct, like the faces of starlets in old movies.

A nurse from the hospital called and asked her to come in.

I've had my checkup this week, my sister said.

The doctor wants to see you, the nurse replied.

So my sister went back to the hospital, took off her clothes, put on the paper gown, and sat down on the crackling papered examining table. Soon the doctor came in. His face had a yellowish tinge, his eyes were bloodshot, and sweat glittered in his hair. He closed the door, sat on a wheeled stool, and cleared his throat.

Jessica waited, swinging her legs.

He said, I've been thinking. I've been thinking very hard, and I— You see, I've been all over the world. I've seen things, things you cannot possibly imagine, the incredible things human beings are capable of enduring, and—Let me begin again. Sometimes things happen that change a person's view of the world forever, epiphanic moments, turning points. There comes a time in a man's life when he must make a decision, a choice that will change his life forever—two roads diverge in a . . . a . . . a forest—have you ever read Robert Frost? Do you understand what I am trying to say, at all?

No, she said.

Let me put it a different way, he said. I want to try a new treatment. He pulled on rubber gloves, took her face in his hands. Close your eyes, he said. She did, but her lids were so thin, she could see him still. He inspected her face carefully, took a deep breath, and kissed her.

But . . . she said.

Don't worry, he said. Don't worry about a thing.

He touched her shoulders and knees. He kissed her toes. They came off in his hands. She giggled. He did not; he had no sense of humor.

He was very serious. He wrapped his arms twice around her and squeezed.

He kissed her nipples. They puckered like paper, then flaked off like paint.

She opened her eyes. His mouth looked as if he had been eating powdered doughnuts. Don't stop now, she said.

So my sister made love that afternoon in a hospital examining room with a doctor who was not as young as he looked but not as old as he felt. Afterward she lay still. It was four o'clock. The sky was darkening to violet, the trees were dark scratches in the window. The streetlights came on. His clothes lay in heaps on the floor.

Now what, she said.

He licked at the bits of skin on his lips and said, We do it again.

I want you to do something for me, she said. You have to promise to do it.

I promise, he said. She gave him detailed instructions. Then he reached for her again; he groped around for her. She was barely there at all and the room suddenly seemed so dark. But he did find her, bits of her. He grabbed at her by the handful, they made love again, and outside snow began to fall, heavy white flakes falling off the face of the sky. They fell and they fell and they did not stop falling.

The children walking home from school looked up and caught snowflakes on their tongues. Their mothers had told them not to—acid rain, pollution, it's just not clean anymore—but they did it anyway.

In the beginning of December the man showed up at our door.

We had all been hoping that my sister would come home for Christmas break, but we had not heard from her for weeks. I was in the house alone on a Tuesday morning; it was 10:25 or so. I was watching my Tuesday-morning programs, I was wearing the striped shirt, and the doorbell rang. I swung open the door, and there stood a tall black-haired man, uneven stubble on his chin and neck, hunching his shoulders up in his coat as if he was cold, but with sweat making small bright dots on his face.

Hello. You must want to speak to my parents, I said. They're not here. Could you come back another time? I started to close the door. He caught the door, then leaned so close, I could hear air whistling in his nose.

I'm here to see you, he said.

Who are you? I asked.

He told me. He told me several things.

Where's Jessica now? I cried. Where is she? What have you done to her?

He laughed like an engine that wouldn't quite catch. She's gone, he said.

Gone? Where? I said.

Gone, he said, nowhere, everywhere, dust, dust, dust. I backed away from him, and he stepped with me into the hallway.

I thought of something to say: It's your fault, then, that she's gone. You're her doctor, so why didn't you cure her? He stepped closer; I backed away again.

Your sister asked me to come here. I'm going to take you places you've never been before, he said, easing nearer.

Oh no, I said, I can't leave here. I just can't. I can't go anywhere just now. Maybe a week from Thursday, now maybe that could work.

No, you're coming right now. I promised your sister, no excuses. Come along, I want to tell you a little story about your sister and I don't have much time.

You don't understand. *I* don't have time. I can't, not now, I told him. Stop it, I said.

I'll take all necessary precautions. You don't need to worry, he said, and stepped so close, I could smell his breath.

But—there are so many things left undone, I said. There are so many things I need to do.

This is true, he said. This is very, very true. Your sister said the same thing.

BARREN

When the women stopped having babies, we were all relieved, at first. We stopped seeing pregnant women on the streets, and mothers with babies in arms, babies in strollers, babies in cunningly designed backpacks and front packs and duffel bags. It was a relief not to hear the whimpers of babies from the back rows of theaters and churches and poetry readings. We were no longer embarrassed by the sight of women breast-feeding in public places. No more swollen, fertile women on the bus or in the grocery store, prompting us to lewd contemplations of how they got that way.

That is, we were relieved at first. We'd seen the statistics, the percentages: the overpopulation, the overcrowding, teen pregnancies, infant mortality rates, Down's syndrome, projected college tuition costs, the price of toddler-size sweatshirts in department stores. We were glad to be excused from these pressures and considerations, at least for a while.

But right from the start there were people who did not share these feelings: freshly married young couples, monarchs in need of heirs, great bovine maternal women whose only desire in life was to drop child after child. These people rushed to the gynecologists, the urologists; they crammed the waiting rooms and hallways and parking lots and harassed the receptionists. "What's the problem?" they asked. "Why this sudden stubborn barrenness? What's wrong with *these?*" they said, grabbing various parts of their bodies and shaking them. And the doctors spent nightmare weeks inspecting hundreds of seemingly perfect, healthy reproductive parts. No one could say what was wrong, why ovum and sperm refused to embrace each other, why the cells would not divide.

There were a few isolated births, which were hushed up as quickly as possible: newborns who looked like kittens or guppies, with gills like fish and tails like monkeys. The doctors did tests; they looked in their microscopes and chewed their nails. "What is it?" they said. "Something in the air, the water? Artificial sweeteners? Invisible rays? Some kind of biological warfare?"

The people rushed next to the adoption agencies, demanding children of any color, any degree of health. But the adoption agents shook their heads; there were no children to be had. Even the countries that normally produced a surplus of babies—China, India, Mexico—even these sources had dried up.

People recalled stories of inner-city neighborhoods where teenage mothers left unwanted babies in garbage cans. So for a time the desperate ones rioted through back alleys and city dumps, sifting through garbage, fighting with one another over every hopeful bundle of rags, every rotten grapefruit fuzzed with mold. They unearthed many things of interest to the local police, but no children.

Some people tried to snatch the half-grown children of others. Other people were determined to conceive—day and night they tried and the cities echoed with heavy breathing and rigorous grinding, bedsprings squealing and the headboard knocking the wall, a grim, unceasing machine.

Nothing worked. We were glad when people began to admit defeat.

Men and women, exhausted by their sleepless nights and chafed skin, began to look around them and notice the peace, the quiet, the silence of a world without children.

We all bought pets, which we coddled and pampered and took to bed with us at night.

We tried to settle into a life without babies, but it seemed that as time went on, we grew more and more conscious of their absence. Baby culture became the newest trend. Fashion models walked the runways in disposable diapers, shaking rattles, sucking pacifiers and bottles. New bands produced songs that were a strange mixture of music-box lullabies, gurgles, coos, and a deep rhythmic thrumming like a distant heartbeat. We spoke of feedings instead of mealtimes; we took naps during the day and woke, crying, at odd hours of the night.

The most popular drug on the streets was a substance nicknamed "milk"; it caused drowsiness, pastel-colored hallucinations, and a feeling of peace and security that did not otherwise exist in a hectic modern world.

When we contemplated the future, we became frightened. Were we the last of the human race? Were we dying out like dinosaurs? Were we the peak of civilization, the final product of thousands of years of evolution? Were we the end? Such thoughts were hard to bear for long. Some people set about writing memoirs and records, but most of us clutched one another and wept, and drooled, and slept.

Each sunrise came like a promise and a threat. We watched the horizons, waiting for the hordes that we knew would come to take over the world. We waited and wondered. Would monkeys take over the world when we were gone? Dolphins? Rats? Insects? Invisible single-celled organisms reducing our planet to a giant petri dish of sludge? Would aliens land the moment all people were dead and out of the way?

We had always suspected aliens.

We imagined them, thousands of years hence, inspecting our bones and books, musing and arguing. What is the meaning of this knee brace, lacrosse stick, eggbeater, fire hydrant, wedding ring? What sort of people were these? Why did they have to die?

Nothing happened. We grew older. Our lives moved slowly, without event. There were no wars. What was worth fighting for? We no longer cared about improving our cities, our schools, our roads, our role models. The government fell idle. There was no reason to argue about abortions, or cigarettes, or religion in public schools.

All we wanted was to finish out our lives comfortably, and with a minimum of thought.

We watched television, watched the actors grow older and older, watched them try to supplant themselves with surgery and makeup. The child roles on sitcoms had to be filled with midgets or talented apes. We preferred to watch reruns.

We grew old, old, older; we considered moving to a retirement community, but in the end we didn't bother because the whole country, the whole world had become a retirement community—minus the golf courses, swimming pools, and pottery classes.

We all retired, deserted our jobs; no one came to fill them; the machinery of our cities ground to a halt.

We stayed in our homes, dying or waiting to die.

It was the chilly autumn of our lives, and some of us returned to sex, out of boredom, not for the act itself but for the springtime memories it sparked.

And then a strange thing happened.

The women began to swell up. They swelled up like melons in August. We watched it happen in terror and fascination. We knew that when a woman in her eighties begins to swell, the cause is usually a tumor of terrible malignancy, growing unchecked.

The women touched themselves as they lay in bed, measuring the hard foreign growth with their fingers.

We held their hands and waited for them to die.

But they didn't die. Their breasts swelled and their hair thickened. They ate voraciously, vomited, laughed, cried, screamed with temper, and grew bigger and bigger. They wrapped themselves in mysterious smiles; they daydreamed at windows, chin in hand.

And then the babies were born, one after another after another. Ninety-year-old doctors and midwives and nurses did the best they could, slowly hurrying from house to house. Neighborhoods that had been silent for years now broke apart with shrieks and groans and cries of encouragement. The women strained with flaccid muscles and brittle bones, and the babies clawed their way to the surface, wet and steaming and releasing thin wails like the whistle of a teakettle. They were born with their eyes open.

Some of the mothers did not survive. Most of the babies did.

We wrapped our children in old shirts and pillowcases. We handed them to the women to nurse. The babies of dead mothers were parceled out among the living. The world was filled with sucking sounds.

Our children were beautiful, remarkable, we thought. They looked around, they grasped fingers. Some already had hair, some already had teeth.

We did not think about the future. We thought only about our children, we hovered over them and watched the way they held their arms out to us, the way they pumped their legs like frogs swim-kicking. They looked at us with eyes that had not yet settled into lifelong colors. They watched our faces, curious.

We tried not to think, but deep down we knew that we would die before we could teach our children to read. Perhaps we would die before we could teach them to speak. How will our children survive, and how will they communicate, and organize themselves? Who will teach them about taxes, calories, the inalienable rights of man?

Will they pick up right where we left off, or will they abandon our ruined cities and start out afresh, a new race, a new breed of beast?

Will they remember us?

But we tried not to think about these things, we tried not to ask such questions. We focused on our joy, on this marvelous burst of life after the long barren time. We held our children, their warm, growing bodies. We tried to ignore our inner feelings of settling, of silt sinking to the bottom of a river, the feeling of sap drying up and branches snapping, the signals of a body preparing to rest.

We looked at our children constantly, hoping to imprint our faces on their memories. We cradled their heads: tufts of hair, the soft skull bones, that precious gray matter. We drenched them in words, we tried to explain about fire, about gravity and relatively and art, Europe, Africa, the sun, moon, stars; we showed them pictures of grandparents, we read them poetry. We tried to explain who they were, who *we* were. We hoped they understood.

And yet we knew. Yes, we knew that the gap of years separated our children from us as completely as if a body of water lay between us, and we knew we could not cross it and would soon be washed away by the flood, and only our children would cross over into a new world.

LESSONS

Welcome to our school. Please take a look around before the students arrive. Here is your classroom; mine is just across the hall. If you need anything, just call. But remember that your room and mine are sound-proof because they are so close to the gym; thus, if your door is closed, or mine, then I will not hear you.

The desk in the front of the room is yours. Feel free to put your things in the drawers. One drawer locks with a key. The others do not lock. Do not put anything valuable in these drawers. Even the locked drawer is vulnerable. Children are clever.

Note the windows along the northern wall. I see you want to open them; yes, the room is stuffy, but opening the windows is not advisable. The air on this side of the building is bad, pollution, exhaust from the trucks on the street. You are downwind from the garbage Dumpsters, which are often not closed properly. You should keep the windows closed. In fact, it is advisable to close the venetian blinds, as well. This is a safe school, I assure you, but this is not a safe neighborhood. There have been several incidents in the area recently. These incidents have not involved the school; however, it is best not to allow oneself to be visible to the outside world; it is best to avoid being an unsuspecting target.

The walls seem bare, I know, but one can work wonders with construction paper, decorated calendars, and science posters and such. Just bear in mind that we may not use tape or tacks or nails or glue or screws on these walls; the school has been recently painted; our principal is insistent.

Be aware of your appearance; the children tend to observe closely and will quickly pick up on any disorder in your appearance. A stain on your skirt or a see-through blouse or unshaven legs can be your downfall. Do not give them too much information: Use your clothes to disguise the shape of your body, your height, the position of moles. Be especially aware of your back. The classic standing-at-the-blackboard pose is particularly vulnerable. Avoid it whenever possible.

If you have a husband or children, do not put their photographs on your desk. You do not need to take unnecessary risks.

The children pass through metal detectors as they enter the school. Nevertheless, they sometimes manage to bring forbidden items into the school. Do not ask me how; the system has its weakness; we are doing our best. If you should see one of these items, poking out of a pocket, perhaps, or concealed in a pants cuff, do not become alarmed. Do not make a fuss. If they threaten you with one of these items, do not act frightened. These children, like wild animals, can smell fear. Speak calmly and firmly, make no sudden movements, and press this alarm button behind your desk.

On the first day it is traditional to give the children a lecture about cheating and plagiarism. This is merely tradition, hardly necessary; it is highly unlikely that these children would read any great works of literature, much less bother to copy them.

Do not be disturbed by the appearances of the children, or the smell. Do not be put off by the ancient, ugly looks on their faces, the piercings and scars, the dilated pupils, the alcoholic tremors, the tracks on their arms, their rank breath, their pregnant bellies. They may act older, world-weary and all-knowing, but do not be fooled. They are mere children; they are here to learn.

Down the hall there is the faculty lounge, where we may smoke and drink coffee during the lunch hour. Beer is available, too; this is against the rules, but the principal turns a blind eye, knowing that some of us need a little something extra to get through the day.

In the lounge we also exchange gossip, about the students and about the other teachers. It is a harmless pastime, a sharing of information. Our favorite topic of conversation is to discuss what we have overheard the students saying about us. Last year the children labeled Ms. Liston a lesbian and invented extravagant tales about Mr. Aiken, the science teacher. We overhear these things in the hallways, in the bathrooms. They give us something to laugh about.

Last year I overheard two girls discussing Ms. Wendell. One girl said, "I heard that she had the insides of her breasts removed." And the other said, "Yes, her boobs are completely empty, and they have these little zippers on them. Once I saw her in the girls' room; she had unzipped them and was stuffing them full of toilet paper."

When I repeated this in the smoke of the faculty lounge, we all had a good laugh; some were laughing so hard, they were tearing. Ms. Wendell was one of these. Later in the semester she was plagued by toilet paper: in her desk, enveloping her car, one night adorning her house, though teachers' addresses are kept strictly confidential.

The culprits were never found, though several students were disciplined as examples. Nevertheless, Ms. Wendell, who in fact had had a recent mastectomy, decided to leave us.

You are her replacement.

You see how the children are arriving; they come all at once, in a wave. You see the gum, the Walkman radios, the T-shirts printed with curse words? These must be confiscated. Do you see how they move in groups, speak in indecipherable slang? You must watch them closely. They are growing and changing even as you look at them, hairs sprouting, bones spreading, sexual parts expanding, their little brains growing toward the dark like fungus. They are monstrous creatures. Who knows how they will end up?

My classroom is filling with them now. The final bell is about to ring. Why is your room still empty?

Your students must be late, all of them. You will have to discipline them, all thirty of them, when they arrive.

There is the bell. I must close the door now, keep out the noise so my students can concentrate.

Call me if you need me.

TRAIN

We're sitting on the subway in a car full of stories. The people sit stony-faced, with their stories in their laps or their pockets or in plastic shopping bags at their feet.

There's a young man sitting in a wheelchair in the space by the door. A kid really, with mustard-colored hair and a shabby leather jacket. He has faded blue jeans and dull underground skin. The wheelchair looks like an old one. It's like a bicycle folded in on itself. He wears gloves to protect his hands from the wheels.

You wonder what's wrong with his legs. They look all right, not misshapen. He wears jeans faded in the knees, like anyone else. His sneakers are beat-up and dirty.

Dirty sneakers? Maybe he can walk after all. It's just an act. When no one's looking, he jumps out of the wheelchair, folds it up under his arm, and sprints away. Maybe he picks pockets, steals car radios, sells drugs, and the chair is a disguise.

His face is not sinister. His lip twitches as if he might smile.

More likely it's some tragic TV sitcom kind of story. It's prom night, in a car, his date in pink sequins and chiffon. His hair is slicked back and shiny, and the rented shirt won't stay tucked; it pops out above the cummerbund. They are driving to a party after the dance. He is student body president, captain of the basketball team. She puts her hand on his leg as he drives. The road curves around a bend. There is a drop-off, a steep slope on their right. A car swerves around the corner. Driver drunk. It smashes into them; they spin and roll. Clouds scud across the sky. The moon blazes like a spotlight.

The car lies in the bottom of the ravine, flattened like a beer can. She sits bolt upright, eyes open and congealing. Blood trickles across her face. Artistic, almost. It melds with her makeup. Her hand, growing cold, lies still on his thigh. He is unconscious, or wishes he was. Later he is a hero and a martyr. When he wheels himself up to the podium to give his graduation speech, people applaud wildly, tears in their eyes. Girls hover around him, fascinated. Later in private they ask one another, "Is it just his legs paralyzed, or everything from the waist down?" He rises above the accident and is noble, or else he bogs down and becomes bitter.

Maybe it happened the other way. He was the one drunk and weaving and crashed into two kids, who became heroes. Now he lives alone, drinks often, and every screech of the tires below him reminds him of screaming brakes and a shattering impact.

He does not look bitter. His lips twitch again. This time he does laugh. He holds his stomach, gasping. The people around him look away and pretend not to notice. They are thinking, Poor guy, a cripple and a screw loose upstairs, too! Some of them are thinking, Get the freak off the train before he hurts someone.

He laughs again and his stomach jerks around by itself. Then a head pokes out of his half-zipped jacket. It's a flop-eared puppy, which he strokes with one finger. How would he catch it if it jumped out of his jacket and ran away? At the next stop he braces himself against the jolt and cradles the shaggy second head sticking out of his chest like a tumor.

A woman in a yellow-striped dress steps on and sits nearby. She sits slowly, carefully, leaning back and lowering herself with bent knees. She has brown curling hair held away from her face with bobby pins. Her stomach is huge; about nine puppies could fit inside her. You look at a woman like that and wonder about the man who made her that way.

Inside her a live thing swims around and around in the dark. He looks like a tadpole with arms and legs. He swims in somersaults, chasing his tail, and he thinks about Einstein and time and space. It is all lucid and plain to him now. His universe is timeless and limited. He will forget it all in the shock of breaking out into daylight. In twenty years he will think about Einstein again and the equations will seem somehow familiar. On his physics midterm he will chew his pencil, struggling to remember, and he will feel as if his mind is running in circles, chasing its tail.

That is twenty years from now. What about eight months ago? The somersaulting tadpole thing in her belly, who put it there? A man with a chest full of thick black hair. Eight months ago he leans over her, resting himself on his elbows in a dark windowless room on a bed that is too small to be a double bed—it is more of a one-and-a-half bed. He brushes creepers of curly hair away from her face. Her eyes are closed. He cannot not tell what she is thinking.

He is thinking only how hot it is, how they are both sweating and their sweat makes their bodies sticky and slippery at the same time. He eases himself down beside her and lays his hand on her stomach. He is not thinking of what he has just planted there. He is thinking of the grass that needs to be mowed, and of the ache in his back, and of Ed, his neighbor, who has a glorious riding mower, bright green with springs in the seat, and it runs smooth as a golf cart. "You ought to get yourself one," Ed had said earlier that day. "It's so damn comfortable, I don't want to get off. So relaxing, I tell you, it's better than a vibrating bed. The only thing it doesn't have is air-conditioning."

She lies with her eyes closed, the ends of her hair tickling her face. The bobby pins have come out. They lie somewhere in the bottom of the bed. When she moves, they prick her legs. She thinks not of sweat or her belly but of Jason, the son of the neighbors across the street. Jason has come back after college jobless and homeless, plans to live in his parents' house while he writes a novel, or a screenplay. He takes energetic walks around the block at odd hours. He is *finding* himself, he says.

She met him one morning two weeks ago when he came across the street to apologize for backing into her mailbox. It was flattened like a beer can, the door hanging open like a jaw dropped in surprise. She saw that he had haunted Hamlet eyes. She invited him in for a cup of coffee. Jason crossed his long legs and they talked about movies and he said, "Movies are crap these days. I watch them and think, Hey, I could write much better. I know I could, don't you think so?" She said yes, and she was pleased that he seemed pleased. It surprised her that he valued her opinion. She had never gone to college, and though she had told no one in the neighborhood, she felt that lack clung to her like an inferior smell.

He put a hand cautiously on her knee and rubbed his thumb back and forth. She leaned forward and they sat breathing in each other's faces for a long moment. They sank down and kissed like two teenagers on the dining room floor. It felt like a dangerous thing to do. The wineglasses and china in glass-fronted cupboards quivered and rattled. Every now and then they knocked against the dining room table with a thud and a grunt. The table leaves flapped like wings. Nothing broke. Jason apologized again about the mailbox and left. She went back to the table, where their two coffee cups sat side by side, full. It was only ten o'clock. She realized she was still wearing her nightgown.

She has not seen him since. He is not really, technically, her lover, but she likes to think of him that way, with that word. She thinks of him when she is in the shower or washing dishes. A delicious little secret. She tries to pretend her husband is Jason, especially at night, when it is dark. Even then it is quite a stretch. She has to close her eyes and concentrate. She thinks of Jason on the night her son is conceived. While her husband dreams of lawn mowers, she clenches her eyes shut and thinks, If I think about him hard enough, maybe he will feel it and think about me.

What is Jason thinking? He is in a bar downtown, dark and smoky, lit with orange lights and neon beer signs. He is talking to a sixteen-year-old girl wearing her mother's makeup and pearl earrings. She is pretty, Jason thinks, but not pretty enough. Whenever he meets a girl, he tries to imagine her as the lead in his movie. He's decided he wants a red-haired heroine. This girl in the bar is blond. She watches him intently, focusing first on his left eye, then his right. He thinks he should leave. He thinks of the typewriter in his room at home and the pile of blank paper. He decides to stay a bit longer and have another beer.

Sometime later he leaves the bar and stumbles to his car. The girl goes with him. Maybe blond hair is all right after all. He helps her into his car and starts driving; he's not sure where to go and he doesn't want to take her back to his parents' house, but he's driving fast anyway, as if driving will help him think, and they are swerving round a bend and are suddenly dazzled by oncoming headlights. The girl is clutching her purse because there is nothing else to grab, and Jason thinks of rattling, crashing dishes as the car rolls down the hill.

The pregnant woman in the yellow-striped dress sits lumped on the subway seat. If Jason had not died in the car accident, he might have been the one to father the tadpole inside. She could still pretend. But she knows the baby will come out with fuzzy black hair like her husband's chest. It will be her husband's son. He will not write screenplays; he will play with Erector sets and bicycles, and he will mow the lawn.

You can tell all this from the way she sits there looking wistful. Other pregnant women look flushed and swollen and content. But she looks wistful and dissatisfied, as if nursing a disappointment. She purses her lips and studies her dark reflection in the window opposite her.

Next to her sits a balding man with a square, plain face. He wears dark new jeans with the cuffs tucked into socks. He leans over, holding a book close to his nose, with his elbows on his knees. It is a thick book; he has almost reached the end. What is he reading? He takes a tube of Chap Stick from his pocket and runs it around and around and around his lips, never taking his eyes from the book.

It is a psycho-killer mystery-thriller and he's almost to the end, where the slavering cannibalistic killer is lurking in the shadows, holding an ax, lying in wait for a tall red-haired woman who puts away her groceries while miles away a fearless detective gasps as he sees the clues fall into place and realizes the identity of the mystery serial killer who will strike again any minute now. The Chap Stick goes round and round; the bald man's lips are shiny with it. Absently he rubs his fingers in it and smears it across his face. The red-haired woman hears breathing and she pauses before the open refrigerator with a carton of milk in her hand.

The bald-headed man works as a bartender in an Irish pub downtown. There is a certain dark, greasy man who usually comes into the bar every evening. The man sits on the same stool and drinks whiskey every night. He comes and goes alone and keeps his eyes downcast. This whiskey drinker closely resembles the description of the psycho murderer in the book. Even more suspicious, he has not showed up at the bar for his whiskey for the past three days. Where has he been? Killing people serially, no doubt. Where is he now? Perhaps lurking in the shadows of a beautiful woman's kitchen.

He has to keep reading, has to find out what happens. Will the murderer kill the red-haired woman, hack her up, and eat her liver, then go back to the bar to have a drink and leave a big tip? Or will the book end with him dead, never to return to the bar, and the brave detective in the arms of the red-haired woman? He must keep reading, keep reading. He rubs his greasy lips together. The train lurches; the pregnant woman jostles his elbow, making him drop the book. Quick! Quick! Find the page! Find the place again! He feels that somehow the story will go on happening whether he is reading it or not, and he fears by the time he finds his place again, he will find the woman dead and groceries scattered over the floor, blood splattered across the page.

The train lurches to a halt and he looks up, dazed. He realizes he has missed his stop.

Across from them slouches a man with a pointed face and huge protruding eyes. His dark hair grows down on his forehead in a widow's peak. His sneakers are huge, glaring white, and untied. Who is he? A vampire, of course.

He is a mild-mannered modern-day kind of vampire. He has no wings. He casually walks on air, with his hands in his pockets, whistling. It sounds like mourning doves in the morning: *ooooh oooh ooooh*. His favorite victims are little girls, twelve or thirteen years old. When he finds one asleep, with her bedroom window open, he slips in and helps himself. He doesn't pierce her neck with his fangs; he just nicks it lightly. The next morning she wakes up with a pinkish bruise. At school her friends stare at her throat with fascination and envy. "Who gave you that hickey?" they ask her in whispers. "Go on, who? Who?" The girl shrugs her shoulders and smiles mysteriously, which drives her friends crazy. She becomes a kind of celebrity among them, long after the bruise has faded.

The vampire indulges in small pleasures. He takes single socks from clothes dryers. He sits in movies, talking loudly, slurping a soda, and laughing during the weepy parts. Then he makes himself invisible. He loves making anonymous phone calls, and uses old tired lines like "Is your refrigerator running?" Then he hangs up and laughs.

Now he slouches on the subway and looks forward to getting home, where he will make himself a Bloody Mary and watch TV and cut his toenails.

Next to him sits a woman, very old. Between her thick-soled orthopedic shoes lies a shopping bag. The bag is making a wet spot on the floor. She looks as if she were made of strings inside. They pull tight against the skin at her throat and on the backs of her hands.

Her face is a mass of lines. Some run parallel, some intersect in a patchwork, and some radiate out like sun rays. Suns at the corners of her eyes. Her hair is gray, held back with plastic child's barrettes. She wears a black wool coat.

It is warm on the subway. She pushes the sleeves up to her elbows. She has small gray numbers on her arm, numbers that speak of an unspeakable place.

She thinks about what is in the bag. It is a fish wrapped in paper, leaking wetness onto the floor of the subway car. An evil fish. This is what she will do with it.

She will take it home tonight and fry it. She will call up her seven sons and tell them to come join her for dinner because she has something important to say. She is normally a woman of few words. Her sons have learned to take those few words seriously. All seven leave their wives and children in their homes scattered across the city and they come to eat at their mother's table.

She will kiss each one on the cheek as he comes in. She will stand on her toes, and the sons will have to bend down. Adam has a scratchy beard now. Matt looks just like his father, same bent nose and heavy brows. Aaron has a round bare spot on the top of his head that she can see only when he sits down. They are all tall men. They will crowd the little apartment built for one. They will step on one another's big feet and their big words will crowd against one another up near the ceiling, filling the room with noise. The youngest, Alexander, will lurk in a corner as usual. He has never married, doesn't even date. His brothers speculate about his private habits behind his back.

They will sit down around the table with a bumping of elbows and scraping of chairs on the floor. She will put pieces of fish on their plates and then one on her own. The sons will all fall silent and wait for her to speak, leaving the fish steaming on their plates. She will sit up straight and say, "I want to see all of you together this one time more before I go. And I want to give you my gifts now."

She puts a large yellow envelope next to her plate. The brothers will look at one another. Their wave of shock at the first sentence ("Oh, no, Mother, don't say that") will be followed by a wave of curiosity. What's in the envelope? She has always kept her business affairs secret from them, so they all wonder about a secret hoard. The seven look at the one envelope and wonder who will be the chosen one to receive it.

She will open her mouth, but before she can speak again, Aaron will cry out, "If you're worried about your health, Mother, you should come and live with Lena and me. We've invited you before. . . ." His offer will be quickly echoed by his brothers. Their offers will heat up into an argument over the fitness of their homes: "Mother can't stay with you. Those rickety porch stairs—she'll break her neck." . . . "Beth works and so do you—no one would ever be around for her." . . . "Mother needs peace and quiet. And your kids, they can't settle down—they're at that age, always a racket.". . . . "My kids? What's wrong with my kids? At least *I* didn't go marry a shiksa. You know Mother couldn't stand to live with her."

Even Alexander breaks in, saying, "I could move in here if Mother needed someone. It wouldn't be a problem. . . ." Aaron will turn on him then, saying, "Oh, that's great. Then you can bring your *friends* around all the time; Mother would love that." Some of the brothers will snicker; others will stare at their plates, embarrassed.

They all surreptitiously eye the yellow envelope, trying to gauge its weight and thickness. They resume their debate, each attacking his brothers, each fighting for the right to house his mother's body. They will trample one another, hoping to win the mother's favor and the golden envelope. Matt knocks Seth's elbow hard to get him to shut up. Anonymous heavy feet kick under the table. The dishes rattle.

Their mother will sit quietly among them, feet planted on the floor in her orthopedic shoes. She will look at the fish congealing on her plate. She will swallow a forkful. A slender translucent bone, curved like a fingernail clipping, will lodge in a tender place in her throat. A tickle in the throat, the straining for breath, and her heart will give up—gently, quietly.

Some minutes later the brothers will turn away from their argument, to find her slumped in her chair, supported by its strong arms, her head tipped at an odd angle. The room will erupt into a confusion of thudding large feet and raised voices that do not rouse her.

The contents of the yellow envelope will be revealed weeks later in a meeting with their mother's lawyer. At the sight of the envelope, the brothers will shudder and glance at one another under lowered lids and think of that night of greed and cold fish.

The lawyer will open it and remove photographs of her husband— cardboard-mounted, black and white, mustache curled and gallant, one elbow propped against his new Ford. Pictures of her cousins as children, in ringlets and lace, in their garden in a Polish village. Yellowed notecards bearing recipes passed along from her mother and great-aunts. The thin gold necklace, a gift from her grandfather on her thirteenth birthday—the one thing she managed to keep safe, hidden in her mouth, in the place where all else was lost. Newspaper clippings and letters. Bits and snippets of people far away and long gone—plus several hundred coupons, neatly trimmed and sorted and held together with rubber bands. This is her legacy, poured out in a jumble on the lawyer's desk.

The few stocks her husband bought when they first came to this country—those have grown and multiplied, the lawyer says. The stock will be parceled out equally among her grandchildren. What about her sons? The contents of the yellow envelope are for them.

There in the lawyer's office they will read the letter crumpled in the bottom of the envelope. Reading it, they can hear her voice, measured and slow:

> Dear boys, Here I give you my memories. They are the only important things I have to give you. You have already what I cannot give you. You have one another to turn to in your time of need. You are not alone. That is the important thing. Take care of each other. P.S. These coupons are no use to me, but they are good money, so it is silly to throw them away—maybe you can use them.

The brothers will avoid one another's eyes. They will look down at the desk, turning things over in their fingers: the photographs, the gold chain, the notecards, the coupons—delicate scraps torn from the page of a day long ago.

She thinks about these things happening as she sits on the subway, the fish leaking wetness out of the bag between her feet. Does she really know what will happen in the hours and weeks to come? She knows. She does. She had an inkling of it this afternoon, when she bought the fish. She saw right away that it had a milky, evil eye. It looked at her as it lay on the ice in the case in the fish market. She went to the counter and made her order. The fish seller began to wrap up the evil fish for her. When she asked him for a different one, he muttered, "This's fine. They're all the same; they're all fine," with his lip stuck out.

So she took it, the evil fish with the one ticklish bone inside it. Now she sits on the train, thinking that maybe she is meant to have it. It is her turn, her time to go. She decides to invite her sons to dinner, to make her farewells.

The cloudy-eyed fish, so cold, so pale, lying in ice—it makes her think of her sister Lottie, so white, so cold, with violet circles under her eyes and veins standing out on her temples and scalp, the nipples blue against her ribs. Lottie, who lay limp and bony in her arms in the place without hope, whose eyes turned cold and glassy as she lay and the life sighed out of her with a small sound like *oh*.

Her story is there in her face for anyone who cares to read it.

You'd like to follow her home tonight and take the bone from her plate. And the vampire. Follow the firefly glow of his cigarette as he floats through suburban neighborhoods. The yellow-striped woman carrying the heavy physicist within. Hold her arm as she plods up the stairs on swollen ankles. Kiss her, whisper words of tenderness into the curly hair. Sit beside the balding man with his book, ride back and forth as he keeps reading, reading, keeps missing his stop as he tries to finish.

We would like to follow them all as they climb the stairs to the twilight street level, follow their trails of pebbles and crumbs along the sidewalks, stand with them on the stoop as they fumble for keys and wait to be invited into a warm interior space. But the closeness is confined to this small moving place, this train car, this point in space and time between here and there where we are drawn together before flying apart. There is where we began, with the *whoosh* of sliding doors.

Here is our stop.

PERMANENT WAVE

Mrs. Maris Wakefield lay there, covered by a plastic sheet, hands folded neatly together. She was waiting to have her hair done.

She heard a door open and a slight dark-haired man approached her slowly, an uncertain smile on his face. She saw the bottles he carried, the bag of clips and curlers, the hair dryer trailing its cord.

"Where's Darren?" she cried.

"Darren couldn't make it," he said. "He asked me to come instead. I'm Gabe."

"But I wanted Darren. Darren always does my hair."

"He wanted me to tell you he's sorry. He just couldn't. This was so sudden, so last minute, you know. He didn't expect it. He told me exactly what you want done."

"Darren's been doing my hair for fifteen years," she said.

"We'll be just fine, Mrs. Wakefield," Gabe said.

"You don't know me. You don't know what I need done."

"Darren told me exactly—"

"Don't touch me. Please. I'm sorry, but I'm going to wait for Darren.

If he's unavailable, I'm going to stay right here until he becomes available. You tell him to come as soon as he finishes whatever it is he's doing. It can't be that important—"

"Darren said he really couldn't bring himself to come," Gabe said. "Oh."

The fluorescent lights droned, as if hornets were trapped inside. The ceiling was made up of tiles, each decorated with little dots, sixteen across and twenty down. That meant 320 dots per tile; how many for the whole ceiling? She could multiply it out, but perhaps it would be better to count them all, dot by dot, to make sure that none of them was missed. There might be one tile with one extra dot; to overlook it would be a terrible thing.

"In that case," she said slowly, "I guess you'd better get started."

"All right, Mrs. Wakefield."

"I guess I don't have a choice, do I?"

His hands were busy, rattling about in his bag. "Well, under the circumstances—"

"It's just that Darren and I had so much to *discuss*," she broke in.

"I know." His hands hovered around her head. He did not seem to know where to begin.

"He knows me so well, you see. He always has such good advice. About my sister. And my children. He's never met them, but it's as if he had."

"Yes." He was patting at her hair. The stiff, puffy curls were flattened here and there; he fluffed them out gently.

"Darren's very empathetic," she said. "He can *empathize*. He's very sensitive. He's a very bright man. I always told him he could be much more than a barber, if he set his mind to it."

Now Gabe was wetting down her hair. His hands stroked over her scalp. It was soothing; she could almost pretend they were Darren's hands and everything was the same as usual.

"Of course he didn't like me to call him a barber," she added. "He said he was a *stylist*. A hair*stylist*. He always got very offended about it. He's very sensitive."

"Yes, I've known Darren for several years now," Gabe said, studying her head carefully.

She was glad she could not see herself; she knew that with her hair wet and slicked down, she looked like a soggy just-hatched chick.

"Darren has the most wonderful *hands*," she said suddenly. "He could have been a doctor. Or a violinist. Or a . . . a harp player or something. I always said he had untapped potential." Darren's fingers, she recalled, were long, graceful, unnaturally flexible, as if he'd been blessed with extra joints. The nails were perfect ovals sunk deep in the flesh.

Gabe's hands fluttered about her face. They were blunt and knobby, she noted with disapproval, and crisscrossed with ugly raised veins, blue and purple like a road map. She thought Gabe was much younger than Darren, and skinnier. She decided she did not like his hunched-shouldered posture, his tight pants, the way he frowned and glared at the top of her head as if he were performing brain surgery. There were bright patches on either side of his nose; here he was, sweating, and she was not even warm.

"Darren told me he used to have dark hair, like yours," she said. "But I've never seen it like that; he always keeps it dyed the most beautiful gold color. Like a field of wheat in the sun. You should try it. It might suit you." She did not like dark hair.

Gabe stepped back. "Have you ever seen a field of wheat in the sun?" he said thoughtfully.

"No, I guess not," she said. "But I can imagine it as well as anything. Perhaps I've seen it in a movie. A lovely shining gold. I once asked him to try it on me, but he said it wouldn't suit my coloring. He always said I had lovely hair. My hair started to turn very early, when I was in my thirties, and I was always ashamed of it, but Darren said it had a lovely silvery sheen and I should be proud of it. That's what he called it, a 'silvery sheen.' He'd say I belonged on the silver screen."

"Quite a tongue twister," Gabe said.

"He has a way with words," she said fiercely. "Few people do. You could learn something from him."

Gabe kept his eyes on her hair. He had his tongue between his teeth, like a child coloring with crayons. He did not inspire confidence.

"I really needed to see Darren today," she said after a minute. "You see, I really wanted to look all right, today of all days. All the family is coming in, you see, and Darren was going to help me with my makeup, cover up the spots and everything."

"I can do your makeup, Mrs. Wakefield. Darren told me what to do."

"All the family will be here, my children will be here. Even April, my daughter, will be coming, and she hasn't come for years. So I wanted to look my best. For her."

"You're going to look just fine. Don't worry about a thing."

"It's more than that," she said angrily. "I have some final things to take care of, things that need to be settled. I thought Darren would help me make some decisions, give me some advice on a few last things."

"You could tell me. Maybe I can help." He was yanking on her hair, twisting small bunches around the plastic curlers.

"I can't believe he would desert me at a time like this," she said.

She heard him sigh, and he touched her on the shoulder. If Darren was here, he would pat her cheek and smile at her in the mirror. But Darren was not here, and there was no mirror. Nothing is right, she thought. Everything around her seemed askew, and the wrong color, and it was to late to put it all right.

"He's not deserting you. This is a difficult time. Try to pretend I'm Darren, and tell me about it. It might give you some peace of mind," he said.

"How can I have peace of mind, with my daughter coming, and some stranger ruining my hair, the house probably a mess and everything all undone?"

"Why hasn't your daughter visited for so long?"

"Oh, April. We've quarreled, this and that, for I don't know how many years. Ever since she was a teenager. She has red hair. Red hair, can you imagine? Where did it come from? My husband liked to make jokes—about the milkman, you know, even when the children were in the room, can you believe? The last time April came, she brought along *that man*. I don't even remember his name, just think of him as *that man*, and I disliked him right away. I could tell, he had a shifty eye and a soft mouth. I can always tell an indecisive man by his mouth, and this man's mouth had no bite at all. I told April to get rid of him, but she wouldn't listen, took off with him for the West Coast."

"And then what?"

"What do you think? Of course *that man* runs off with another woman, some woman even older than my April, and with two teenaged children, can you imagine? And one of the children has some disease, is in a wheelchair, can't speak or even lift his head. This is what he leaves my April for. I heard he even married her. I've hardly talked to April since, just on holidays and her birthday. She says a few sentences to me, then hangs up the phone so fast, like she's afraid to hear 'I *told you so.*'"

"Is that really the reason?"

"Of course, she doesn't like to admit that I'm right. I'm just trying to help. I just want her to be happy, after all. She's not so young anymore. I want her to marry a nice doctor and have some nice children. Is that so terrible? Her brothers did all right. I don't know what's the matter with her."

"Maybe she's just taking her time."

"A few years back I thought Darren would be perfect for her. He's so handsome, and always dresses so nicely, and says such pretty things. I showed him pictures of April, and he said she was lovely. He thinks it's wonderful the way she makes bowls and vases that are so beautiful, people buy them and put them in their homes for decoration without even putting flowers or anything in them. April always let her hair hang in her face; I thought if they got married, her hair would always look nice, and they would have beautiful children with gold hair and long fingers, and I would pay for the piano lessons so they could get started early on music careers. It was a perfect match, but when I told

Darren about it, he was very sweet and said he was *that way* and didn't like women."

Gabe was working at the back of her hair; she couldn't see his face.

"Of course I knew *that*," she said. "I'm not stupid, you know. I just thought that maybe, if he met her, if they really liked each other, maybe he would change his mind."

"Things don't always work out the way you want them to," Gabe said.

"Darren never said things like that. I never heard a cliché cross his lips," she said sharply.

"Sorry," Gabe muttered. His dark hair stood up in damp spikes; he was sweating again. He circled her head with light dancing steps, darting in now and then, like a boxer.

She realized she was making him nervous. She didn't want him hacking off a chunk of her hair, by accident or out of spite. She looked up at the ceiling. The dots called out to be counted. They were tiny open mouths, crying out, Don't forget me! Don't forget me! There were so many of them, how would she ever keep track? She felt a sudden swoop of panic.

"I'm a little anxious, that's all. Don't mind me," she told Gabe after a moment. "I wish I could talk to April today, tell her that I love her, that I'm not disappointed in her. But it's too late for that."

"I'm sure she knows."

"I should have told her ages ago. I should have done it last week. Yesterday."

"You shouldn't worry yourself with *should have*'s and *what if*'s, Mrs. Wakefield. You'll drive yourself crazy."

"I hope I look all right, at least. All these people coming, all the people in the world I know and care about are coming, and they will all be *looking* at me. I don't want them to remember me looking like a mess."

"Looks aren't what's important," Gabe said. A second later he smiled apologetically and said, "Sorry. Seems like clichés are the only things I can think of to say at times like this."

"You remind me of my husband," she said. "He's been gone six years now, and I can hardly remember anything he ever said. I guess he never said anything memorable his entire life. I remember *him*, of course. Just nothing he said."

Gabe turned on the hair dryer. A high-pitched whine rose up to meet the buzz of the lights. Somewhere air-conditioning thrummed. Gabe breathed near her face; he had a slight cold, a whistle in his nose.

"He had a very *solid* presence," she said when Gabe turned off the hair dryer. "You could always feel it, like being in a dark room with a big heavy piece of furniture that you couldn't see but knew was there. Like swimming in the ocean with a blue whale beneath you. A safe feeling."

"Have you ever swum with a blue whale?"

"No, of course not. I might like to, though. There are many things I would still like to do."

"Sure. We all feel like that."

"I think I left the water running. I think I left the lights on."

"Someone will turn them off."

"My husband always took care of those things. He always locked the doors at night. When he was gone, I always forgot to do it. For years now I've been sleeping in an unlocked house."

"You're lucky nothing ever happened."

"I wasn't afraid. With my husband gone, and the children elsewhere, there wasn't anything to worry about."

"I'm almost done," Gabe said. "Your hair looks great, it really does. Darren couldn't have done better."

He looked terribly young to her suddenly; with his face hovering near hers, he was like a child waiting to be kissed good night. His eyes flitted from her face, to her hair, back to her face, like a child drinking in one last look at his mother before she turns out the light. She felt suddenly lonely, for him, for herself.

"Do you have someone? A wife, or someone?" she asked.

"I had someone," Gabe said. He drew away, uncapped a can of hair spray, and gave her hair a few stinging blasts; he did not bother to shield her eyes. "He's gone now."

"I'm sorry," she said. Then: "How long ago?"

"Not so long," he said.

"What was he like?"

"Oh, about my size. Very thin in the end. Long, straight black hair, cheekbones like an Indian. Very distinctive."

"Do you miss him?"

"Very much."

"Perhaps I'll see him sometime."

"Yes." He stepped back, admired her from a distance.

"Do I really look all right?"

"Yes, you do. You really do."

"What will they think? Will I disappoint them?"

"No." He removed the plastic sheet, shook it out.

"Will they remember me?"

"Definitely."

"Tell Darren I understand why he couldn't come. Tell him I wasn't angry, will you?"

"Sure."

"Tell him, oh, I had something special to tell him, and now I forget what, something important—"

"I'm sure he knows, Mrs. Wakefield."

"It's Maris. Maris. I never liked it much."

"I like it. But I should be leaving now. Your family's coming and everything."

"Please, stay another minute. I'm a little nervous. I'm not ready for this, I don't want to go. I have some important things left to say."

"Nobody's ever ready, Maris."

"I wish I'd met you sooner, Gabe. You seem like a nice young man."

"Yes, me, too."

He was walking away. She wanted to clutch at his sleeve but couldn't. "Don't leave just yet, Gabe. I don't think you're quite done yet. My hair, it's not quite right. . . ."

And she thought of what she wanted to say, but by then it was too late; they both heard the sound of footsteps, a herd of footsteps rumbling slowly down the hall, the rustle of flowers held too tightly, the thick, heavy air rolling forward like thunderheads, the reluctant approach, the clicking in throats, these people who held their faces in their hands as if bearing them forward to present to her, good-byes already painted on the lips and the open mouths, with soft sobs rising up and trailing after in limp banners like a rain-soaked parade.

BRUNO

Bruno, next door, roars when he gargles, roars when he brushes, growls through his teeth as he lathers his face.

Every morning the sound of his routine comes through the wall and into the room where a man and a woman lie together.

The wallpaper has roses on it. It is yellowed like parchment and is peeling. They lie side by side on their backs, with their heads sharing the pillow. A square of sunlight falls on them like an extra sheet. They lie looking up at the ceiling, which sags a bit toward the center of the room. They listen to the sounds next door.

They are new in the apartment. They have never seen the neighbor, but Bruno is the name on the mailbox downstairs and on the tag by the door. Bruno? Mr. Bruno? Mrs. Bruno? They know his bathroom sits tight against their bedroom, with the wall pinched between.

Their first morning in the apartment the rough coughing next door woke them up. The sound was so close. It was in the room with them almost. She pressed against her husband, half-startled. He did not open his eyes but remarked that they would not be needing an alarm clock here. She could hear the words rumbling deep in his chest.

Later they both got up and put on their clothes. He drew on his shoes and laced them carefully and then said he would go next door and ask their neighbor to be a little quieter in the mornings. He stamped his feet as he said this. His name was Josef. People called him Jack. He liked to get things done.

She was called Celia, and she told him, "Don't do it. It would be impolite," she said. She felt as if they were the ones trespassing, eavesdropping on the man's private affairs.

He combed his hair with water so it would stay flat. "All right, then, if that's what you think," he said. "If you don't mind rhinoceroses grunting next door, I don't, either." They bumped noses as they kissed, and she laughed and said, "No, I don't mind rhinoceroses."

So they did nothing that first time, and now it is a habit. Every morning, early, they listen to the coughing and splashing of the man next door, whom they have never seen.

What is he doing over there? His voice is deep and loud and hearty. It rings and echoes against bathroom tiles. The wall quivers, vibrates against the headboard of their bed. They lie with their arms and legs tangled and their faces close together. They try to picture what the Bruno next door looks like.

Jack says Bruno is a small man with a big dog who pants into the bathroom, drinks from the toilet, jumps up to put his forepaws on the sink and breathe at his dog reflection in the mirror. All while his master sleeps. Jack's profile is smooth and polished-looking. Celia sometimes thinks that if she tapped the skin, it would crack.

She says Bruno is huge, with thick arms and a broad chest. Strong still but not so young; the voice is deep, so he must be older, but not too old. All the hair on his head and his chest is still black and curly.

"Black and curly. Sounds like a poodle," Jack says, folding his hands over his pale, sunken chest. "Your picture sounds like mine," he says.

Celia thinks again and says, "He is not a dog. He has a big thick neck and big heavy hands and a big broad face, such a big face that it takes him a long time to shave it. That's what he does every morning for so long. And his mouth, so big that he has twice as many teeth as most people, so it takes twice as long to brush. A big barrel chest and the music pours out in a stream like the organ-grinder's box."

She laughs at the thought of a huge face atop spindly legs, a curly dwarf poodle-man. Jack does not; he brushes Celia's hair away from his mouth. He tells her it is time to get up.

Jack has a violin and he dreams of a place in the orchestra. Now he mends watches and gives music lessons to small boys who cannot sit still. At night he practices with a mute on his strings so as not to disturb the neighbors.

Celia sings. She will not do it if Jack asks. He makes her shy. She does it when she is alone, walking somewhere or taking the trash outside. The alley behind the apartment makes her voice sound rounder and hollower, like blowing into an empty bottle. It's nothing important. She also has secretarial skills.

In the morning they dress and leave, one to mend and one to type. Celia has her hair pinned up or pulled back or twisted around. Her dresses are stiff and fasten firmly at the throat. Jack's jacket is old and limp and he wears gloves even when it is not very cold—to protect his hands. At night when they return, it is dark outside. The harsh light of bare bulbs makes their small rooms look barren and empty. They are quiet. They eat and then Jack retreats with the violin.

The early mornings are the best time. That is when Celia has her hair down and her throat free; Jack can see the hollow just above her collar-bone. And Jack's hair is light and dry, not plastered down on his head. The sun makes a square that falls against the two curves of their bodies.

Sometimes in the morning they come together and Celia's hair falls all around like water and the headboard knocks against the wall. And as if in answer, Bruno, on the other side of the wall, is louder than ever. He grunts and hums, a thick, robust sound. He splashes about, slaps water against himself. The pipes sing with him; he must have the water on full blast. The echoes rattle and roll against the tiles.

When Celia and Jack fall apart, the noise peters out. They hear him turn off the tap, rinse his mouth, let out one final sigh. The slap of a wet towel dropped to the floor. Heavy receding footsteps. *Drip drip drip* goes the leaky faucet. They lie side by side, breathing deeply, staring up at the sagging ceiling and peeling roses. The sunlight falls in a warm white patch on the sheet.

They both think of the puddles on the floor and the wide-mouthed, bare-chested man splashing and bellowing next door.

It happens more than once, their neighbor's morning toilette rising and falling in a crescendo that matches their own. Jack growls, "That guy is eavesdropping; he's acting obscene. I'm going to stop it."

Celia laughs; she thinks it is a strange coincidence, that's all. She rolls onto her stomach, facing the wall, and calls, "*Good Morning, Mr. Bruno.*" Jack sits up stiffly and tells her to stop. She kicks up her heels and looks away. It doesn't matter; they can hear that the bathroom is empty.

More than once Jack stops by their neighbor's door. In the mornings, on his way to work. In the evenings, with the hallway darkened by twilight and shadows. Each time he knocks on the door, then pounds with his fists. No one answers. Not a dog. No one at all. He rattles the knob. He picks with a fingernail at the yellowed label next to the broken doorbell, the label that reads BRUNO.

He knocks; no one answers. He abandons the idea, but the thought of their invisible prying neighbor drives him back to kick at the door again.

He turns from fury to furtiveness. He moves the bed from the wall so it will not knock. He breathes softly and speaks in whispers. But their neighbor knows, somehow, and always during their intimate morning moments he appears and stomps around. His coughs like a rooster's crow, his throat clearing like a benediction, his deep joyous hum as he pats on shaving lather. Jack grits his teeth. The sound grates on him.

Celia looks at his squeezed-shut eyes. She sits up and sings a little at the wall. A silly wordless thing. And Bruno answers, an echoing hum. A tuneless rumble really. Perhaps a random noise. But she would like to think he answers. She sings out again, and again the rumbling almost replies. Jack's eyes are closed, his mouth lies in a straight line except for one corner, which twitches, twitches, like the tail of a rattlesnake.

The next morning she sings to Bruno again and the walls tremble with his reply. Jack is on his stomach, flattening himself into the mattress, crushed by the sun on his back.

The following morning they fight. They lie apart, not looking at each other, but up at the sagging ceiling, which threatens to burst and rain down upon them. They jab at each other with sharp little words. He is hot and sneering; she is cold and bitter. He wants to play his violin where people will understand and appreciate it. She wants a child and a place to raise it. A child! He laughs, thinking of the hateful wriggling boys he teaches, who whack each other with their bows. Both have the covers pulled up to their chins and beads of sweat creeping across their foreheads. Neither wants to be the first to get out of bed and be bare and vulnerable to the other.

On the other side of the wall Bruno hacks and coughs violently. He crashes against the sink, spitting. They hear him but try not to. Eventually they turn their backs to each other and get dressed. Jack is limp and colorless, cheeks sunken. Celia's hair is ragged, will not stay in the hairpins, sags down lopsided.

They are both late for work that day.

Next morning and the morning after and the morning after that, too, they lie unmoving in side-by-side identical positions, like cookie cutters or snow angels. They are silent, their profiles neatly aligned, awake and waiting for the time when they can get up.

The sounds from their neighbor are weak and raspy. He wheezes and shuffles with whispered grunts. When he turns on the water, it whines through the pipes.

Finally after another sleepless night they argue again, Jack standing at this side of the bed, Celia at that. The bed is between them; their words form storm clouds above it. Jack looks thin and drawn in and dried up. His hair stands up all over his head. His pajama pants sag, so Celia can see the elastic waistband of his underwear. His eyes are sunken and his hands flap about, lost with nothing in them.

Celia stands with her feet apart, swaying. The bed looks so small, how did they ever fit in it at the same time? The wallpaper, peeling and curling. And Jack waving his arms like a windmill scarecrow. As their voices rise once again, Bruno begins coughing and banging about.

His voice is louder than ever, raucous. It rises to drown out Jack, falls when she tries to speak. Jack is trying to make a point, crying, "Can't you see, Celia? See, Celia?" Horrible refrain, See-Celia, See-Celia, until the words are meaningless. Bruno bellows against him, water gushes, the walls tremble, and Jack turns toward the sound and cries, "*You and your coughing! You can choke on it!*" and flings a shoe against the wall.

The shoe hits the wall with a thud and there is sudden silence. Then another thud, or an echo, on the other side of the wall.

Jack and Celia stare at each other for a startled, prickling moment across the room. Then they cannot look at each other again. They stare instead at the shoe splayed out, tongue flapping loose, in the center of the bed.

Celia sees him carried out the next day. A tiny shrunken man, very old. The size of a child. Gray hair scattered across a brown-spotted eggshell. A mouth puckered and pursed. She stands in the shadows with other curious neighbors as the stretcher is carried away.

He never comes back to the apartment.

Celia leaves the apartment that night. She never comes back, either.

Not much later, she has a child. She calls him Bruno and sings songs to him that she makes up. And years later when he asks about his father, she tells him about a thick-necked, broad-shouldered, boisterous man.

Jack stays on in the apartment. He is still there years later. Still there. The neighbors say he spends a lot of time in the bathroom, washing his face, brushing his teeth, staring at his reflection in the mirror.

The couple next door wishes he would be a little more quiet in the morning.

BURNED

There was this man once. You might have seen him before, you might have seen him once on the street. He might have brushed you, barely, veering as he rounded a corner. You might have seen him on your TV; he always seemed to get caught in the background of events. It was his strange fate always to be walking past the car accident or the demonstration, or sitting behind the kid in the stands who caught the runaway home-run ball when the cameras were rolling.

A man like that looks weathered and unwashed. He has a mustache that droops into his mouth. He blends in. When you see him on the street, you look once and not again; there's nothing more to see. Or maybe you swerved to give him room to pass, more than enough room, room for five of him to go by. And even as you took the trouble to do that, you didn't look at him.

It's because of the lines on his face: lines like seams, as if something had blown him apart once and he'd been pieced back together.

You don't want to know what made him a patchwork man with worn-down heels on his shoes. You say everyone has a blowup back in his life somewhere. The heels of your own shoes are worn down, but you're not complaining.

Maybe so. But this man was different.

This man once lived in a place where he could see the horizon all around. In that flat place, people moved slowly and were never surprised by anything. They could see far, far, far all around. Long before a thing arrived, the people could see it approaching, see the dot in the distance, kicking up dust.

The sky there made up for the flatness of the land. The sky made cloud mountains that lay on the horizon. It made bleeding violet and pink stripes like a bad watercolor painting. It made a daytime blue too big and bright to look at. The colors in the sky were bright and loud; each tried to shout its name louder than the others, like layers of graffiti.

The people who lived there, they developed squint lines early, those fine lines radiating from the corners of their lids. They all had those same eyes. It made them look related. A stranger passing through might stop in the grocery store to pick up some Cokes, and he would say, "Haven't I seen you before?" Or: "I just bought some gas down the road from a man who must have been your brother, or was it your cousin?" The man behind the counter would stretch his lips wide and shake his head. He'd heard it all before.

The buildings in this place were low and faded and scattered about, none tall enough to interrupt the sky. The sky was a dome that came down to meet the earth on all sides, like a circus tent pegged down tight.

Here, now, you don't see a sky like that. These buildings are too high, too close. Here the sky is only a little bit of something, a little hole between this building and that one. A little piece, like a bit of laundry strung between the two rooftops. You could almost touch it from a fire escape. It is nothing much here. But there, in that other place, the sky was everything.

There, the buildings knew better than to scrape the sky. They sagged and settled with a creaking of boards. The stores and gas stations huddled in clumps along the highway. The dull-colored houses were spread farther out.

The highway was yellow-striped bleached asphalt that poured in from the distance and rolled through town and vanished on the other horizon. That highway was like a zipper holding together the two flat halves of the earth. Up close it was a straight glittering strip, but in the distance it wavered and rippled before dropping off the edge of the world. The sun made it too hot for bare feet.

This man used to live there, in that place next to the highway under the sky. He had not been born there. He had blown in accidentally and stuck there like a bug on a windshield. He stayed long enough for the squint lines to grow on him.

The people there ceased to notice him, which was their way of accepting him. He did not stir up dust. He was a young scarecrow man in patched jeans who stopped sometimes in the evenings to stare up at the sky. The old ones on front porches watched him and thought, That one won't make any waves.

He worked in the gas station pumping gas and wiping dust off windshields. He moved into an abandoned house that was crumbling bit by bit. A dog without a name lived underneath the front porch. They both came out on the porch sometimes to sniff the morning air or look at the moon. They stood alike, with necks stretched back and eyes slitted. The dog was missing a piece of his leg, but he got by all right.

When he first started working, he put on the jacket left behind by the former gas station attendant. It had a patch on it that read JIM, so that was what people called him. It was not his name, but it stuck.

So he went along like that, spending his days with nearsighted Mr. Carson, who owned the gas station, spending his nights in dreamless sleep in the one room in his house where the roof was whole. Until something new blew into town.

The people could see it coming long before it arrived, the dusty, rumbling Greyhound bus. It rolled in that evening as the sky unleashed a wave of red. The bus stopped for gas and some of the sleep-crumpled passengers stumbled out to stretch.

A towheaded girl in a T-shirt climbed down and stepped out of the shade of the bus. Her eyes were the steady, far-seeing kind. She was about eighteen but had the wise, unblinking look of someone much older. She was on that bus, on her way to find a better place. She stepped out and looked up, up, up at the impossible red-painted sky. She looked out at the sharp edge where the sky met the earth, and then at the dark silhouettes of the crouching buildings. She looked at the highway stretching out on her right, and at the fat man stretching his legs on her left. Then she noticed the man standing beside the gas pumps.

She looked at the man in Jim's jacket. He looked at her. She did not get back on the bus.

Some say it didn't really happen. They say, "Love at first sight only happens in stories. It didn't really happen like that."

She stayed. She did.

Some would like to believe it was some freak accident that kept her there. Maybe she went to use the gas station bathroom and the door got stuck and the bus left without her. Or she went out behind the gas station to look at the sky and a three-legged dog cornered her there next to the Dumpster, growling, and would not let her leave until it was too late. Or she decided to stay to visit an old distant cousin she had heard about, not knowing that the cousin was long dead and her old house was now occupied by a silent stranger.

These things might make you believe, but they were not what happened. What happened was that she got off the bus and did not get back on. She did not even retrieve her suitcase. Strange girl, to be so sure.

Do you think what she did was foolish? Do you think she was brave? She did not feel brave. She had reached her destination, that was all. It had come up sooner than she expected, it had taken her by surprise.

They stood and watched the bus vanish in the distance, and above them, the sky blushed and glowed and swelled. Then they looked at each other. He looked into her left eye and saw the whole enormous sweep of sky and himself, too, reflected there.

They stood and looked at each other. She was too young; she felt a pull but did not know what it was. And he was one who all along had slid along unfeeling, had let life slide off his back like water off a duck. Now this stopped him dead in his tracks.

Now they had come together not on purpose and not by accident. She slid in beside him as if she had always been there, yet it was a terribly new thing.

They began with fumbling, in starts and stops. They clung to each other fiercely, ravenously sometimes. It was such a strange new thing. Sometimes they were peaceful; they had all the time in the world; they could walk about in a slow warm way or sit still for hours doing nothing.

When they were together, a warm haze came down before their eyes. It coated everything red, like the world seen through a glass of wine. They thought it was something only the two of them could see. But the old ones on front porches saw the windows of the rotting house glowing scarlet. They watched and rocked in their chairs.

Those two, they had long conversations with just their eyes. They took long wordless walks. Even when they were not touching, they could not be pried apart. If you have never cleaved to someone in that way, you would not understand.

But you want to know what happened next, what went wrong. Did he leave her? Did she leave him? Did she lie to him, cheat on him, maybe sleep with Carson from the gas station? You want her to slip up, don't you? She doesn't seem real to you yet; she is too perfect. You want to see her make a mistake.

But she didn't slip up. That is not what happened.

What happened was they loved too hard and strong too soon. The man went to his job at the gas station later and later in the mornings so he could be with her. Then he did not go at all. He could not eat and could not sleep. He became jealous of every minute she spent away from him.

His jealousy was a sick greenish glow. He grew suspicious of the people who said good morning to her on the street. He envied the lame dog because she seemed to love the dog. He was jealous of the sun and the sky and the stars because she loved these things. He watched her hand smoothing a sheet or slapping at a fly or pushing back her hair and he envied all these things because they knew her touch.

His jealousy grew until he could not stand for her to look in a mirror or eat or brush her hair because these things meant that she was not thinking of him. She was thinking of other things or other people or even herself. And her dreams! They were not of him. He knew this because she murmured names in her sleep and kicked her feet as if running. He could not stand for her to sleep.

He did not want her to talk to other people. He would not let her leave the house. He tried to drive away the dog, but the dog would not leave. He would have torn down the sky if he could.

His love became a new kind, a fierce, possessive clutching kind of love, but not so strong as before. Jealousy had put a flicker in the flame.

And her? She kept loving him as from the start. When he grew suspicious, she tried to love him even harder than before. She wanted to prove herself, but he only thought she was hiding something. She grew tired. Her love stayed bright, but it buzzed and sputtered like a dying neon sign.

Can't you see, they still loved each other? They had been surprised by the love and then it turned on them. And still they loved, desperately. They were were like drowning swimmers clutching at each other, each trying to hold the other above the water's surface, yet as one tries to draw breath, the other smothers her with a kiss. And all the while they are dragging each other down, down, down.

You are thinking, They never loved each other. She was aimless, a drifter, a runaway. She had nothing. Not even her suitcase. She needed a place to stay. And him—he was alone; he just wanted to get laid. They had an arrangement, and they tired of it after a while. They never loved. They used each other until they got used up. Like a tube of toothpaste. That's all.

But you are wrong. They still loved each other. That was why neither left the house that had become a silent battlefield. The house trembled and threatened to collapse, but they never noticed. They waged war from room to room and the air around them crackled crimson and orange and green. The old ones on porches watched the fireworks from afar and shook their heads.

Finally she grew so tired that she broke the silence. She said, "You are taking years off my life."

And he was.

Every day she became a little smaller, a little drier. The veins reared up on the backs of her hands. Her pale hair grew paler. The skin around her eyes turned delicate and papery. Her lips drew in. Her bones stuck out.

Day by day the flesh fell away from her face, so the skin was looser. It fell in folds. The wrinkles began around her eyes and branched across her cheeks and temples. They were not squint lines, for she never saw the sun. The color seeped out of her eyes.

He did not notice, tried not to notice, until her teeth began to loosen. That day as they sat facing each other in the sunless house, one of her lower front teeth dropped from her mouth. It bounced on the floor and then lay still. She put her hand to her mouth. They both stared at the tooth. That was when she said it: "You are taking years off my life."

He said nothing, but he looked at the hand, so gnarled now, that she held to her mouth. There would be a space there now if she moved her hand. And there was the tooth on the floor. He got up and tried to kick it away, but he must have missed, because it lay still, as if fastened to the floor. He grunted deep in his throat and thudded out of the house.

That was her chance to escape. As he strode off in a straight line across the flat, empty earth, she might have crept from the house. She might have made it to the highway. She might have found a ride with a trucker into the next town, four hours down the road. She might have found another bus to take her away, another Greyhound like the one that brought her in.

But by then she was so old. She could not walk without holding on to the backs of furniture. Could she still see? As she leaned against the door frame with the door flapping open, could she see the distant whisper of movement in the shadows that was the old ones rocking on their porches?

Could she see the sun orange and huge, sinking down, blackening the edges of things? When you watch the sun sink like that, you can almost see the ground tip, you can almost see the world turn beneath you. But could she? Did she feel the tilt? Did she hear the chairs and tables sliding across the floor as the world turned a little too quickly? Could she see the dark figure of a man shrinking in the distance?

The man walked and then ran away from the house. He had not stopped for his shoes. He ran with his eyes closed. Nothing rose up to trip him. His own breath rasped in his ears and his heart knocked about like a wild bird in a cage. Then he stopped and turned and looked back.

He saw the house dark and unsteady, leaning against the sky. He saw the sun sinking behind it, flaming, dragging darkness across the sky behind its descent. As the sun went down, the flat earth seemed to rise before it and the house leapt upward. The world lurched and bucked beneath him, knocking him off his feet.

Then the house began to burn. He thought the sun had passed behind the house, making it glow like that. But no, the sun had already set and the house was glowing by itself. First the windows glowed, lit from within, then the roof collapsed and burst into flame, a brilliant red-orange fire that arched into the sky.

He tried to run back, but he could not. The world still seemed tilted. It had not righted itself. He struggled uphill, weaving and panting.

He fell, staggered to his feet, and fell again. He flung himself against the ground as if he could push it back down into flatness. He ran again, darkness rushing across the earth behind him, and the only light was the reddish afterglow in the sky, and the curling flames leaping up to meet it.

Before he reached the house, it seemed to explode—but softly, gently, like a bubble popping. The flames streamed upward, higher, dancing. Orange flames spreading with the smell of burning roses, white too-bright fire like the midday sun, a weaving green streak that carried with it the smell of burning hair. A geyser of fire, a weaving column reaching for the sky. The flames did not crackle; they rushed and roared like heavy breathing. Maybe it was his own breath roaring in his ears.

And then it was over. The last of the flames streamed upward and disappeared into the sky. And that was all. No smoke. Only a sprinkling of ash, some blackened nails. He squatted in the ash for hours, sifting through it with his fingers, searching for an earring, a spoon, a nail file, anything that might have survived. The stars were pinpricks of white light. All night they needled him in the back as he knelt in the dust.

When morning light began to seep across the sky, he stood up, creaking. The world had steadied itself; it was again an endless flatness. His hands, his face, his hair were gray. With ash maybe. His tongue clung, like a dried cake of clay, to the roof of his mouth. His eyes were too dry and sunken in for blinking. He started walking.

He followed the highway. Which direction? It did not matter. He left behind the empty space where his house had stood, left behind the gas station where he had been Jim, left behind the squint-eyed people who were not his people. He walked. They disappeared behind him, swallowed up by the big clear cloudless blue. He kept walking and everything looked the same. The flat emptiness on either side was unchanging and the highway stretched away from him as far as ever. There was no difference between walking and standing still. Occasionally a car zoomed out of the distance, rending the air and the quiet. Then it disappeared and the stillness and silence mended themselves.

Along toward evening a truck pulled over. The driver called to him to get in. When the man came closer, the driver got a good look at his ravaged empty face and bare feet, and he regretted the offer. But it was too late; the man had already swung himself into the cab. He sat stiffly in the seat, as if his back would not bend. And his eyes closed slowly, haltingly, as if the lids had rusted to their sockets.

He was not really missed by the people he left behind. They noticed the absence of the house and wondered about it. Those old ones who had watched the red light building and boiling inside the house, they knew what had happened. They had seen it coming. But they rocked and said nothing. And the rest of the people, they only noticed the missing house (it was on its last legs anyway) and the missing Jim (Carson said he had turned unreliable, footloose) and the runaway girl, and they remembered that night for the most spectacular sunset anyone had seen in years.

That is how he came here, to this place. He is looking for her. She could be dead. She might not be. Perhaps she took the three-legged dog with her and left. He does not know where to look, so he looks everywhere. That's what he was doing when he brushed by you on the street—he was scanning the crowds, searching for her.

He does not know exactly what to look for. How old is she now? The last time he'd seen her, she'd been so old. Ancient. And yet she had been eighteen when she came to him. What is she now? Is he looking for an old woman, a young one, a middle-aged one? Has she dyed her hair? Has she had the tooth replaced? He has been searching for years. By the calendar, she should be twenty-nine by now. The dog must be dead.

Is he looking for a young face? An old one? Is it a face that now buries itself in the shoulder of another? He looks for the eye that can hold him and all of the wide, deep sky reflected in its dark pool.

The sky is another reason he is here. Here the sky is subdued, ignored. Here he can hide from the sky, so different from the bright sweep he once knew. The sky that saw him and does not forget and makes him ache deep inside.

That is how his face came to be like cracked drought land. Do you believe that? Do you want to hear more?

Go ahead and ask him. Ask him what happens next.

HERSHEL

When I was your age, back in the old country, they didn't make babies the way they do now. Back then people didn't dirty their hands in the business; they went to the baby-maker instead.

These days, these young people, they all want to do it themselves; they'd buy the do-it-yourself kit if there were such a thing. They don't trust anybody else to do it for them. And most of them aren't any good at it—baby making requires skill and training. These modern babies they turn out today, some of them are all wrong, and the parents keep them anyway. That's why the world's all mixed up these days. I haven't seen a baby in the last twenty years that could hold a candle to Hershel's.

Who was Hershel? He was the baby-maker in our village. He did wonderful work. People came for miles around to buy his babies. He was a good man, never cheated customers. They bought babies by the pound back then, and Hershel always gave them exactly what they wanted, not an ounce more or less.

Most people got one at about six and a half to seven pounds. A baby was a large purchase; people saved for years to buy one. Some-times a very poor couple would buy a small one. Hershel didn't rec-ommend this; the small ones were scrawny and underdone and often died. He made no guarantees. Once the baby left his hands, that was it. You couldn't bring it back.

Hershel seldom left his workshop. He rose with the cocks and worked all day. When the stars came out, you could see in his window the orange glow of a candle as he tinkered away far into the night. People had to come to the workshop to place their orders. It was a large stone building in the middle of the village and it looked like a bakery, with large ovens and chimneys like fingers pointing at the sky, puffing out white smoke and a sweet yeasty smell.

Sometimes a woman came alone to order her baby. More often she made it a big occasion, with most of the family tagging along. As Hershel emerged from the steam to greet her, the woman would say, Hershel, make me a baby. And Hershel would nod and say, God will-ing.

And then he would take the grease pencil from behind his ear and begin to make notes. A boy or a girl this time? he would say. How large? What color? And the woman might say, Brown curls, please, and a nose like my sister Sarah's, and a special mole in a special place so that I will always know she is mine. Hershel would write it all down and say, No guarantees, remember, no returns.

The parents would give him the money, and nine months later to the day, the baby would be finished. Sometimes it was what they had ordered. More often it wasn't. But it didn't matter, because Hershel's babies were such wondrous things that people fell in love with them instantly and forgot the specifications they had made. The woman cradling her new baby in her arms would say, Oh, I *did* want a boy after all, and I *did* want black hair, not brown, and *look* at his little nose like a sideways potato! Thank you, thank you, Hershel.

And Hershel would blush and stare at the floor and say, It is the hand of God. Whether he was being modest or whether it was an excuse for his mistakes, I do not know. I only know how wonderful the babies were, how fresh and new and perfect as he wrapped them up and handed them over the counter to the parents.

Once the babies passed over the counter, Hershel washed his hands of them. He said he was not responsible for how they turned out. He said once, I only make the outsides. The parents make the insides. I make only the seed. If they cultivate it, then it will flourish.

Did he ever miss the babies once they were gone? We often wondered. Hershel had no wife, no children of his own. His work occupied all of his time. He lived in a little room in the back of his workshop, empty save a bed and a table and a prayer book. He was not an old man, though he stooped and shuffled like one. His eyes were unreadable behind the thick glasses.

He was not secretive or mysterious about his work. He was fair to customers, never cheating them by filling their babies with water to seem heavier, as I have heard crooked baby-makers do. Hershel allowed anyone to come into his workshop to watch him work. During my childhood I spent many hours there, watching. The other boys came, too, and the girl named Alina. We felt more at home there than any other place.

The place was lush and steamy. The babies were sensitive and needed warmth to grow. Hershel began by making dough. He stirred together powders and liquids in a big wooden bowl, carefully testing its consistency. We did not know what went into the dough and could not ask, for as he mixed and poured, Hershel chanted prayers, one after another in a torrent, sometimes with his eyes closed.

When the dough was golden pink and about the consistency of an earlobe (Hershel once let us touch the dough, making us wash our hands first), Hershel then began to knead it. This was wonderful to watch. Though a slight man, Hershel had thick muscular arms built up over years of kneading. We watched the dough somersault and dance, and the ropes of muscles stood out on his arms and the sweat ran down his cheek, and we boys looked at one another and said, *That's* what I want to be when I grow up.

Then Hershel placed the dough in a bowl and covered it and left it to rise. When it grew to twice its size, he punched it down again. Twice he did this. Then he rolled up his sleeves, wiped his glasses, and began the most wonderful part. With his strong, sensitive hands, he began to shape the dough into a baby, chanting prayers all the while. As he shaped the head and neck and belly, he prayed for the things he could not shape: the heart and the mind and the soul. He caressed arms and legs into shape, he twisted fingers and toes and patted cheeks into place. Soon the complete body lay before him, dusted with flour. Except for the ears, which he had left as buds. They would uncurl and bloom during the baking.

Then he would slide the baby on its back into the oven. The ovens were clean and white and were kept at exactly 98.6 degrees all year round. The babies shifted and bubbled as they baked, rocking about on their backs. Some stretched; others curled up. Hershel checked them conscientiously but did not disturb them. After nine months (he kept careful records) he would draw them out either by the head or the feet. Nothing could compare to the sight of a new baby fresh from the oven, crisp at the fingernails, crying from the cold as Hershel held him aloft, checking for any mistakes in his handiwork.

I am Hershel's work. That probably explains why I've turned out so well.

Hershel claimed to have no bond to us. He said he had merely prepared us for our rightful parents, just a step along the way. Nevertheless, we were all attached to him. As children we brought him gifts: a flower, a drawing. Once I brought him a bird, frozen, cupped in my mittens. A pet for you, Hershel. Put him in the oven, bring him back! I said. He shook his head sadly.

When we were older, my friends and I supplied him with firewood for the great ovens. We invited him to our homes for holiday meals. He seldom accepted. He was a solitary man. Sometimes, though, we would glimpse him in the window, looking up from his prayer book to watch us tumbling in the snow.

Hershel never picked favorites. But secretly I hoped that he had liked me (even a little bit) more than the others, that he had blessed me with an extra stroke, a pinch, a little more attention than the others, in the making. I'm sure the others hoped the same thing, too: that Hershel had given them something special, an extra ingredient.

I thought, sometimes, that he watched me more than the others.

As I grew older, I began to look forward to the time when Hershel would make a child for me. But then the trouble came. We did not know then that it was a mere hint of what was to come.

The girl named Alina, she was beautiful. She was about my age, with hair to her waist and shining eyes. Hershel had made her, and I sometimes thought jealously that perhaps *she* was a favorite, for how could she be so beautiful if he had not worked longer on her and given her some extra spice?

As children we had played together. She had been daring, quick on her feet, skipping along the top rails of fences or turning cartwheels. Now that she was older she had to wear long skirts and cover her hair, but she was the same laughing red-lipped Alina dancing about on her long new legs, gypsyish and wild.

I dreamed of her. We all did. I remember waking in the night to hear my younger brother whisper *Alina!* in his sleep. He was only fifteen and still a boy. I lay awake, burning with jealousy over the fact that she could be dancing in another's head.

And then—I don't remember how it happened, how the man first saw her. Perhaps he was out hunting for sport and came through our village. Perhaps Alina was in the city visiting her relatives and he saw her there. Where doesn't matter. The man took one look at her and wanted her for his own.

It all happened so quickly. How could she refuse? He was a wealthy landowner with connections in the government. Her family was poor. He had ice-blue eyes and a set of iron teeth. He was very powerful. He owned everything. She had no choice really.

Then again, he was rich. He was powerful. He may have been handsome. So . . . she married. I do not know if she wished it or not. But she was gone and we all missed her. The clouds came down, the snow fell, and the sky did not clear. We suffered terrible nightmares.

And then we heard stories. We heard that he was cruel. That he left her alone for days. That he beat her. That he did not love her as a man loves a woman, but as a man loves a horse that is beautiful and good to ride. As the stories trickled out to us, we suffered for her.

Then suddenly she came back, wearing a long coat and a veil over her face. She did not go home to her parents. She went instead to Hershel's workshop. She burst in from the cold, dropped a heavy, clinking bundle on the counter, and said, Hershel, make me a man.

She looked at him and she knew he would not refuse. She saw that, like the rest of us, he loved her. But he could not act on his love because he was almost a father to her, and he could not love a daughter as a husband. And yet still he loved, and he dreamed, and his dreams spread to all the men and boys he had ever made, so that they all woke in the night with a chorus of *Alina!*

How did she know it? Perhaps suffering had sharpened her eyes. Perhaps Hershel had given her something extra that let her know his thoughts. She said, Make me a man. And he silently nodded.

She pushed the bundle toward him and said, Two hundred pounds' worth; I will be back in nine months.

She looked hard at him, her face chiseled sharp by desperation, and he longed to press again the cheek he had once pressed into shape. But she was gone.

Hershel rolled up his sleeves and began. He refused other orders and worked only on Alina's man. He worked for days in a frenzy, without eating or sleeping or praying. All his love for Alina and all his years of experience he poured into the colossal mound of dough. He kneaded it, wrestled with it, massaged it, the sweat rolling unchecked down his face and dripping in the dough. The massive body took shape beneath his hands. He labored over the face, carving out nostrils with his fingernails. When he was finished, the man was over six and a half feet tall. I don't know how he got it into the oven.

When Alina returned, she looked more ravaged than before. Again she wore the veil. Again she went directly to Hershel's workshop. Wordlessly, Hershel led forth the man. Alina stared.

He was a giant, and smooth and beautiful as a piece of Roman statuary. Hershel had no clothes to fit him, so the man stood wrapped in a sheet. The eyes were iridescent, like fish scales. Each muscle bulged firm and strong, and they lay together snugly like bricks forming a wall. Hershel had even drawn the lines in his palms promising long life and happiness.

Alina did not thank Hershel. She merely took the giant by the hand and led him into the night. Hershel dusted his floured hands against his apron and closed his eyes. He saw again her face as it had been a moment before, eyes lit up with joy. That moment, he thought, that look, it was worth any price. If he couldn't love her, Hershel thought, then at least she could be loved by something made by his hands.

I wish I could have told him that he had made *me*, and I could have loved her, too.

The news of what happened next, in the great house in the city, traveled back to us quickly. Such news always does.

Alina quietly led the man to her bedroom in the house of her husband. Her husband, she thought, was away. But the husband came upon them, the two of them, in the bed together, late in the night.

Alina was not frightened at first. Her husband was a slight man, and no match for her giant.

But her man lay unmoving, breathing deep and slow. The husband thundered closer and rolled his colorless eyes and shouted threats and obscenities. Alina then clutched at the man, called to him, tried to rouse him—but still he lay sleeping like a slab. And as she screamed and pounded on him and forcibly turned his face to her, she sobbed and cursed Hershel, for she saw in her hands the wide-eyed, uncomprehending smile of a newborn. And then her husband cut them both down with his sword.

That was the end of Hershel. As soon as he heard the news he closed his doors. The ovens went cold. And he disappeared without saying good-bye to all his children. We followed his footprints in the snow, but they stopped abruptly, like a sentence interrupted. We could not find him.

We grieved. The whole village did. For Hershel. For Alina. For the hundreds of beautiful unborn children that had been taken from us.

And we became frightened, for we learned that the other baby-makers in the surrounding villages were also disappearing, closing up their shops and leaving, or suffering strange accidents, or just *gone* suddenly, with food going cold on the table and the chair tipped over backward and the window broken. What about our *children?* we cried, but it was only the beginning, only a hint of the larger tide turning and building and washing over us, the days and years of blackness, of madness that you would not believe if I told you.

Afterward your grandmother and I had to make your father by ourselves. It was an awkward, newfangled thing for us. But I think he turned out all right. And then your father and mother, they managed pretty well with you. Your ears did not turn out quite as well as mine, I think. But they are good ears. They listen well.